Mrs. Winchester's Biographer

Deanna Lynn Sletten

Mrs. Winchester's Biographer

Copyright 2023 © Deanna Lynn Sletten

ISBN-13: 978-1-941212-74-5

Cover Designer: Deborah Bradseth

Novels by

Deanna Lynn Sletten

Sarah Lockwood Pardee Winchester's Family

Leonard Pardee (1807 - 1869) ·············· **Sarah Burns** (1808 - 1880)

- Sarah E. Pardee (1831 - 1832)

- Mary Augusta Pardee ·············· William W. Converse
  (1833 - 1884)   (1834 - 1889)

- Antoinette E. "Nettie" ·············· Homer Baxter Sprague
  Pardee (1834 - 1913)   (1829 - 1913)
    - Charles Homer Sprague
    - Sarah Antoinette Sprague
    - William Pardee Sprague
    - Goldwin Smith Sprague

- Leonard Morehouse ·············· Sarah H. Domkee
  Pardee (1837 - 1910)   (1838 - 1912)
    - Sarah "Sadie" Catherine Pardee
    - Louise Beecher Pardee

- Sarah "Sallie" Lockwood ·············· William Wirt Winchester
  Pardee (1839 - 1922)   (1837 - 1881)
    - Annie Pardee Winchester (1866)

- Isabelle "Belle" Campbell ·············· Louis Merriman
  Pardee (1843 - 1920)   (1845 - 1908)
    - Marion "Daisy" Isabel Merriman ····· Frederick A. Marriott III
      (1869 - 1949)
        - Margaret Marriott (1903 - 1961)
    - William Winchester Merriman

- Estelle L. Pardee ······························ George Lyon Gerard
  (1845 - 1894)
    - Sarah "Saidee" Louise Gerard
    - George Leonard Gerard

Mrs. Winchester's Biographer

CHAPTER ONE

May 1918

Olivia Anne Collins tried not to wring her gloved hands as the black automobile pulled up to the front door of the beautiful Atherton, California home. Peering out the window, she was immediately impressed by the landscape around the entrance. A lush green lawn spread out around the home with giant shade trees spreading cooling shadows over it. Gardens of colorful flowers were artfully placed around the yard, and purple wisteria draped beautifully over the walls of the pristine white house.

Olivia stared at the home with both admiration and trepidation. This was the home of the grand lady. She was excited to meet Mrs. Sarah Winchester but also frightened of what the esteemed lady would think of her.

Taking a breath, Olivia ran her hand over her striped skirt to press away a stray wrinkle, then raised it to the nape of her neck, smoothing her already perfect auburn chignon. Her slender fingers touched the small hat tentatively, ensuring it still sat securely on her head. As she did this, the uniformed driver came around to her side of the motorcar, opened the door, and graciously offered his own gloved hand to help her out.

"Ready, Miss?" he asked, smiling down at her.

Olivia nodded and accepted his help. She stepped onto the cement patio and ensured she was steady before letting go of the driver's hand. He nodded and smiled again, then returned to the driver's seat.

Olivia turned toward the stairs that led to the front door. Smoothing her skirt once again, she thought she caught movement from a large window on the right. The draperies swayed. Had someone been watching her, or was she just imagining it?

Despite the day's comfortable temperature and the gentle cooling breeze, Olivia suddenly grew warm. Her hand went instinctively to her stomach as it knotted within. She needed all the strength she could muster to get through this interview and, hopefully, secure a place for herself. Otherwise, she wasn't sure what would become of her.

Steeling herself, Olivia stood straighter and walked up the four steps to the front door. Before she even touched the brass knocker, it opened.

"Miss Collins?" a woman asked, smiling. "We've been expecting you. Please come inside."

"Thank you." Olivia followed her into the polished tile entryway. The woman wore an outfit similar to Olivia's—a sensible striped skirt falling nearly to the ankles with a billowy crape blouse and waist sash. It was the perfect working woman's outfit, easy to wear and move in.

"I'm Miss Sivera," the woman said. "Mrs. Winchester's secretary. She has asked to see you right away, so please follow me."

Olivia nodded, and the heels of her oxford shoes clicked

on the tile floor as she walked across it. They took a right at an open archway that led into a large living room. A left turn took them through another doorway into an office.

"Mrs. Winchester. Miss Collins is here," Miss Sivera said softly.

Olivia had been waiting days for this meeting and had tried to imagine what Mrs. Winchester would be like. Of course, she'd heard the stories but had also heard only good things about her from Sarah's lawyer, Samuel Franklin Lieb. Yet, nothing had prepared her for the sight of the diminutive woman who turned from the front window and gazed at her with bright eyes.

"Thank you, Henrietta," Mrs. Winchester's soft voice said.

Miss Sivera nodded, turned, and left them.

Olivia stood still, unsure if she should approach Mrs. Winchester or wait to be approached. Despite her small stature, the older woman looked formative. She wore an outdated long, dark dress with a high collar and full sleeves. Her round face was wrinkled yet pixie-like, and her gray hair was pulled up in a loose bun. After a moment of studying Olivia, Mrs. Winchester gave her a small smile and walked slowly toward her.

"It's nice to finally meet you," Mrs. Winchester said, offering her hand with effort. Even though she was in the house, Mrs. Winchester wore gloves just like Olivia was wearing.

Olivia was not tall by any means at five feet, two inches, but she felt she towered over the elderly woman as she reached for her hand and held it gently. She'd been told Mrs. Winchester had painful arthritis, which was one reason she needed assistance. So, Olivia shook her hand with care before letting it go.

"Thank you for seeing me," Olivia said. "I'm very honored to meet you."

Her statement caused another impish grin on the older lady's face. "I'm not so scary in person, am I?" she asked.

Olivia startled.

"It's fine, dear. I know what people say about me. Please, let's sit," Mrs. Winchester said. She walked to a set of white and black striped settees that faced each other with a beautifully carved Asian-inspired table between them. As both ladies sat, Miss Sivera entered the room with a tea tray and set it on the table.

"Thank you, Henrietta," Mrs. Winchester said. She turned to Olivia. "Would you mind serving? I'm afraid I'd spill if I did."

"Of course." Olivia was thankful to keep her hands busy. She removed her gloves, setting them aside with her small bag, and then began to pour the tea. "You have a lovely home, Mrs. Winchester. And such beautiful landscaping."

"Thank you, dear. That's very kind. I have the most wonderful people who work for me and keep my gardens and house exactly as I like it."

Olivia set a teacup closer to Mrs. Winchester and poured one for herself. There were cookies on the tray as well, but she thought it best to not eat while they were speaking.

"I prefer coffee, to tell the truth," Mrs. Winchester said, then sighed. "But it doesn't agree with me, I'm afraid. There is so much we start to deny ourselves as we age."

"I can understand that," Olivia said, thinking of how she'd felt over the last few months and the foods that suddenly made her ill.

Mrs. Winchester nodded. "Frank Lieb tells me he and your family have been acquainted for many years."

The interview had begun. Olivia nodded. "Yes. Long before

I was born. My parents moved from Ohio to California at the same time Mr. Lieb did. They were from the same county and were farmers. Although by then, Mr. Lieb had earned his law degree. My father had great respect for him, and as the group traveled west, they spoke often."

"How interesting," Mrs. Winchester said, her face lighting up. "I met Mr. Lieb after moving here, and he's been a great help to me over the years. But I hadn't known of his Ohio roots until recently. Where are your parents now, if you don't mind me asking."

Olivia didn't mind. She knew Mrs. Winchester would want as many details as possible before deciding her fate. "They live north of San Francisco on their original orchard farm. I come from a large family—eleven children—and was the second youngest. After years on the farm, I craved to do more. My parents encouraged me about leaving home and learning a new skill to support myself."

"Ah, a woman with spirit," Mrs. Winchester said. "I commend you for taking your fate into your own hands."

This surprised and pleased Olivia. "Thank you. My parents were a bit wary, though, and consulted Mr. Lieb on where I could find a suitable school and boarding house. He and his lovely wife, Lida, invited me into their home until a proper place could be found."

"That doesn't surprise me," Mrs. Winchester said. "They are very kind people."

Olivia lifted her teacup to her lips and quietly sipped. The tea was delicious and helped to calm her nerves. She noticed that Mrs. Winchester's cup was still untouched. "I attended school for a year to learn Gregg Shorthand and typing," Olivia continued. "After I successfully completed the course, Mr. Lieb recommended me to a colleague's law firm as part of their new secretarial staff. That was in 1916. I was employed there until recently."

Mrs. Winchester folded her gloved hands in her lap. "And that is precisely why I was very interested when Mr. Lieb recommended you to me. I'd been looking for someone to help me with my new project, and here you are."

Olivia's brows rose. "Project?"

"Yes, dear. Henrietta is my personal secretary and companion, but I already have her working too much to add another project to her list. So, I need someone who can take dictation and type for me. Does that sound interesting to you?"

"Why, yes," Olivia said, her heart fluttering with excitement. "That would be perfect for me."

Mrs. Winchester's face grew solemn. "I understand you are in a delicate predicament. Mr. Lieb, however, holds your character in the utmost regard, and I trust his judgment."

Olivia's excitement faded. She'd known they'd have to discuss this, and embarrassment deepened the shade of her creamy cheeks as her blue eyes dropped to the floor. "I'm afraid I put myself in an untoward position and am deeply embarrassed by my actions," she said sadly.

"My dear," Mrs. Winchester said gently. "I'm not here to judge you. I, of all people, know how it feels to be judged by others who know nothing about me. I merely wish to bring this out in the open—just between us—so we can come up with a workable solution."

Olivia dared to raise her eyes and saw the kind look on the older woman's face. Her compassion propelled her to explain. "I allowed a dishonest man to coax me into an awkward position by professing his love and admiration of me," Olivia said. "I thought he was being honest and true, but he was not. We both worked at the firm—he was a lawyer's assistant, and I was a typist—and I truly believed he wanted to marry me. Now I am left to pick up the pieces alone."

"The cad," Mrs. Winchester said with disgust. "Mr. Lieb assured me that he was fired without anyone's knowledge of why, so there is at least that."

Olivia nodded. It still hadn't helped her predicament. She'd gone to Mr. Lieb when she had no one else to turn to and had asked his advice on what she should do. He'd been professional and kind and thought he might have a solution.

"How far along are you, my dear?" Mrs. Winchester asked.

Not wanting to appear weak, Olivia looked her in the eye. "Four months. The baby should be due sometime in October."

"How old are you, Olivia?"

Olivia swallowed hard. She was no longer sure how the interview was progressing. "Twenty-two, ma'am."

"Twenty-two," Mrs. Winchester said dreamily. "I was still keeping company with my sweet William at that age, and we married a year later." Her face softened. "No one should be judged harshly for a mistake made so young. And a baby is the greatest gift of all."

Olivia was stunned by her understanding. Most women her age would have judged her harshly, but Mrs. Winchester was full of gentle kindness. "I promise you I will act with the utmost propriety if I come to work for you," Olivia said. "If you can find it in your heart to trust me."

Mrs. Winchester smiled. Olivia noticed all her smiles were closed-mouthed, yet they still held warmth and kindness. "I believe you, dear. I think you and I will get along just fine."

Feeling elated again, Olivia dared to ask. "Are you saying you are hiring me?"

The elderly lady nodded. "Yes. I am. And I believe you
and I will have such a wonderful time working on my project.
Granted—it will be work—but I can tell you are up to the
task."

"Oh, thank you very much, Mrs. Winchester. I won't let
you down," Olivia said, feeling near tears. She had worried
about what would become of her and her baby. Despite the
circumstances, she'd known she couldn't have given her baby
up for adoption because it was a part of her. And she hadn't
wanted to bring shame on her family, who thought so highly of
her accomplishments. Mrs. Winchester had saved her.

"Now," Mrs. Winchester said, all business again. "We must
come up with a story so as not to raise any question about you
or your baby's legitimacy. I am not one to lie in general, but a
little white lie will protect you. How would you like to kill off
your husband?"

"Excuse me?" Olivia asked. "My husband?"

"Yes, dear. In this day and age, with the war in Europe
and that dreaded Spanish Flu starting to circulate around the
globe, it's easy to make a pretend husband disappear." She
grinned mischievously.

"And you're willing to lie for me?" Olivia asked, stunned
by her candor.

"To protect you and the baby, yes. Mr. Lieb and I discussed
the possibility, and he agreed. We will tell the staff and everyone else we were mistaken and you are Mrs. Collins, not Miss,
and that your husband passed away recently."

Olivia pondered this. The man who'd seduced her had
no idea she was expecting because he'd been dismissed and
left town soon afterward. In fact, only Mr. Lieb and Mrs.
Winchester were privy to her indiscretion. So, there'd be no

one to discredit the fact that she had been married and her husband died. Glancing up at Mrs. Winchester, she saw she was waiting patiently for her reply.

"Perhaps he came home injured from the war recently and then, after a time, passed?" Olivia suggested. "Then I wouldn't have to make up too many details."

"Yes," Mrs. Winchester said, seeming to ponder the story. "A white lie shouldn't be complicated. She smiled warmly. "From this moment on, you are the young widow, Mrs. Collins. I will let Mr. Lieb know our plan."

"Thank you," Olivia said softly. "You are too kind to help me, and I promise I will not disappoint you."

"I believe you won't," Mrs. Winchester said, slowly standing. "We will have a room ready for you here tomorrow. I'll have the driver take you home so you can pack your things. Shall we start work the day after tomorrow?"

Olivia stood. "Yes, ma'am. That will be fine."

"Wonderful." Mrs. Winchester rang a bell that sat on the end table, and Henrietta arrived a moment later. "Henrietta. It seems I was in error. Mrs. Collins, not Miss, will be joining our staff beginning tomorrow. It seems her husband has recently passed. Will you be so kind as to show her around tomorrow when she returns?"

Miss Sivera's expression remained neutral as she nodded. "Of course, Madame," she said, then turned to Olivia. "I'm pleased you will be joining us."

"Thank you." Olivia wondered if Miss Sivera believed the story. She guessed it didn't matter one way or the other. If Mrs. Winchester said it was true, then it was.

As she followed the secretary out of the room, Olivia was elated that she was now employed and had a place to live. She desperately hoped that she and Mrs. Winchester would get along nicely as she already felt a personal connection with her and was thankful for her understanding.

For the first time in weeks, Olivia felt safe to plan a future.

Chapter Two

Today

"Mom, I'm here," Morgan called out as she entered her parents' house. She dropped her backpack in a chair in the living room and walked toward the kitchen. "Where are you?"

"I'm in here," Annie Connors called out.

Morgan found her in the kitchen with boxes piled around her. The garage door was open, and more boxes sat just inside it. "Wow. I didn't know you still had this much of grandma's stuff."

Annie sighed as she pushed her shoulder-length brown hair out of her face. "It's a lot. Even though we'd gone through everything before she went into assisted living, there were still things we didn't know what to do with."

Morgan dropped onto one of the kitchen table's chairs. It was Sunday, and she was tired from her busy week at work. Even though Saturday had been her day off, Morgan had spent it reviewing her new author's manuscript, making notes for the editor. But she'd promised her mother she'd help her today, so here she was.

"Doesn't Uncle Andy want any of grandma's things?" Morgan asked, peering into a box that held a pile of crocheted doilies.

"Not really. And his wife doesn't either," Annie said. "Can you imagine one of these lace doilies sitting under a lamp in their ultra-modern house?"

Morgan laughed. "No, I can't imagine that any more than I can having them under my lamps."

Annie smiled at the thought as she looked at her daughter. "You look cute today. Did you get a new haircut?"

Morgan reached up to her short blond hair and ran her fingers through it. It was styled in a pixie cut that accentuated her oval face. "No. I haven't had a cut in a while. It's a little longer right now. I'm not sure if I want to grow it out a little or cut it all off again."

"You'll look adorable either way," Annie said. "How can you not with that petite figure and impish face?"

"You make me sound like a garden gnome."

"A cute one," Annie teased.

Morgan sighed. "It's hard enough getting the men in my office to take me seriously at my height. I don't need to look like a gnome."

"Believe me, dear. You don't."

"Hey, sweet pea! You're home." Morgan's father entered the kitchen and wrapped his arms around her from behind. "I haven't seen you in a while."

"Hi, Dad," she said, smiling up at him. "They keep me busy at work, just like you."

"Not for long," Dean said, heading to the fridge and pulling out a water bottle. He offered one to Morgan, who nodded yes. "Three more years, and I'm out of there."

"I have one more month, and I'm done," Annie piped up cheerfully. "Thirty-five years of teaching history to middle schoolers is long enough."

"You say that now but you'll miss it," Morgan said. "I know you—you love to be busy."

Annie smiled. "I'll miss the kids, but honestly, I will find other things to keep me busy."

Dean glanced into the garage. "Do you want me to bring those boxes inside here?"

"Yes," Annie said. "You can stack them over by the wall. This is going to take all day."

Morgan helped her dad carry the rest of the boxes inside so they could close the garage door. It was a warm May day in San Jose, and there was no sense in losing the home's cool air into the garage.

As her mom chose boxes to open, Morgan glanced around. Her parents had done a few updates to the house over the years, and it looked nice. She and her brother, Chris, had grown up in the four-bedroom, three-bath house, and it had changed a lot since they were children. The house had a big backyard because it was a corner lot, and all their friends used to hang out there. With home prices rising steadily in California, she was sure this house was worth a lot more than her parents had paid for it.

"So, when you both are retired, will you sell the house and move somewhere else?" Morgan asked, curious. She hadn't really thought of it before, but with her living in San Francisco and her brother and his family down in San Diego, maybe her parents were ready for a change.

"We haven't thought about that yet," Dean said, looking through one of Grandma Kathleen's photo albums. "This house would sell for a lot right now, but buying something else would be just as expensive."

Annie rolled her eyes. "The prices around here are ridiculous. If we hadn't bought this twenty-five years ago, we'd never have been able to afford a house. It's crazy."

"You might want to move to San Diego to be closer to Chris and his kids," Morgan said. "Being near the ocean would be nice."

"It would be nice," Dean said. "But those prices are high too. I think we'll travel a little first and then see what we want to do. It's still three years away."

Morgan nodded. She knew how crazy prices of houses were. Even renting in San Francisco was nearly impossible. When she'd acquired her position at Generation Publishing seven years before, she'd struggled to find a nice apartment in a safe neighborhood. She'd scored a one-bedroom place in an old Victorian house that had been remodeled as rentals and had lived there ever since. She liked the older neighborhood and the many vintage homes that lined the streets. And she could take the bus to work if she wanted to or even walk. But it was still costly.

Dean disappeared into the family room to watch TV as Morgan and Annie started digging through Grandma Kathleen's things.

Annie carefully went through a box of Haviland china that had belonged to her mother and her Grandmother Rose. Some of the plates were chipped after all these years, but the pattern was beautiful.

"I don't suppose you'd want Grandma Rose's china," Annie asked, lifting a plate up to show Morgan. It's from the 1940s."

Morgan looked up from the box of news clippings she'd been studying. "It's pretty, but I don't know what I'd do with it. My little apartment has nowhere to store it, and I doubt I'd ever use it."

Annie nodded. "This is why I still have this stuff. It's antique, and it meant a lot to my mother and grandmother, but I don't really have space for it either."

"I can see why that would be hard. But if it has no meaning to you, there's no sense in keeping it."

"Yes, I suppose you're right." Annie sighed.

"Have you asked Chris and Amy if they'd want any of these things?" Morgan asked. Amy loved a mixture of new and old and had a very eclectic style.

"I mentioned we were going through Grandma's things to Chris, but he sounded like he wasn't interested. Maybe I could send a few pics to Amy and see if these would interest her. She already has her grandmother's china in the cupboard, but who knows?" Annie took a few pictures of the set and sent them off.

"There's a whole shoebox of old newspaper clippings here," Morgan said, looking through them. "Some from the early 1900s."

"Oh, yeah. I forgot about those." Annie glanced over at the box. "I think they're a mixture of clippings from your Great-Great-Grandmother Olivia on down. Probably wedding announcements, birth notices, and such."

Morgan lifted out an old, yellow newspaper clipping. "Mrs. Sarah L. Winchester Is Taken by Death," she read out loud. She looked up at her mother. "That's an odd clipping for someone to keep."

"Oh, not really," Annie said. "It's probably Olivia's. She worked for Sarah Winchester in the early 1900s."

Morgan stared at her mother, stunned. "Great-Great-Grandma Olivia worked for the crazy lady who built the weird house?"

Annie shook her head. "Your Grandma Olivia would hate hearing you call Sarah Winchester a crazy lady. She had great admiration for her former employer. Olivia despised all the bad publicity given to Sarah over the years."

Morgan sat back in her chair. "I've never heard anyone talk about a relative of ours working for Sarah Winchester before. Why am I just hearing this now?"

Annie shrugged. "I don't know. I guess we just never talked about it. Olivia died before you were born. She was ninety-two when she passed. And you were six when her daughter, Rose, died, so I doubt you remember her either."

Morgan frowned as she thought back. She didn't remember meeting her Great-Grandma Rose. Of course, she remembered Grandma Kathleen, who'd recently died. But she'd never heard her talk about a relative who'd worked for Mrs. Winchester. "What did Olivia do for Mrs. Winchester?"

"Well, I think she was a kind of secretary or something. She typed up a manuscript for her. Here, let me look." Annie opened a few boxes and searched. Finally, she pulled out a box that was the size of 8 ½ x 11 paper. "This might be it." She set the box on the table in front of Morgan.

Morgan tentatively lifted the box's lid. Inside, it was filled to the top with typewritten pages, obviously done on an old typewriter. The paper looked thin, and the type-print had faded. Morgan read the title on the top page in stunned disbelief. "Mrs. Sarah Lockwood Pardee Winchester, Autobiography, 1922."

Once again, Morgan's eyes lifted to her mother. "Is this real?"

Annie laughed. "Of course, it's real. I mean, I've never read it, but if my mother, grandmother, and great-grandmother said

Olivia typed it up for Mrs. Winchester, then I believe them."

"Why haven't you read it?" Morgan asked. That was the first thing she wanted to do.

"I was never offered the chance. By the time I knew it existed, the paper was so old that I suppose Grandma Rose didn't want it handled. I don't know if anyone has read it, to tell the truth."

Morgan leaned closer to her mother. "Aren't you curious about what it contains?"

"A little, sure," Annie said. "I guess I just never thought about it. And your Grandmother Rose never offered. She kept it up high in her closet, then after she passed, my mom got it and just put it away too."

"Mom, do you realize how important this is? An actual autobiography of Sarah Winchester? People would want to read this." Morgan's heart pounded. This lost manuscript would be the perfect project for her to take to her boss for publication.

"Well," Annie hesitated. "The story I was told was that no one gave Olivia permission to take it, let alone publish it. That's why she kept it hidden."

Morgan's excitement deflated. If her great-great-grandmother had taken the manuscript without permission, then it made sense why she kept quiet about it. But surely, after a hundred years, would it matter? "Do you mind if I take it home and read it?"

"Of course not," Annie said. "In fact, keep it. It's been passed down to so many generations and is just hidden away. Someone should look it over."

Morgan carefully placed the box cover over the manuscript, then found some string to tie around the box. There was no way she was going to risk it falling and scattering. "I'll take these newspaper clippings, too," she told her mother. "Maybe I can do some research on Olivia and find out more about her role with Sarah Winchester."

"That's a great idea," Annie said, growing excited. "In fact, I've always wanted to do some research on our family tree. Maybe that will be my project this summer after I retire."

They continued going through boxes and marking which ones to keep, which to give away, and which to try to sell. But throughout the whole process, all Morgan could think about was going home, curling up on the sofa, and reading the old manuscript. She could hardly wait.

CHAPTER THREE

May 1918

Olivia was excited when she returned to Mrs. Winchester's house the next day carrying her two suitcases. The elderly lady had sent a car and her personal driver for her. Olivia felt like a queen, being driven to the prestigious Atherton neighborhood in a chauffeured limousine.

As before, Miss Sivera greeted Olivia at the front door and showed her the way to her room.

"I'm so sorry about the loss of your husband," Miss Sivera said as they walked up the stairs to the second floor. "There are so many young widows because of this terrible war."

"Thank you," Olivia said. "It was a shock. We'd married before he left for Europe, and then he returned wounded a few months later. Unfortunately, his injuries grew worse, and he passed."

Miss Sivera shook her head sympathetically. "How awful. I hope our boys come home soon." Down a long hallway, she opened the door to a bedroom suite. "I hope you'll like this room. Mrs. Winchester picked it out for you."

Olivia entered, expecting a typical servant's room, and was mesmerized by the size and beautiful decorations. "It's wonderful," she said, gazing around. It was a large room with a bed, nightstands, and a dressing table on one end and a sitting room on the other. A fireplace sat between the large windows overlooking the backyard. The bed quilt and chairs were burgundy velveteen, and lovely patterned chintz curtains covered the windows. Plush rugs were scattered over the gleaming oak floor.

Miss Sivera smiled. "You also have a private bathroom." She pointed to the door next to where they'd entered. "Mrs. Winchester thought this would afford you privacy when you worked and when the baby came."

Olivia's brows rose at the mention of the baby. "Oh. She told you?"

"Yes, she confided in me. Mrs. Winchester and I are quite close, and she trusts me completely. She felt I needed to know in case you need any assistance." The secretary frowned. "I hope you don't mind."

"No, of course not," Olivia said quickly. "It will be obvious soon anyway."

Miss Sivera's expression softened. "I think it's wonderful that you'll be able to live and work here while you're expecting. It's the perfect job for you now that you're on your own. You'll find Mrs. Winchester has a big heart and gives readily. I'm sure you'll love working with her."

"I feel like I will, too," Olivia said.

"Well. I'll let you get settled in. The staff dines at six o'clock in the dining room off the kitchen. Breakfast each morning is buffet style between six and nine since we have varying schedules. And lunch is at noon. You're welcome, of course, to find snacks in the kitchen whenever you're hungry. We always have plenty of fresh fruit and vegetables from the San Jose house, and our cook is constantly baking. You'll like our chief, Mr. Nakmo. He's a very hard worker and is quite friendly. And Mrs. Murphy is a lively one. She works in the kitchen too. Please, make yourself at home."

"They sound lovely," Oliva said. "Do you dine with the staff also?"

"I dine with Mrs. Winchester, often at the table in her bedroom but sometimes in the main dining room when she feels well enough," Miss Sivera said. "But please don't feel offended by that. Mrs. Winchester is very self-conscious of her failing teeth, and that's why she dines with just me."

"Oh, I see," Olivia said. That explained why Mrs. Winchester hadn't smiled widely or sipped her tea the day before. "Has she not been feeling well?"

Miss Sivera folded her hands in front of her. "Mrs. Winchester's health has been rather up and down lately. A few years ago, we thought we were going to lose her to multiple health issues. But she regained her health and now has good and bad days. It's up to the staff to ensure she doesn't overwork herself." She smiled again. "I don't know how much you've heard of Mrs. Winchester, but she loves to keep busy. I think working with you on her project will lift her spirits and not be too taxing. At least, I hope so."

Olivia nodded. She was excited to get started with her work for her new employer.

After Miss Sivera left, Olivia went to work hanging her clothing in the wardrobe and placing her personal items on the dressing table and in the lovely bathroom. This room was a luxury for her. At the boarding house, she was always rushing in the tiny bathroom so as not to make others wait. And her room had been a small box compared to this room.

After unpacking, she walked over to the desk and lifted the dust cover off the brand-new Underwood typewriter sitting there. The black paint gleamed under the lights. She opened the center desk drawer finding pencils, erasers, and extra typewriter ribbons. Pulling out a side drawer, she found two reams of white paper and a package of carbon paper. Her heart soared. At the office where she'd worked, they were always running around looking for supplies. Here, she had all the supplies she needed.

After exploring her new room, Olivia wondered if it would be proper for her to take a walk around the house. It was still too early for dinner, but she could wander the backyard and stretch her legs. Miss Sivera had told her to make herself at home.

Slipping on a pair of comfortable shoes, Olivia stepped out into the hallway. Plush rug runners covered the oak floors, and wooden cabinets appeared in spots along the hallway. Curious, Olivia opened a cabinet door and saw they contained linens and towels.

Olivia headed toward the opposite end of the house from which she'd come earlier. She thought there must be a servant's staircase that led down to the kitchen, and back door, below.

She found the staircase that went both up and down from the second floor. Olivia supposed there were servant's rooms on the third floor, like many grand houses. She walked down the stairs and soon heard voices rising from the kitchen.

"Well, now. You must be Mrs. Winchester's new girl," a woman said as Olivia hesitantly entered the busy kitchen. A Japanese man was cutting up vegetables, and the woman who spoke to her had her hands in dough. Olivia was surprised at how big and open the kitchen was, with two long stretches of windows to let in the light and a cross breeze.

"Good afternoon," Olivia greeted the smiling woman. "I'm Miss, er, Mrs. Collins."

"Well, it's nice to meet you, Mrs. Collins," the woman said with an Irish brogue. "I'd shake your hand, but I'm up to my elbows in pastry dough. But don't be shy. Sit on down and join us. I can talk and work at the same time."

The man behind her laughed but kept chopping as Olivia perched on a metal stool by the counter.

"Don't mind him," the woman said with a grin. "I'm Mrs. Murphy, but please feel free to call me Alice. Back there is Mr. Nakmo. He's chief cook and bottle washer." She chuckled.

"It's nice to meet you both," Olivia said. "It smells delicious in here."

Mr. Nakmo glanced up and smiled at her, then hurried back to work.

"He's not one for talking, but he's an excellent chef," Alice said. "I'm more of your basic cook, but I make an apple pie to die for."

Olivia smiled. "I believe you." She immediately liked Alice. She wasn't much taller than Olivia, and her figure was round under her apron. Her dark red hair was pulled up in a bun, and her green eyes shone brightly when she spoke.

"Are you hungry, dear?" Alice asked. "I just took these cinnamon crisps out of the oven. Here, try one." She slid a plate of delicious-looking cookies toward Olivia. Unable to resist, she took one and bit into it.

"Oh, these are wonderful," Olivia crooned.

"Yessire. You and I are going to get along quite well," Alice said, grinning.

After a time, Olivia excused herself and went out the door to the back patio. Another young Japanese man had hurried into the kitchen by then and was vigorously washing the pots and pans in the large trough-like sink. Olivia was surprised at how many people worked at the house, and she hadn't even met them all yet.

Outside, it was cooling down for the day, and it felt wonderful walking around the grounds. The lawns were lush and green, and as she circled the house, she admired the many flower beds and shrubs. In the distance, she saw another beautiful home. Other homes were sprinkled about, but Mrs. Winchester owned enough land around hers to be set apart from them.

Olivia passed an older Chinese gentleman working in one of the rose beds. He turned and smiled at her, then went back to work. She thought of complimenting him on how beautiful the flowers were but decided not to bother him. Maybe he'd be inside for dinner later, and she would meet him and tell him then.

Returning to the porch outside the kitchen, Olivia leaned against the retaining wall and admired the view. She wanted desperately to fit in here and become a permanent part of the staff. So far, everyone had been friendly and inviting. This would be the perfect place for her to work and raise her baby. No one would question her status, and she would no longer have to worry if she'd make enough money to feed herself and a child.

She'd do everything in her power to work hard and make herself useful for Mrs. Winchester.

* * *

Dinner that night with the other staff was like eating with one big happy family. Besides the people Olivia had already met, the housekeeper, Mae Shelby, and a woman who acted as Mrs. Winchester's nurse, Maud Merrill, were at the table along with Misa Hurata, a quiet Japanese woman who worked as Mrs. Winchester's dresser. Mr. Nakmo and the gardener Olivia had seen earlier ate in the kitchen. A young man rushed back and forth, bringing in plates and bowls of food.

Alice had motioned for Olivia to sit beside her, and she introduced her to the group. They all said hello as they looked at Olivia with interest, but soon everyone focused on eating the delicious meal.

"The Ushios have a home on the property and eat their meals there," Alice told her. "They are a pleasant couple. You'll see Tomo in and out of the house. She works as a personal maid for Mrs. Winchester. Rikitaro works with Charlie in the gardens."

"Mrs. Winchester has quite a large staff," Olivia said. Having grown up on a farm where the children and parents worked, she wasn't used to how the wealthy lived. Her head had spun enough when she'd stayed a while with Frank Lieb and his wife and seen the enormous staff they employed.

"Oh, yes. It seems like it, but compared to some of the wealthy people around here, Mrs. Winchester has a small staff. Llanada Villa has even more people than we do, even though Mrs. Winchester hasn't lived there in years."

Olivia's brows rose. "Llanada Villa?"

Alice was slicing a tender piece of chicken as she spoke. "The ranch near San Jose." She lowered her voice. "You know, the big house that all the newspapers write about. The crazy house," she whispered, rolling her eyes. "It's a sight to see, but there's nothing crazy going on there. Mrs. Winchester just loves her projects."

Olivia smiled as she ate the delicious chicken, rice, and vegetable medley. That's why she was here—for one of Mrs. Winchester's projects.

After dinner—and the delicious apple pie dessert Alice had made—Olivia offered to help clean up, but Alice shook her head. "You were hired as a secretary, not for the kitchen. Enjoy the status." She winked. "As time goes by, I'm sure we'll let you get your hands dirty."

With nothing more to do, Olivia said good evening to everyone and walked up the staircase to the second floor. Miss Sivera was just coming down the hallway, carrying a food tray.

"Ah, Mrs. Collins. I'm glad I ran into you. How has your first day been?" the secretary asked.

"Quite nice, thank you," Olivia replied. "The staff here are so kind and welcoming. And I just enjoyed a delicious dinner."

Miss Sivera smiled. "I'm so happy to hear that. We do have a wonderful staff. Mrs. Winchester has asked that you meet her tomorrow morning in the downstairs office at ten."

"Thank you," Olivia said. "I'm looking forward to working with her."

"I know she is eager to work with you, too," Miss Sivera said. "Goodnight."

"Goodnight." Olivia continued to her bedroom. She still couldn't believe she lived in this fine house and would be working for the grand lady herself.

That night as she lay in the comfortable bed, Olivia felt something rolling in her stomach. Her hand went to her belly, and again, she felt a flutter and a roll. It was a strange feeling, but she knew it wasn't her dinner protesting. It was the first movement of her baby. It had been easy to ignore the fact that she was expecting, even after she'd had many mornings of sickness. But now, it was all too real, and she couldn't help but smile.

* * *

Olivia was up and dressed early so she could eat breakfast before her workday began. She ate eggs, bacon, and toast as Alice kept her company, then hurried back to her room. If she remembered correctly, Mrs. Winchester expected her to take shorthand while she spoke, so she searched the other desk drawers in her room for a notepad. There, in the bottom drawer, were several notepads. She lifted one out and selected two pencils to take to the office with her.

Precisely at ten, Olivia walked through the living room downstairs and into the office. Mrs. Winchester looked up at her from behind the desk.

"Good morning, Mrs. Collins," she said, smiling. "Right on time. I like that."

"Good morning, ma'am," Olivia said. She'd heard Miss Sivera call Mrs. Winchester "Madame," but she didn't feel comfortable using that term. Today, Mrs. Winchester wore another dark gown that fell to the floor with long sleeves but without a high neck. Instead, she had a lovely paisley scarf tied around the neck, and she wasn't wearing gloves. Olivia could clearly see how gnarled the older woman's hands were. They looked painful.

"Please, come sit," Mrs. Winchester said, waving a hand toward a wide leather chair in front of the desk. "I was just going through this box of newspaper clippings to remind myself why I decided to begin this new project."

Olivia sat, placing the notepad in her lap, and waited quietly for Mrs. Winchester to continue.

"The newspapers have been quite unflattering about me over these past decades," Mrs. Winchester stated, looking perturbed. "All I've done is mind my own business and work on my projects, but they've insisted on being busybodies and telling falsehoods." She pulled out several clippings and laid them on her desk. "Mrs. S. L. Winchester Continues to Build Her House Because She's Afraid of Death," she read out loud. "Ridiculous. They accuse me of communing with ghosts, of feeling guilty over the men who've died because of the Winchester rifles, and of holding sèances in the house at midnight every night. They've called me a snob and have even gone so far as to say I had a nervous breakdown after the big earthquake and that I am mentally ill. Why, they even killed me off a few years ago, and my poor family in New Haven was grief-stricken until they learned it was a lie." Mrs. Winchester shook her head in disgust. "And we won't even speak about how they maligned my beloved houseboat in Burlingame, saying I was afraid a great flood would come and kill us all. Many wealthy families had houseboats on the water as vacation homes. But I'm the crazy one."

"That's terrible," Olivia said, stunned by how much had been written about this petite little lady. Of course, she'd heard some of it over the years but hadn't really paid much attention.

Mrs. Winchester scooped up the clippings and dropped them in the box. "I've ignored them as much as I could over the years. It's just ridiculous gossip. But now, I think it's time to share my story—my true story—so at least family and friends will remember me as I really was, not as some crazy old lady."

"I think that's an excellent idea," Olivia said, lifting her notepad. "I'm excited to help you with it."

Mrs. Winchester smiled over at Olivia, her eyes sparkling. "I'm happy to hear you say that, dear. It will take some time, as I tire easily these days, but you and I have time to spare."

"I'll work here as long as you wish me to," Olivia said, meaning every word. She liked Mrs. Winchester. She admired her spirit.

Mrs. Winchester sat back in her chair, looking less stressed and more relaxed. "You can begin writing, dear. I may ramble on because starting from the beginning isn't always easy. As we put this together, perhaps you can set it in some semblance of order."

"I'll be happy to," Olivia said. She held her pencil at the ready.

"I was not the first Sarah to be born to my parents," Mrs. Winchester began. "They named their first child Sarah, after my mother, but the poor child died a year after birth from cholera." She sighed. "I can feel their pain, believe me. I was the fourth child born, with two sisters and a brother ahead of me and two younger sisters afterward. That made me much like a middle child. My older sisters bonded, and my younger sisters also did. My brother had no use for any of us, frankly. My parents named me Sarah, but because my father's mother, Sally, had recently died, the family nicknamed me Sallie. All of my family, and the Winchester family as well, have always called me Sallie." She smiled, remembering.

"My father, Leonard Pardee, had been a woodworker by trade but lost his first business due to the financial era. He managed the City Bathing House in New Haven, Connecticut, for ten years before he was able to establish a carpentry business again. I was about eight years old at the time we moved to the Court Street house, and my father's business was right next door. When I was fourteen, we moved again to a more upscale neighborhood near a larger building for my father's business. Thanks to the popularity of Victorian-style homes, my father's business grew. And I have to say, I was in my element there. For the first time in my life, something other than books interested me. I fell in love with woodworking."

CHAPTER FOUR

Sarah – 1853

Sarah entered Leonard Pardee & Company after a short walk over from their house and headed directly to her father's office. "Papa," she said, nearly breathless. "Mama says lunch is ready."

"Oh, Sallie, dear." Leonard smiled up from his desk strewn with paperwork. "It's noon already?" He stood and stretched, then grabbed his suit coat from the back of his chair, slipping it on. "I guess we should go up to the house and eat."

"Oh, I've already eaten," Sarah said. "Would you mind if I walk around and look at the craftsmen's work?" At fourteen, Sarah was a cute, petite young woman, and her father could never deny her anything when she gave him an impish grin.

"Yes, of course," he said, walking with her out of the office. Leonard called out into the workshop. "Lunchtime, gentlemen!"

The shop was filled with workers running various machines, sanding, and painting. Many of the men stopped what they were doing and headed to their worktables to pull out their packed lunches.

"Don't disturb the men," Leonard warned Sarah, as he

always did. "And do not touch any of the equipment. But go ahead and look over their work. I know how much you love it."

"Thank you, Papa," she said, beaming. As her father took his leave, Sarah walked among the many worktables, eyeing the items that had been created that day. Her father's business supplied many of the decorative trims used to create unique exteriors for luxurious Victorian-style homes. They also made decorative moldings and hand-carved oak and walnut doors for the interiors. But Sarah's favorite pieces of all were the many gingerbread trims made to turn a plain house into a fairy-tale house.

"Well, good afternoon, Miss Pardee," one of the craftsmen said cheerfully. He wasn't eating his lunch but instead was sanding a beautifully turned gable ornament with small spindles and scrolling along the edges.

"Good afternoon, Mr. Waverly," Sarah said, smiling. He was an older man with salt and pepper hair and a kind face. Mr. Waverly always took the time to show Sarah his latest pieces. "That's a beautiful gable trim you're working on."

"Thank you," he said. "These spindles were tricky because they're so thin. But I think it turned out nicely. It'll fit perfectly at the point of the rooftop of a lovely Victorian house."

"What color did they request it to be painted?" Sarah asked, intrigued. She loved how the newer homes were being painted in so many cheerful colors like yellow, red, robin egg blue, and even green. Although a white house with black trim could look quite regal too.

Mr. Waverly grinned. "Pink."

This took Sarah by surprise. "You mean like soft baby pink?"

He nodded.

"An interesting choice," she said, not wishing to appear rude. "I wonder what color the house is going to be?"

"I can only imagine," Mr. Waverly said. "It seems people keep trying to outdo each other with their decorations and colors. I believe this person may have gone a bit batty."

Sarah laughed. "Perhaps. Or maybe they are just very creative."

"If you say so, Miss," he said with a chuckle.

Sarah continued walking among the tables, greeting the craftsmen who'd taken time out to eat lunch and perusing their work. She loved being in her father's factory. She enjoyed the camaraderie of the workmen and the smell of freshly cut wood. Sarah didn't even mind the noise of the lathe and the other sounds of men sawing and sanding. If only she'd been born a boy, she could learn to do many of these things herself.

Finally, she tore herself away from the workshop and made her way up to their comfortable home. Her elder sisters, Mary and Nettie, were sitting on a bench outside under a tree, enjoying the beautiful day. They had notepads in their laps and glanced up as Sarah approached.

"Well, here comes our little carpenter," Mary said, giggling at her joke. Nettie giggled along. "I don't know what intrigues you so much about the factory. Look at you! You have sawdust on the hem of your skirt."

Sarah looked down at her hem, unconcerned, and shook the sawdust from her skirt. She raised her eyes to her sisters. They were two years apart in age, but you'd think they'd been born twins. Ever since Sarah could remember, they'd always been attached at the hip and had done everything together, having no time for her.

"What are you two working on?" Sarah asked politely to

change the subject.

"We're planning our wedding, of course," Mary said. "These things don't work themselves out. You really should help us with this instead of going to the factory and being around all the workmen."

"I like the factory," Sarah said. "The men are kind to me, and they make such interesting pieces that are shipped all over the country."

Nettie rolled her eyes. "That's not women's work, Sallie. That's men's work. Father shouldn't let you be around there."

Sarah sighed. Her sisters were always trying to tell her what to do. They were both engaged to be married and had insisted on a double wedding. Sarah didn't know if she'd ever marry, but if she did, she wasn't going to plan a big event and definitely wouldn't plan it with one of her sisters.

"My French tutor will be here soon," Sarah said. "Have fun planning your wedding." She hurried to the house. Sarah really didn't care about her French lessons, although she was doing quite well. She just didn't want to hear again about Mary and Nettie's wedding.

"Sallie, dear," Sarah's mother called as Sarah walked through the kitchen toward the study. "After your French lesson, will you come and help me prepare dinner? The Reverend Hill is joining us tonight, as well as your sisters' beaus. We have so much to do."

Her mother looked tired, and even at her young age, Sarah felt sympathy for her. The elder Sarah was a petite woman like her daughter, with dark hair and brown eyes. She'd given birth to seven children, six of which had lived, and spent her days caring for their big family. Generally, her mother was a strong, positive influence on the family, but young Sarah could tell her mother, at times, was overwhelmed. She tried to help as much as she could.

"Yes, Mother," she said agreeably.

Her mother smiled at her. "Thank you, dear. I wish all the children were as helpful as you."

As Sarah headed to the study, she also wished that. Her older sisters had become so self-involved in their own lives and weddings, and her younger sisters were busy with school and friends. Her only brother Leonard, at age sixteen, begrudgingly worked beside his father at the business, even though Sarah knew he didn't want to. Sarah was too old to go to her sisters' school, so she was tutored at home, making her available to help her mother.

That evening at dinner, the Reverend Benjamin Hill and Nettie's fiancé, Homer Sprague, had a lively conversation over the abolishment of slavery, among other topics. Reverend Hill had been a good friend of the family—as well as being their Reverend at the Baptist Church the family attended—since Sarah's father and mother met at a revival meeting in 1828. Both of her parents had been raised Puritans, but as the Puritan faith began to fade and young people were looking for new paths to follow, Reverend Hill came along and changed the lives of many in New Haven. Sarah's parents were also emphatic about new ideas and the rights of others, and they invited many people with varying views into their home.

Sarah listened quietly to the lively debate, taking it all in. She enjoyed hearing everyone's opinions on the different subjects, except for Homer's. Even though she agreed with much of what he said, he was too emphatic and emotional about his views. The Pardees encouraged the entire family to voice their thoughts, but Homer didn't stop there. He always took everything to the extreme and would ram an opinion down your throat if he could. Sarah couldn't understand what her sister Nettie saw in the outspoken Yale graduate.

"Well, we all know Mr. Spragues views on everything," Reverend Hill said with a chuckle. He turned to Mary's fiancé, William Converse. "What are your thoughts, young man?"

William glanced up from his plate and smiled warmly. "I agree that everyone should be free to live their lives as they choose. Isn't that what we'd all want?"

Sarah dropped her eyes and tried not to giggle. She liked William so much more than Homer. He was a quiet man who didn't force his ideas on anyone. And he found humor in everything.

"There, we all agree that the best life is a free life," Sarah's father said. "Now, if we can get the rest of the country to agree with us, the world would be a better place."

"It will take a war to do that," Homer muttered from his end of the table. "A bloody one at that. Mark my words."

"They are therefore marked," Sarah's mother said, standing. "Sallie, will you help me bring in the pie for dessert?"

Sarah and her sisters stood to clear the table as the men continued discussing events in New Haven. Once in the kitchen, Mary remarked, "That's my William. Always affable and to the point."

Nettie stared at her with piercing dark eyes. "I like that Homer is passionate about his beliefs. There's nothing wrong with that."

"Now, girls," the elder Sarah said soothingly. "Both men are good in their own way. Let's not debate who is better than the other. You have both made fine matches."

Young Sarah bit her tongue as she cut the apple pie and set

the pieces on dessert plates. She was afraid she might make a disparaging remark about Nettie's choice of husband. Around the older sisters, it was best to stay quiet.

After the guests had left and Sarah had helped put the younger children to bed, she sneaked off to her favorite reading spot in her father's study. Taking a book from the shelves, she crawled into the bay window alcove and let the drapes fall around her. From here, she could watch as night settled over their yard and read one of the many books she loved.

As she sat there propped up by thick pillows, Sarah thought about her sisters' husbands-to-be and wondered who she'd eventually marry. She knew her father was proud that he could give his daughters the best of everything now that his factory was successful. The big wedding for the two sisters was seen as a high achievement for the Pardee family. But Sarah wasn't interested in having the wedding of the season or marrying a man of status. She wanted to fall in love like her parents did, with someone who shared her same values and ideas. Maybe she'd marry a young craftsman from the factory who made beautiful decorations for homes. Or maybe she'd meet an architect who'd studied at Yale, and they could collaborate on the house they would build. Sarah sighed. She felt invisible most of the time. Who on earth would even notice her? One thing was for certain—Sarah wanted a partner in life who she would feel equal to, much like her parents. They valued each other's opinions and expressed their feelings freely. Sarah could only hope to find the same kind of partnership.

Sighing again, she opened her book and was soon immersed in the story with all thoughts of marriage pushed aside.

CHAPTER FIVE

1918

Mrs. Winchester stopped speaking, and Olivia held her pencil still. She'd been writing non-stop for almost two hours but had been so immersed in the older lady's childhood that it hadn't seemed like work.

"I think we'll stop there for the day," Mrs. Winchester said. "I may lose my voice if I continue."

"Yes, ma'am," Olivia said.

"If you would type up what you've written today, I'd like to read through it this evening," Mrs. Winchester told her. Slowly, she stood from her desk, using one hand to steady herself.

"I'll have it to you this afternoon," Olivia said, standing also. Her first instinct was to run around the desk and help steady her employer, but then she thought better of it. Mrs. Winchester was a proud woman and might not like being treated like an invalid by her secretary.

"Go along and have your lunch first," Mrs. Winchester said. "There's no rush. I'll read it this evening before bed, so you have all day. Shall we meet again at ten tomorrow morning?"

"Yes, ma'am. That will be fine." Olivia nodded and turned to leave the room. Miss Sivera entered as she left, and the two women smiled and nodded to each other.

Olivia joined the other staff ladies for lunch, sitting again with Alice, who always had something interesting to talk about. Mr. Nakmo and Charlie were once again eating in the kitchen.

"Don't the men like to eat with the ladies?" Olivia asked quietly. She didn't want to offend anyone but was curious why they stayed in the kitchen.

Alice waved her hand through the air. "They find our chatter boring. I think they like to talk about things they believe aren't proper to speak of in front of women. They are very traditional men."

Olivia couldn't blame them. She supposed two men would find a table full of women a little boring.

"How was your first day of work with Mrs. Winchester?" Alice asked, buttering a fluffy biscuit.

"It was interesting," Olivia said. "We're working on her life story and started with her childhood. It seems her parents were very progressive thinkers for the time."

"That doesn't surprise me," Alice said. "Mrs. Winchester has lived an interesting life and made all her own choices since moving to California decades ago. I'm so happy she's putting her life story on paper. So many people say such terrible things about her. It's aggravating."

"Yes," Olivia agreed. "I think it's a good idea too."

After lunch, Olivia took a walk around the yard to enjoy the warm day and stretch her legs. She loved the open yard and gardens and all the space. How lovely to have the kind of money that afforded a lifestyle like this. That was only something she could dream of.

She passed Charlie Yen working on yet another flower garden, and she smiled at him and nodded. He did the same but went back to work again. He seemed like a friendly person. Maybe she'd be able to strike up a conversation with him at some point.

Finally, Olivia went inside through the kitchen. Alice stopped her for a moment and offered her a plate of butter cookies and a glass of iced tea to take upstairs with her. "For your afternoon snack," Alice said with a wink. Olivia thanked her for her thoughtfulness and gratefully carried the food up to her room. From the look in Alice's eyes, Olivia wondered if she already knew she was expecting a baby. It was either that, or she thought Olivia needed fattening up. That thought made Olivia chuckle. She'd be big soon enough.

Despite the day's warmth, Olivia's room was cool and comfortable. She left her door open and unlatched the windows so the breeze would flow through. She'd be typing at her desk, so she didn't mind if someone saw her as they walked down the hallway.

Sitting at the desk, she lifted the dust cover from the type-writer and once again felt elated at seeing the new machine. She would be the first person to type on it. It seemed so unreal after using the beat-up machines at the law office.

Olivia opened the drawer and pulled out a clean sheet of paper, then carefully rolled it in, making sure it was perfectly straight. Glancing down inside the drawer, Olivia noticed the carbon paper again. She thought a moment. When she typed letters for the lawyers, she'd always made a carbon copy so it could be filed away. Perhaps she should do the same with Mrs. Winchester's manuscript. Just in case something happened to the original.

After a moment's thought, she decided she should and rolled the paper out of the typewriter. Placing a sheet of carbon paper between two sheets of paper, she once again rolled the paper through the machine and straightened it. Stopping again, she thought of how to format the sheets. She assumed this was to be read like a manuscript, so she started the first line halfway down the sheet and titled it Chapter One.

Taking a deep breath, Olivia opened her shorthand notebook and studied the writing on the page. Learning shorthand had been difficult at first for Olivia, with all the squiggles and lines that seemed to make no sense. It was like learning a different language. But she'd worked hard and slowly got the grasp of it. After a couple of years of taking dictation and reading her own shorthand, she'd made adjustments to what she'd learned, and it had helped make reading it easier. It was odd to glance at lines and curlicues and actually make words from them. Now, she carefully reread the first page to ensure her writing made sense. It did.

Placing her fingers over the typewriter keys, she began to type.

Olivia had loved learning to type. She could translate her dictation from her eyes to her fingertips and onto paper as if by magic. Sometimes, she found herself daydreaming as she typed, yet she was still able to place the words perfectly on the page. It was as if the typewriter was an extension of her.

Finishing the first page, she looked it over carefully for any mistakes before pulling it from the carriage. Feeling like someone was watching her, Olivia glanced at the door and saw the housekeeper, Mae, standing there with fresh towels in her arms.

"I'm so sorry to disturb you, Mrs. Collins," Mae said,

looking startled at having been caught watching her. "I came
to put clean towels in your bathroom."

"Thank you," Olivia said.

Mae hurried into the bathroom and came out a few seconds
later carrying the used towels. She stopped and watched as
Olivia placed new paper into the typewriter. "Your fingers do
fly over that machine," Mae said, sounding impressed. "I was
mesmerized at how quickly you type."

"Oh, thank you," Olivia said. "I've had much practice. It
isn't difficult to learn."

Mae shook her head. "Oh, I could never move my fingers as
fast as you do. Why, even Henrietta doesn't type that quickly,
and she types letters for Mrs. Winchester all the time."

This made Olivia smile. "That's very kind of you to say.
Please let me know if I can help in any way to make your work
easier around here. I can place my dirty towels in the laundry
for you if that would help, or collect clean ones on my own."

Mae grinned. "No, ma'am. That's my job. You just keep
typing like that for Mrs. Winchester. We all have our jobs to
do here." She nodded and smiled again, then hurried down the
hallway.

Olivia sat still a moment, thinking about both Alice and
Mae. She'd offered to help both women, but they had refused.
It felt strange being waited on. But as they both had said, it was
their job, and they took pride in doing their work well. Mrs.
Winchester had a wonderful staff, that was for certain.

Setting the new sheet of paper straight in the carriage,
Olivia returned to typing Mrs. Winchester's story.

* * *

After Olivia had finished typing that day's work, she closed her bedroom door and laid down on the bed to rest her eyes. Even though she was no longer experiencing morning sickness with her pregnancy, there were days she felt incredibly tired. Plus, sitting on the chair for so long this morning and then again to type had caused pain in her lower back. She hadn't gained much weight yet, and she wondered how she'd manage once she was farther along. Would sitting become unbearable? She hoped not, as she didn't want to disappoint Mrs. Winchester.

With the cool breeze coming through the windows, Olivia fell into a deep sleep. She awoke two hours later—nearly dinner time—and was surprised she'd slept so long. She hurried into her bathroom to fix any stray hairs from her chignon and smoothed out her blouse and skirt. Slipping on her low-heeled pumps, she went to her desk and lifted the sheets of paper she'd clipped together for Mrs. Winchester. Olivia had placed the carbon copies in the bottom drawer of her desk in case they were needed.

She left her room and walked down the hallway toward the back staircase, suddenly realizing she didn't know where to deliver Mrs. Winchester's sheets. She turned, wondering if her bedroom was on this floor, and that was when she saw Miss Sivera coming out a door down the hallway.

"Ah, Mrs. Collins," Miss Sivera said, walking toward her. "I was just going down to pick up Madame's dinner. She asked me to tell you that you can deliver your work to her room before dinner if it's ready."

"Oh, good," Olivia said. "I wasn't sure where to go. Is it the room you just came out of?"

"That's my room," the secretary said. "I'm sorry. I should have pointed out where my and Mrs. Winchester's rooms were.

Her room is down past mine, closest to the staircase. Just knock and announce yourself. She's sitting at the table waiting for dinner."

"Thank you." Olivia turned and walked down the hall. Lifting the timepiece that hung from a chain around her neck, she saw it was nearly six. Olivia was a bit worried that Mrs. Winchester had thought she'd dallied away her time all day. She should have tried to get the papers to her earlier before falling asleep.

Taking a moment to compose herself, Olivia knocked on the elderly woman's door.

"Come in," a small voice said.

Olivia entered, placing a smile on her face. "Good evening, Mrs. Winchester. I have your papers here. I'm sorry I didn't get them to you earlier."

"Oh, Mrs. Collins. I'm happy to see you." Mrs. Winchester set aside the magazine she'd been perusing. "Quite honestly, I rested all afternoon, so you're not late at all. I hope you took some time to rest also."

Olivia felt her face flush. "Frankly, yes, I did. I'm afraid I napped too long, though."

"Dear. You are carrying another human being. You need all the rest you can get. Don't even think twice about it."

Her words touched Olivia's heart. This woman truly was a dear person. "Here is today's work," she said, trying to be professional even though all she wanted to do was hug the older woman.

"Wonderful. I can't wait to read what we did today. If it's possible, perhaps you can bring the papers to me each evening around this time. It will give me time to enjoy reading them."

"I'd be happy to," Olivia said. "It won't be any trouble at all."

"Good. Have a lovely evening, dear. I hope you enjoy your dinner. Mr. Nakmo and Mrs. Murphy always feed us well."

"I'm sure I will enjoy it, thank you," Olivia said. "I hope you have a good evening as well."

Mrs. Winchester gave her a small smile of appreciation, then turned her attention to the papers. Olivia left, opening the door just in time for Miss Sivera to enter with a tray of food.

"Enjoy your evening," Miss Sivera said.

Olivia thanked her and hurried down the hallway to the stairs.

* * *

Just as the day before, Olivia woke up early and had breakfast so she would be to work on time. She was greeted cheerfully at breakfast by the group of women and enjoyed another delicious meal. After only three days, she already felt comfortable with all the other employees who worked there. It was such a relief to feel at home here.

Olivia entered the office just as the clock struck ten but was surprised to see that a gentleman was sitting in the seat across from Mrs. Winchester, and Miss Sivera was there also.

"Oh, I'm so sorry to interrupt," Olivia exclaimed, embarrassed she'd walked in on the group. She turned to leave, but Miss Sivera called out to her.

"Mrs. Collins. Please don't leave. We were just finishing up."

Heart pounding, Olivia turned around again and faced the group. The gentleman stood politely, making her feel even more self-conscious. She shouldn't have rushed in the way she had. Of course, a woman as significant as Mrs. Winchester would have other business to attend to besides her projects.

Miss Sivera approached Olivia. "We were expecting you," she said, placing her arm through Olivia's and leading her to the desk. "Mrs. Winchester needs another witness to her signature on these documents, and we were hoping you'd be willing to do so."

"Oh, yes. I'd be happy to," Olivia said, stunned they'd ask her to do such an important task.

"Wonderful," the gentleman said.

"Mrs. Collins," Mrs. Winchester spoke up. "This is Daniel Stanley, a very important assistant to Frank Lieb. We had a few matters that needed settling. Mr. Stanley, this is my lovely new secretary, Mrs. Collins."

Mr. Stanley offered his hand to Olivia. "It's very nice to meet you, Mrs. Collins. Mrs. Winchester speaks very highly of your work."

Olivia's eyes rose to the warmest pair of brown eyes she'd ever seen. Mr. Stanley was quite a bit taller than her and had a young face framed in wavy chestnut hair. When he shook her hand, it was warm and smooth. Were his eyes actually twinkling? She suddenly felt her face flush and immediately hoped he hadn't noticed. "It's very nice to meet you, too, Mr. Stanley."

"So, shall we sign some papers?" Mrs. Winchester said.

Reluctantly, Olivia released Mr. Stanley's hand, but not before he smiled widely at her, showing perfectly straight teeth.

"Yes, I suppose I need to get back to the office at some point today," he said teasingly. "Although I prefer being here with you kind ladies."

"Flattery will get you nowhere," Mrs. Winchester said but smiled as she did. "And you can stay as long as you want. You know you're always welcome."

Mr. Stanley smiled back at her, then got down to business. Both Miss Sivera and Olivia signed underneath Mrs. Winchester's signature on all the pages. Olivia wasn't sure what the paperwork was for—they looked to be financial papers—but she was only there to witness, so it didn't matter. Once everything was signed, Mr. Stanley placed the paperwork carefully into folders and slid them into his briefcase.

"It's always a pleasure to come here and see you, Mrs. Winchester. I'm happy we were able to finish all this for you," he said, standing to shake her hand.

"Thank you for coming all this way, Daniel," the elderly woman said. "I'm sure Mr. Lieb appreciates not having to come out here."

"I don't mind the trip at all," he said. Turning to Olivia, he smiled again. "It was nice meeting you. I'm sure I'll see you again soon."

Olivia nodded, not trusting herself to speak. She'd never been tongue-tied in front of a man before, but he made her feel completely off balance.

Miss Sivera escorted him from the room, and in a moment, he was gone.

"Mr. Stanley is such a fine young man," Mrs. Winchester said. "And Mr. Lieb tells me he's his greatest asset at the firm."

Olivia turned back toward the desk, suddenly aware she'd been watching the gentleman leave. "Oh, yes. He seems like a nice gentleman."

"Had you never been introduced before?" Mrs. Winchester asked. "I thought you may have met him when you lived with the Liebs."

"No. We've never met," she said. Collecting her wits, Olivia walked over to the chair Mr. Stanley had just vacated and sat.

"Well, now," Mrs. Winchester said, all business. "Shall we get to work?"

Olivia nodded, opened her notepad, and held her pencil ready. Despite his leaving, she could still feel the warmth of Daniel Stanley's brown eyes upon her.

CHAPTER SIX

1859

Sarah stood quietly beside her brother, Leonard, and her two younger sisters, Belle and Estelle, as the group of people mingled on the lawn of the First Baptist Church. There had been a gathering that Wednesday evening of the church members, more as a social event than a religious one. Belle, at age sixteen, had insisted they go so she could see her friends. And, of course, if Belle went, Estelle, now fourteen, did also.

Sarah, however, always felt uncomfortable at these gatherings. She could hold her own with a small group of people and speak freely, but with so many surrounding her, she became mute. Unlike gregarious Belle, who said and did whatever came into her head and regretted nothing. In many ways, Belle was the antithesis of Sarah, yet Sarah also admired her ability to stand out in a crowd and not care.

"Well, as I live and breathe," Leonard said, a slow smile appearing on his face. "It's been a while since I've seen you."

Sarah turned and saw a young man approaching them. He was at least a foot taller than her and quite lean, with neatly combed auburn hair and a pale complexion. His long, mutton-chop whiskers seemed out of place on his kind-looking face. And when his eyes met hers, she was surprised at what a lovely shade of blue they were. When he smiled, his face lit up, and Sarah couldn't help but smile too.

The man shook Leonard's hand. "It's been a few years, I'd say. How are you faring?"

"I'm doing well," Leonard said. "I've nothing to complain about. I heard you were back from your European tour and working at your father's shirt factory."

"That I am, and I'm happy to be home," the gentleman said. He turned to Sarah, and recognition shone in his eyes. "Why, this can't possibly be young Sallie. Isn't she still a child?" He beamed at her.

Sarah was taken aback that this gentleman knew her. Why could she not place him?

"Sallie," Leonard said. "You remember our old playmate from Court Street, William Winchester."

"Of course," Sarah said, relieved to finally recognize William. She had only been eleven when they'd lived near the Winchesters and hadn't actually been included when Leonard and William palled around together. They'd seemed so much older than her back then, although it was only by two years. But now, when she looked up at William, she remembered he'd always been kind to her when their paths crossed.

"I can't believe you've grown up," William said. "And your younger sisters? They must be young women now, too."

"Yes," Sarah said, glancing around to see where Belle and Estelle were. "They're attending the new secondary school close by."

"How wonderful," William said, smiling at her.

The way William looked at her, Sarah felt she was the only person there. It was both unnerving and exhilarating.

"Perhaps we can get together and have a good talk," Leonard said, unwittingly breaking the connection between Sarah and William.

William turned his gaze back to Leonard. "Yes. I'd like that."

"Sallie. Let's gather the girls, and I'll take you home. Mother is probably wondering where you are."

Sarah reluctantly nodded. She would have liked to speak more with William, although she wasn't even sure what they'd talk about. "It was nice seeing you again, Mr. Winchester," she said politely, using his surname. After all, he was now helping his father run their company and was no longer a childhood playmate.

William reached for her gloved hand. "The pleasure was all mine," he said warmly.

Sarah felt her cheeks flush and lowered her head so he wouldn't see how he'd affected her. Never had she felt this way about a young man's attentions. It was a bewildering new experience for her.

Leonard drove them home in his carriage as Belle complained about leaving early, and Estelle pouted on Belle's behalf. He deposited them safely at home and drove on to his own rented rooms where he now lived. Her brother, for reasons Sarah didn't understand, had no desire to work at or take over his father's business and instead worked in the carriage industry, creating embellishments for beautiful new carriages. Sarah, on the other hand, would have loved to have been given the opportunity to work alongside her father and the other craftsmen. But because she was a young woman, it was not an opportunity she was allowed to have.

"How was the get-together at church this evening?" Sarah's mother asked as the young women entered the house. Now that both Mary and Nettie were married and lived in their own homes, and Leonard had moved out, all that was left was Sarah, her parents, and her two younger sisters. Mary and her husband still lived in New Haven, with William working as the bookkeeper for the Pardee Woodworking Factory. They hadn't been blessed with children yet, but everyone hoped they would be soon. Nettie and Homer lived close by, too, and had two young children, a boy and a girl. Both her mother and Sarah had been honored when the little girl was also named Sarah. But being the eldest daughter in the household now meant that Sarah helped her mother even more than before.

"It was very nice," Sarah answered her mother. She wanted to mention seeing William Winchester after all these years, but Belle interrupted.

"Except Leonard made us leave early," she complained. "I was speaking with the reverend's wife about the treatment of children in factories, and we were rudely pulled away."

The elder Sarah gave Sallie a knowing look and then replied to Belle. "I'm sure you were having a fascinating conversation. But it was generous of Leonard to take you there and bring you home again, so you shouldn't complain."

Sarah knew her sister would complain anyway. She loved being the center of attention.

Belle sighed and flounced upstairs, and Estelle followed her.

"I've just made some tea. Shall we have it in the study, Sallie?" Sarah's mother asked.

"Yes. I'd like that. Is Papa home?"

"He is. I think he went to rest in the study with a book."

Sarah lifted the tea tray for her mother and followed her to her father's study. Even though it was his office, Leonard had never minded the children and his wife using it as a place to read or relax. He looked up and smiled at his daughter when they entered.

"The tea smells wonderful," he said, sitting up slowly and moving his legs from the ottoman to the floor.

Sarah watched him struggle to get comfortable. All his years of working were catching up to him, and at times, his back, legs, and arms hurt him terribly. But her father rarely complained. A little liniment on the affected areas and a bit of heat from a hot water bottle, and he'd say he was good as new.

Sarah poured her father a cup of tea and placed the amount of sugar he enjoyed in it before handing him the cup. She did the same for her mother. The women settled on the settee across from Leonard.

"Was it a good meeting at church tonight?" Leonard asked after taking a sip of his tea.

"It was a nice gathering," Sarah answered. "Many of the younger congregation were there."

He grinned. "I suppose that was the point. I think they are playing at matchmaking with these types of gatherings."

Sarah was startled. She hadn't thought that was the point of bringing the younger church members together. But now that she pondered it, she could see that might be true.

"Well, it doesn't hurt to let the younger generation have a chance to mingle and discuss the topics of the day," Sarah's mother said. "We used to do that, remember, dear?" She smiled at her husband.

"A very long time ago," he said with a chuckle.

"An old friend of ours was there tonight." Sarah tried to sound casual about bringing it up. "William Winchester. He and Leonard spoke for a short time. He's working at his father's clothing business now that he's back in town."

"Oh, yes. William. I remember when the Winchester children were young, and you were all playing together. Such nice children," Sarah's mother said. "How is he faring?"

"He seems to be faring quite well," Sarah said, then added quickly, "From what I heard him tell Leonard."

"Hmm. I see." Her mother sipped her tea and smiled. "He hasn't married yet, has he?"

"Not that I'm aware of," Sarah said, suddenly unsure. She'd assumed he was as unencumbered as Leonard was.

"Interesting," her mother said. "We see the Winchesters in church from time to time. Perhaps we'll see William there on Sunday."

Sarah dipped her head and sipped her tea, but she was smiling. She hoped she saw William at church on Sunday as well.

* * *

Unfortunately, Sarah did not see William Winchester at church the next week, and her mind returned to her other responsibilities. For the past few years, their family had been prosperous enough to have a hired maid to help the elder Sarah with the cooking and cleaning. Ellen Connor was a nice young Irish woman who was friendly and worked hard. Sarah was thankful her mother had help, and this left time for Sarah to work on other projects.

Sarah had always been quite efficient at sewing, and recently, her father had gifted her a beautiful Singer sewing machine. Sarah went right to work learning how to use it and soon became quite proficient in creating clothing for herself and the girls. She spent many days in her room, sewing dresses, blouses, and skirts for Belle, Estelle, her mother, and even Nettie's young children. She loved matching fabrics and creating the latest styles. It was an outlet for her creativity.

She also kept busy, along with Ellen, making delicious treats for the upcoming carnival at her sisters' school.

By the time Sunday rolled around two weeks later, and her mother asked her to set two more places at the table, Sarah's mind was on several different things. Leonard was coming for dinner, and she assumed the Reverend Hill might attend also. Flushed from the late afternoon heat and helping her mother and Ellen in the kitchen, Sarah was surprised when her mother suggested she dress for dinner.

"Dress for dinner?" Sarah asked, looking down at herself. She was dressed properly.

"And you might wish to tidy up your hair," her mother said off-handedly.

Ellen giggled when she saw the confused look on Sarah's young face. After her mother left the room, Ellen whispered, "It seems a young man is coming with Leonard for Sunday dinner."

Sarah's heart beat wildly. Was her brother bringing William home for dinner? She quickly flew up the back staircase and hurried to her room. Staring into her looking glass, she saw that she did look a mess.

Sarah washed her face with cool water from the pitcher at her washstand and combed and pined up the loose strands that had fallen from her bun. Her naturally curly hair gave her trouble in the heat, but she managed to tame the small curls around her forehead and make them look presentable. Opening her armoire, she decided to change into a fresh white blouse with billowy sleeves but kept on her full skirt and low-heeled slippers.

Staring into the dressing table mirror, Sarah decided this was the best she could do. She pinched her cheeks for color, then headed downstairs, holding back her excitement.

Minutes later, Leonard walked into the house with William Winchester in tow. Sarah's brother's booming voice announced their arrival. As she watched from down the hallway, Sarah could tell that the subdued William was uncomfortable with all the ruckus Leonard was making.

"I've brought home the grand William Winchester," Leonard yelled to anyone within earshot.

From the study, the elder Leonard called out to the men to join him, and they disappeared into the room.

When dinner was served, Sarah's mother suggested Sallie sit across from William at the table. Leonard sat next to William, and Belle and Estelle sat on either side of Sallie. Ellen served dinner so the elder Sarah could sit and enjoy her meal.

"We're so happy you could join us, William," Sarah's mother said, passing him the plate of roast beef first. "Tell me, how are your parents faring?"

"They are fine, thank you," William said in his gentle voice. "My mother sends her greetings to you and your family."

"That's very kind of her," Sarah's mother said. "I hear your family will be celebrating a wedding soon."

"Oh, yes," William said, grinning. "My sister Annie and my mother are very excited about the upcoming nuptials." He glanced across the table at Sarah as he spoke, a glint of mischief in his eyes. "In fact, that is all anyone talks about in the house these days."

Sarah smiled back at him. "It was that way when my two older sisters were planning their wedding as well," she said.

Sarah's mother laughed. "It was quite intense. But I'm pleased for your sister. I'm sure she will be very happy."

William nodded. "She seems to be."

"Your father's new factory is impressive," Leonard Sr. said, changing the subject. By now, all the dishes had been passed around, and everyone was enjoying the delicious meal.

"He's very proud of it," William said, slicing some roast beef and dipping it in the gravy he'd put on the side. "We have over 2,000 workers now and 500 sewing machines. It's incredible the scale of output compared to when my father started his business."

Sarah's father chuckled. "I remember the days when Oliver carried a bolt of white fabric to work and cut out the shirts himself. It pleases me to no end that he's accomplished so much over these past years."

"As I hear you have too, sir," William said. "Your factory and business have grown since the early days."

Leonard nodded. "It has, and we feel blessed to have done so well."

The talk turned to other matters, and William remained quiet, listening to the chatter among the family. Occasionally, he'd glance up and meet Sarah's gaze, smile, and then return to his meal. He had such a kind, gentle way about him and was obviously well-educated and well-mannered. But when he smiled at Sarah, she felt herself grow warm inside, which was a pleasant yet unexpected feeling.

As dinner was winding down, Belle spoke up, no longer content with being quiet. "Where do you stand on the abolition of slavery, Mr. Winchester?" she blurted out.

Sarah sucked in her breath, embarrassed her sister would talk so bluntly to someone she didn't know well. They spoke this freely with Reverend Hill and other guests who came to dinner, but Sarah didn't think it was appropriate to bring it up now.

William looked at Belle and considered her question. It hadn't shocked him—he seemed to take it all in stride. "Well, Miss Isabelle, that's a good question. Of course, I do believe that all people should be free to live their lives as they choose."

Sarah relaxed, happy that Belle's question hadn't ruined a perfect evening.

Belle sat back in her chair, looking a little defeated. If she'd wanted to provoke William, she hadn't been able to do so.

"Good answer," Leonard Sr. said, chuckling. "We encourage our children to speak their minds in this house, and we always appreciate when guests do also."

William nodded and smiled, but Sarah noticed he was looking at her.

After dinner, the younger girls were sent up to their rooms for the evening, and the adults went into the study for tea and cakes. Sarah sat beside her mother on the settee and watched as William wandered the room, perusing the many books on the shelves. She liked that he seemed interested in books because she loved books too.

"You have a wonderful collection of books," William said as he returned to the group and sat in a chair near the younger Leonard. He turned to Sarah. "Have you read them all yet?"

Sarah sat up a bit straighter when she realized he'd spoken to her. "I've read a great many of them," she said proudly.

"If I remember correctly, you always had a book with you," William said.

"Yes, she always had her nose in a book," her brother said. "While everyone else was running around, playing, Sallie sat still as a statue under a tree or on a bench and read."

"You could have tried to do a bit more reading yourself," Sarah's mother said, smiling warmly at her only son. "It wouldn't have hurt you."

"I'm just as guilty of hiding out with a book whenever I can," William said, looking over at Sarah. "You can never read enough."

Sarah smiled. She liked that he was trying to make her feel less like a loner because she loved to read.

After dessert, William thanked the elder Pardees for inviting him to dinner and for being so kind. "I hope we see more of each other since we all live so close," William said. "And I'd love to tour your factory if you have the time," he said to Leonard Sr. "I find building and woodworking fascinating."

Sarah's ears perked up at his. Could he really be as interested in building as she was, or was he just being polite?

"Anytime, young man," Leonard said proudly. "Although I should let Sallie give you the tour. She's as much an expert about my factory as I am."

William looked over at Sarah. "That would be wonderful."

"Sallie, dear. Why don't you show William out?" her mother said.

After another round of goodbyes, Sarah walked ahead of William to the front door.

"Thank you again for the lovely meal," William said. "Your family is so warm and inviting."

"Well, except for Belle, I'm afraid. I'm sorry she cornered you like that," Sarah said, feeling unnerved standing so close to William.

He smiled. "She has a mind of her own. How lucky for her. We should all be so willing to speak up."

Sarah couldn't help but laugh. "Imagine if we all said what we thought. What a world that would be."

"Yes. It would be an interesting world then." He walked out the door and onto the porch, then turned. "I was serious about visiting your father's factory. If you have time this week, I'd appreciate a tour."

"Oh, why, yes. Any time," Sarah said, taken off guard.

"Tuesday at one?" he asked, looking hopeful.

"Of course." Sarah's heart was pounding again. It seemed to do that a lot around William. "I will see you then."

William bid her a good evening and walked with long strides down the street toward the Winchester home on Court Street.

As Sarah closed the door, she bumped into her brother, who'd come up behind her. "Goodness, Leo. Why are you so close? You startled me."

Leonard chuckled. "So, did he ask you?"

Sarah was puzzled. "Ask me what?"

"I don't know," Leonard said. "To go walking? Or for a carriage ride. Whatever men ask a young lady to do in order to get to know them better."

"He asked me to give him a tour of Father's factory on Tuesday," Sarah said. "He's interested in seeing it."

Leonard grinned. "Yes. That's what he's interested in. He's a good man, though. You could do a lot worse."

"What does that mean?" Sarah crossed her arms. Had the entire evening been a set-up?

"Nothing at all," Leonard said. "But I saw the interest in his eyes at the church social and again at dinner. Sometimes, a little push is all some people need." He kissed his sister on the cheek and headed out the door. "Goodnight, Sallie."

Sarah watched him leave and then closed the door. She wasn't sure how she felt about the fact that tonight may have been set up to put her and William together. But in the end, that was what she'd wanted. A smile crept up on her lips. She was seeing him on Tuesday, and that made her very happy.

CHAPTER SEVEN

Today

Morgan arrived at work the next morning feeling tired but exhilarated. She'd stayed up late reading the first few chapters of her Grandmother Olivia's manuscript and had been enthralled. There it was in black and white—Sarah Winchester's story. It was the untold story that no one else had written. Morgan couldn't wait to get home that night and continue reading it.

Her first thought was to rush into the editorial director's office and tell her about her amazing manuscript find. But as she made her way to work that morning, the urgency had waned. It would be best if Morgan read the entire book and then did some research to make sure it was authentic. If she tossed it on her boss's desk too early, it might not turn out well.

Morgan walked through their esthetically modern office and sat at her desk in the corner cubicle. She had floor-to-ceiling windows on two sides, which she liked, but the only view was of the other downtown buildings and the street. Still, it was nice to have sunlight around her to make the long, busy days seem less dreary.

She went right to work marking up her latest acquisition, noting parts of the manuscript that she wanted the editor to look closely at. She'd talked extensively with the author about changing a character and pulling another one out, and she wanted to relay those changes to the editor. Morgan believed the story would be more intense and focused with these changes, but the author was on the fence. Since it was a psychological thriller—intense and focused was key.

"So, how was your weekend?" Jonathan Waters asked, poking his head over the divider between their cubicles. He'd been working next to Morgan for four years, and although they weren't best friends, they occasionally went out for lunch and sometimes dinner after work.

"Busy," she said, glancing up. His brown hair was wind-swept from riding his bike to work, and his brown tortoiseshell glasses were a little crooked, which made her smile. He was a tall, lean, good-looking guy with thick brown hair and dark brown eyes. But he seemed unaware of how cute he was.

"What are you smiling about?" he asked.

"Your glasses are crooked. Must have been a good bike ride."

"Oh." He straightened his glasses and laughed. "Yeah. I was almost hit by a limousine, but otherwise, it wasn't a bad ride.

"A limo? Just think. You could have sued some rich person and then given this all up." Morgan stretched out her arms.

"And let you take all my acquisitions? No way." He grinned, then turned around to sit at his desk.

At ten o'clock, Amanda Janowitz's assistant, Gabriela, came around to the cubicles announcing a surprise meeting. "She wants to know what projects you're working on right now," she said to each editor as she passed their cubicles. Gabbie was young, petite, and highly energetic, plus very loyal to Amanda. Yet she was also helpful to the editors, giving them a heads-up whenever she could. Morgan liked Gabbie, but she was always a little too perky in the morning.

Morgan gathered her file on her latest manuscript and, at the last minute, grabbed the file on the new author she was really excited about taking on. She stood in front of Jonathan's cubicle and waited as he did the same.

"Love the surprise meetings," he said, rolling his eyes.

Morgan smiled. Jonathan was a good foot taller than her, and it didn't help that she usually wore sneakers to work instead of heels. They walked together toward the conference room along with the other five editors.

"Okay, ladies and gentlemen. Gather around, sit down," Amanda said from her seat at the head of the large glass conference table. "We have coffee and snacks if you're hungry. But let's get to work fast. I have a phone meeting with the main publishing company in less than an hour, and I need to impress them." She raised her dark eyes rimmed in black glasses to everyone who'd sat down. "Now. Impress me!"

Everyone stopped and stared at each other. Some had already grabbed a coffee, and Brandon, the crime/detective/murder editor, was reaching for a donut. No one wanted to go first.

Amanda sighed. "Jonathan. What are you working on right now?"

Jonathan opened the file in front of him. "I have an interesting author who writes horror but more in the style of Stephen King. The story is creepy and chilling, but his writing style keeps you involved like a true novel."

Amanda snapped her fingers impatiently. "Name? Title?" She had her pen poised over a notepad to take notes.

"Jeffrey Shimms. The Longing."

Amanda's eyes darted up. "The Longing? That sounds like a romance novel."

Jonathan chuckled, but Amanda didn't join in. "We can always change the title. It's about a man who has checked out of life after the murder of his wife, and he's living in a cottage near a deserted lighthouse out on Long Island. But he keeps seeing his wife everywhere and thinks he's going crazy. The question is: is he going crazy, or is someone trying to make him feel like he is? It's an excellent story."

"Hmm. Okay. Who's next?" Amanda said, scanning the group.

Lila tentatively raised her hand. She was the newest team member with only a year under her belt and, at thirty-two, looked more like a young woman of twenty. Morgan knew the poor girl was terrified of Amanda. "I have the cutest cozy mystery series lined up by a new author. It's titled Something to Die For by Andrea Cranst. She's already written the first three books, and they involve a small-town coffee shop, the niece of a nosy older lady, and a silly tuxedo cat."

Morgan cringed when she saw Amanda roll her eyes. What kind of boss rolled her eyes at someone?

"What cozy mystery doesn't involve a coffee shop, nosy lady, and cat? And who said we're buying all three books when we don't even know how the first one will sell?" Amanda asked Lila.

Lila opened her mouth to speak, then closed it again. She flushed, looking embarrassed. "Of course, I'll run it by you and the team first, but it's really good," Lila said softly.

"Next!" Amanda insisted.

Morgan spoke up because it looked like the others were terrified to do so. "I'm working on preparing Andrew Marcus's suspense book, Voices in the Hallway, for developmental editing," she said quickly. Amanda had already approved the purchase, so she was safe. "And I'm reading an excellent suspense novel by a new voice, Luella Perkins. It's titled Where Are The Children? and is fast-moving and intense."

Amanda sat a moment, considering. "Where did you find this Luella Perkins?"

"She has several independently published titles, and her last book hit the top one hundred on Amazon," Morgan said. "Over 10,000 readers follow her on Facebook, and her Instagram following is large, too. I contacted her to see what she was writing next, and she had just finished this manuscript. She's excellent."

"Hmm." Amanda wrote something on her notepad. "You know I hate it when we approach authors, but if she's that good, then we can consider it." She looked over at Brandon, the Crime/Detective editor. "What do you have?"

The rest of the meeting went the same way, with Amanda either ignoring titles she thought weren't worth their time or taking a few notes. They were dismissed abruptly, and everyone filed out of the room collectively heaving a heavy sigh.

Morgan walked across the room to Lila's cubicle and stood in the open doorway. "Don't let her get to you. If you believe in a project, then push for it. Amanda actually respects you more if you fight with her."

Lila looked up, her blue eyes watery. "Thanks. I keep trying, but she's really hard. I think she enjoys making fun of the books I bring her."

"She's not a fan of cozy mysteries. It's not your fault. She'd rather only do suspense/thriller books because they're hot. But we need variety for all readers. And readers love cozy mysteries. Just like they love book club fiction, women's fiction, and family drama. Just keep fighting. You know a good book and author when you see it."

Lila nodded, but she still looked like she could burst into tears at any moment. Morgan headed back to her desk and dropped the file on it with a large thump.

Patrick walked by her cubical. He was the oldest member of the team, other than Amanda, and acquired books in the memoirs and biography genres. He'd come from a larger publisher where he'd been laid off, and he had a chip on his shoulder. "She's a tough cookie, that one," he said. "I don't know how she keeps employees."

"Why do you stay?" Jonathan asked, popping his head over the divider.

"Because I need to work," Patrick said brusquely. "Just like we all need to. But it wouldn't hurt Amanda to be a little nicer."

"She gets a lot of pressure from the top," Morgan said. She didn't want to defend Amanda, but she knew it was true. "I think she feels like her job is on the line every second of the day. And being a woman, she has to be tough."

"Working in publishing used to be fun," Patrick said. "It's cutthroat now. We don't build authors' careers like we used to. We grab the ones already near the top, use them up, and then toss them aside." He shook his head and walked back to his own cubicle.

"Is Lila okay?" Jonathan asked.

"She'll either have to get tougher or find a new job," Morgan said, sitting down. "There's no crying in publishing."

Jonathan snorted. "That's plagiarism."

She laughed. "I'll steal where I have to."

Later that day, Morgan asked Jonathan to join her for a sandwich down the block for lunch. They ordered and found a cramped little table in the corner by the window.

"I want to run something by you," Morgan said. "But you can't tell anyone about this, okay?"

He'd been about to take a bite of his sandwich but stopped. "You're leaving Generation Publishing, aren't you? Shoot. I just got used to sitting near you, and now I'll probably get stuck with Lofty Lucinda or Pouty Patrick next to me."

Morgan laughed. "No. I'm not leaving for another job."

"Whew! That's a relief. Then what secret are you going to tell me?"

"You know who Sarah Winchester is, right?" Morgan asked.

He frowned. "You mean like the Winchester Mansion? The crazy lady who built the house for ghosts?"

Morgan bristled at his description. After having read the first few chapters, she already felt protective of Sarah. "She wasn't crazy. But yes, the woman who built the mansion. What would you think if I said I have a manuscript written decades ago that is the official autobiography of Sarah Winchester?"

His thick brows rose above his glasses. "That's interesting. How do you know Sarah Winchester wrote it?"

Morgan took a breath. "Actually, she dictated it to my Great-Great-Grandmother Olivia. Then Olivia typed it up in a format that reads like an autobiography."

"Really? Your relative worked for Sarah Winchester? When was this?" Jonathan asked, looking interested.

"She worked there sometime around 1918. I haven't read the entire manuscript, and it doesn't include my grandmother's story, so I'm not sure how long she lived with her. They lived and worked at Sarah's Atherton estate then. That's about all I know."

"Winchester lived in Atherton?" Jonathan looked impressed. "That's where all the rich Silicon Valley people live."

"I know. Apparently, Sarah Winchester knew good property when she saw it. So, what do you think? I haven't read the entire manuscript yet, and I was bursting to bring it to Amanda. But now I wonder if that would be a good idea. I plan on reading it first and doing some research, but do you think our publishing company would be interested?"

"Well, first you'd have to make sure you have the right to publish it," Jonathan said. "And frankly, if you're able to, I'd take it to the biggest publisher in the country. Forget Amanda."

Morgan sat back in the hard chair. "I did think about that. It would be hard to work at Generation Publishing, though, if I sell a manuscript to another publisher."

He nodded. "But if that manuscript is as valuable as we both think, you probably wouldn't have to work as an editor anymore." He grinned.

She laughed. "We both know there are very few one-hit wonders in publishing."

Jonathan considered her seriously. "But you do want to write at some point, right? This would be your chance to start a writing career."

Morgan shrugged noncommittally. "I would like to write, but I haven't yet, so who knows if I even have the ability to be a writer."

"Don't sell yourself short, Morgan," Jonathan said. "You know a good book when you see it. The books you choose for the imprint do well. And you have great insight into what changes to make to a book so it will sell. It's not too far of a leap from there to writer."

"Thanks," she said, embarrassed that the conversation had turned to her. "But what do you think about this manuscript?"

"I think it would definitely be a hot commodity once you're able to prove Sarah wrote it and if you have the right to sell it. It's worth looking into. But," he looked into her eyes. "Don't say anything to Amanda until you're sure you want her to publish it. This just might be big."

As Morgan stared back into Jonathan's eyes, she realized she'd never noticed how expressive they were. And she also never realized just how much she valued his advice. Jonathan had always been the quirky guy who worked beside her, rode his bike to work, and wore button-down shirts and jeans to work every day. He read horror, which could seem a bit creepy. But he wasn't that at all. He was an intelligent, mindful person. And he was cute, too.

"Something wrong with my face?" he asked after a few seconds. He grabbed his napkin and wiped his mouth.

"Oh, no," Morgan said, startling herself out of her thoughts. "I was just considering what you said. I think you're right. Thanks."

He smiled. "Any time."

That evening, Morgan curled up in bed to read more of Olivia's manuscript on Sarah Winchester. It was odd thinking that her relative had worked on this and done a nice job writing it. Maybe writing was a family trait. Maybe, if she set her mind to it, Morgan could write her own novel someday. Pushing that thought away, she began to read.

CHAPTER EIGHT

1862

Sarah Lockwood Pardee was getting married. Even she had to pinch herself to believe it. What had started as an innocent tour of her father's factory in 1859 turned into a sweet court-ship between Sarah and William Winchester.

The day of the tour, William had shown great interest in her father's large factory. Sarah could tell he wasn't just being polite—William enjoyed looking over the machinery, the beautiful wood pieces being created, and speaking with the craftsmen about their work. He showed great interest in the pieces Sarah showed him and admitted that he, too, loved the idea of designing and building a home of his own. Sarah was excited to know they shared a bond with their love of wood-working and houses.

From that point on, they spent time together at church socials, taking walks in the neighborhood with Belle or Estelle reluctantly tagging along as a chaperone, or attending dinner invitations from other families in their neighborhood. Sarah's favorite memory of their courtship was the first dinner she was invited to at the Winchester home. Even though she knew Oliver and Jane Winchester through their church, she didn't know them personally. She had thought they might be a formal family in complete contrast to her family's way of life.

When she'd walked through the door, she was instantly hit by how warm and inviting everyone was. William's mother, Jane, greeted her affectionately, as did his sister Annie and a slew of cousins who lived under the roof with them. Then there was Oliver, William's father. Sarah had always thought of him as a rather intense, stern man by the way he carried himself. But he was actually a kind and generous man. Oliver was the complete opposite of William—energetic, robust, and outgoing. He was shorter than his son but made up for it with his big personality. While William was contemplative and spoke quietly, Oliver was open, boisterous, and spoke his mind easily. Sarah liked him immediately and was accepted into the fold as a daughter from the beginning.

As Sarah and William's relationship grew closer, Abraham Lincoln became president, and the southern states began to secede. War was imminent and unfortunately came to pass. Both the Pardee and Winchester families agreed on Lincoln's politics and the stance of the newly formed Republican Party. They both also believed in abolishing slavery. This common ground made it easy for Sarah to fit right into her new family.

Despite the outbreak of the war, William and Sarah married on a warm September day in 1862 at the Baptist Church in New Haven in front of a small gathering. Reverend Benjamin Hill presided over the ceremony, as he had for Sarah's parents and her older sisters. Sarah was the happiest she'd ever been. She knew she and William would have a long, companionable life together. Both were well-educated and easy-tempered and enjoyed many of the same interests. But most of all, William respected Sarah's interests as being just as important as his own. He believed she could do anything she set her mind to, and it was this belief that made her love him dearly.

By the time they'd married, Sarah's brother Leonard had already enlisted in the war and fought at the first battle of Bull Run in Virginia. He served his required three months and returned home, back to his job at the carriage business. He rarely spoke of his time in the war, but his refusal to re-enlist spoke volumes.

As they married, Sarah's brother-in-law Homer Sprague was serving in the war, where he kept a journal with the hope of publishing a book about his experiences. Like everything else in Homer's life, he was outspoken and critical about those who didn't serve and those who only enlisted for the mandatory time.

Sarah, however, was scared she might lose William to the war like so many other young wives had. But after multiple discussions between William and his father, it was decided he wouldn't enlist. William was the only son in the family, and his health wasn't as robust as it could have been. Sarah knew William carried regret for not fighting for what he believed in, but she was greatly relieved.

After their marriage, Sarah and William made their home with the elder Winchesters and their youngest daughter, Jennie, in the Court Street house, along with several other relatives. By the time they'd moved in, William's sister Annie had been married for three years, and they had two sons, Oliver, age two, and Charles, age one. Annie often lived at the house with her children, too, making the house quite crowded. The plan was to build a much larger home on the newly purchased Prospect

Hill property, but with the war raging on, materials were not readily available.

Still, Sarah was happy. She spent her days sewing clothing to be sent to soldiers, volunteering with the local ladies' group rolling bandages and making care packages for soldiers, and helping her mother-in-law in the house. The Winchesters had a full staff of maids, a housekeeper, and a cook, but there was always something that needed tending.

Her evenings were spent listening to her father-in-law's lively conversations about his newest hobby. He and his business partner John Davies had invested in The Volcanic Repeating Arms Company, then purchased the company as it was going bankrupt and renamed it The New Haven Arms Company. Oliver then hired Benjamin T. Henry, a mechanic from his shirt company, to reconfigure the repeating revolver into a rifle, and by 1862, Oliver was sure that their new Henry Repeating Rifle could win the war for the North. But despite his best efforts, he had trouble selling the rifle to military officials.

"It makes no sense at all," Oliver complained as they sat in the study after dinner each evening. "Why would they wish to keep the single-shot carbines over a rifle that could shoot several shots without reloading?"

"It's difficult for some people to see change," William offered as an explanation.

"That is so true," Oliver said, still infuriated. "But this is the gun of the future. Even President Lincoln agreed it would be a much better choice after he'd tested it. Apparently, his generals don't listen to him, either."

Once alone in their bedroom, Sarah commented, "Your father is very passionate about his rifle project. It seems this is more than just a hobby, as everyone first believed."

William shook his head as he readied for bed. "He does get quite intense about it. But our bread and butter is the shirt factory, and I hope he doesn't lose sight of that." He smiled at Sarah. "At least he's left me and Davies' son, Cornelius, to run the factory while he concentrates on his rifles. It's good he's passionate about something else."

Noise from the other rooms filtered through the walls, and Sarah sighed. "I do wish we had a little more privacy here. It's wonderful that your parents are so giving to the other relatives and take care of them, but it gets quite crowded at times."

William moved toward her and wrapped Sarah in his arms. "Once this terrible war is over, the family will be able to build the larger house on that nice property right outside of town. We'll have more room and privacy." He kissed her tenderly on the lips. "And hopefully begin a family of our own."

Sarah smiled up at him. She loved that William wanted children and looked forward to being a father. "Yes. That will be nice."

Their first year of marriage was a busy and happy one despite the terrible news coming from the war. William enjoyed running the shirt business alongside Cornelius, and Sarah was content with her safe, secure life. But almost a year after their marriage, tragedy struck the Winchester family.

Annie was expecting her third child and was staying at her parents' home with her two young boys when her two-year-old, Charles, grew terribly ill. Jane instantly called the doctor, and they did everything they could to care for the young child. But after days of illness, Charles died.

Annie was beside herself, and so was her mother, Jane. Both women wept incessantly, and Sarah did her best to care for them and prepare the funeral for the little boy. Even the boy's father, Charles, who some thought of as cold and stern, was heartbroken at the loss of his namesake.

As they buried their beloved son, Annie's strength waned. She was five months pregnant at the time of young Charles's death, and both Jane and Sarah were afraid she'd lose the baby.

"You must eat to keep up your strength," Sarah told her sister-in-law as she cared for her. "Losing baby Charlie was devastating, but you can't lose this baby too."

Annie had taken to her bed most days after their son's death, and even as Sarah cajoled her to eat, she didn't seem to have the strength to sit up. "I keep seeing his little face, Sallie," Annie said, staring up at the ceiling. "He just stared at me as if begging me to help him, and there was nothing I could do."

Sarah's heart hurt for Annie. She had also tried everything with Charlie and had seen that look of desperation in the young boy's eyes. They had all done what they could, but nothing had helped. Even the doctor wasn't sure what illness had taken his life so quickly.

"I know, dear," Sarah said gently. "I saw how he looked at you. But he loved you so much, and you loved him too. You must get well so you can care for the new baby when it comes."

Still, as the months passed, Annie grew weaker and gained little weight. When she went into labor in January 1864, she was very weak. The doctor came, and they did all they could, but Annie faded and died after giving birth to a tiny little boy whom they named William Winchester Dye.

Sarah took it upon herself to do as much for the baby as she could as the entire family mourned Annie's death. She held the baby often, and a wet nurse was hired to feed little William, but despite it all, the baby didn't thrive and died nineteen days later.

Jane had been overwhelmed by little Charlie's death, but now she was utterly despondent over the death of Annie and the baby. It was too much for one mother to take all at once. As the family mourned, Jane folded inside herself. She spoke little and no longer smiled or joked. All that was left of Annie's little family was her husband, Charles, and their four-year-old son, Oliver.

"I'm afraid for your mother," Sarah told William one night as they lay in bed in the darkened room. "She's so fragile. What if she grows ill and leaves us too?"

William reached for his wife's hand under the covers. "My mother is stronger than even she knows. She grew up with a widowed mother and knows what it takes to survive in a difficult world. She will pull out of this. It'll just take time."

Sarah sighed. She'd wanted so much to have a child of her own, but after everything that had happened, she feared something terrible might happen to her, too. "I'm not sure I could live through the loss of a child," she whispered. "It's so devastating."

William rolled over on his side and wrapped his arms around her. "You are the strongest woman I know," he said seriously. "I truly believe you could live through anything if you set your mind to it."

Sarah hoped he was right because, after the past few months of tragedy, she wasn't sure what she could survive.

* * *

The family went through the motions of life for several months until the pain slowly subsided, although they all knew the feeling of loss of Annie and the children would never be gone completely. Oliver took matters into his own hands and decided to take his wife on a European vacation in early 1865. He would also use the opportunity to show off his Henry Repeating Rifle across Europe. The Civil War at home was winding down, so he set his sights across the ocean. If he could secure contracts overseas, he could make the rifle a success.

On New Year's Day, 1865, Oliver and Jane Winchester set sail for Naples, Italy, and planned to visit several large cities all over Europe. This left Sarah and William to run the household and the shirt factory all on their own for the first time.

Sarah loved the responsibility of running the house. She took her work seriously, organizing the staff, managing the budget, and making the day-to-day decisions. Likewise, William was made full partner along with John Davies's son Cornelius. The shirt factory was now theirs to run as they saw fit, and they worked together perfectly, just as their fathers had.

"Is this what it would be like to have a home of our own?" Sarah asked her husband wistfully as they sat in the study after dinner, enjoying tea and dessert. Jennie, at age eighteen, was still at home, and some of the cousins still resided there, but Sarah enjoyed having fewer people underfoot.

"I believe it is," William said with a smile. He was happier than he'd ever been, feeling free to become the business proprietor he'd always wanted to be. "I'm wondering if we should consider buying some of the Prospect Hill property from my father and building our own home."

Sarah's eyes lit up. "Would that even be possible? Do you think your parents would mind?" Sarah had always dreamed of building her own home and loved the idea.

"I don't see why not," William said. "Hopefully, Father will come home feeling optimistic about his rifle business and will agree it's a good decision for us all."

Sarah hoped that was the case. She loved her in-laws dearly, but a home of their own would be so lovely.

Unfortunately, the happy couple's quiet time in the house was short-lived. By July of 1866, John Davies and William learned that Benjamin Henry was trying to take over Oliver's rifle business and change the name. A telegram was sent to Oliver in Switzerland, and plans were made for him and Jane to return home immediately. Oliver had put his trust in Henry and had given him power of attorney while he was away. Now, that power was being used against him.

The couple returned, and Oliver went right to work doing what he did best—fixing the problem. He quickly had all his personal loans pulled from the company and also pulled out all the Winchester money. Henry hadn't thought his plan through and was suddenly in charge of a bankrupt company. Oliver then set up the Winchester Repeating Arms Company and offered to buy out Henry's loans and take back what belonged to him. From that moment on, the repeating rifle was known as the Winchester Repeating Rifle. Oliver had never wanted his name connected with the guns, but now it was, and he wasn't going to trust an outsider again. The articles of incorporation included the two names he trusted the most—William Wirt Winchester and John Davies.

Sarah's short-lived joy of being the lady of her own house was crushed immediately by the return of the Winchesters. Jane was adamant that she couldn't bear to have Sarah and William move out of their home and live separately from them. The older woman had lost so much already by losing Annie and the two children. Sarah didn't want to break her mother-in-law's heart again.

But by late 1865, a new baby Winchester would be on the way that everyone hoped would bring the family great joy.

Chapter Nine

1918

Olivia wrote the last few words Mrs. Winchester had spoken. She looked up at her employer, waiting to see if there would be more. Today, Mrs. Winchester had sat on the settee instead of behind her desk, stating that she'd been feeling a bit weary lately. Olivia had chosen to sit across from her on the other sofa.

"I think that's all I can manage for today," Mrs. Winchester said, reaching for a glass of water that Miss Sivera had brought her earlier. "There is still too much sorrow to deal with."

Olivia set down her pad of paper and pencil. "I'm so sorry about your sister-in-law and her children." Her heart ached for the family at their great loss despite it being many years ago. "Mrs. Winchester, your mother-in-law, must have carried that pain her entire life."

Mrs. Winchester nodded. "She did." After a moment, she looked over at Olivia. "I hope I didn't upset you with that story. I sometimes forget that you are expecting, too. Believe me, you will have the best medical care when the baby comes, and all will be fine. I've already spoken to my personal doctor, and he will be at our beck and call when your baby comes."

This was news to Olivia. She hadn't thought that far ahead, and here Mrs. Winchester had. "That is very kind of you," she said, touched that the older woman would offer her own doctor's services.

Mrs. Winchester smiled. "I brought you here knowing you were expecting a little one, and it is my responsibility to ensure you and the baby are safe."

Olivia felt near tears. She'd never met such a generous person as Mrs. Winchester. "Thank you," was all she could manage to say.

"You're very welcome, dear. I look forward to reading today's transcript. But now, I believe I'll have Henrietta help me to my room so I can rest a bit. Daisy, my niece, is coming over to have lunch with me."

Olivia stood. "Oh, that's nice. Does she live nearby?"

"Oh, yes. Not far at all. Daisy is the reason I have this lovely Atherton house so I can be near her," Mrs. Winchester said, sounding cheerier than she'd been. "She's Belle's daughter, but I have completely stolen her as my own." She chuckled.

Miss Sivera entered the room and handed Mrs. Winchester a cane. Olivia had never seen the older woman use one before and was always impressed at how Miss Sivera anticipated her employer's needs.

"How was your morning's work?" Miss Sivera asked Olivia cheerfully as she assisted Mrs. Winchester.

"We had a fine morning," Olivia said, smiling back at her. "Mrs. Winchester's life is so interesting."

This made the elderly woman laugh. "I guess some would say so. But we did have a successful morning despite my feeling under the weather." She turned to Olivia as they were leaving the room. "I will see you later tonight, dear. Enjoy your lunch."

"Thank you, ma'am," Olivia said. "Enjoy your visit."

They parted ways in the hallway, with Mrs. Winchester and Miss Sivera heading to the small elevator that would take them to the second floor. Managing steps was no longer an option for the elderly lady. Alice had told Olivia there was also a new elevator installed at the San Jose mansion, even though Mrs. Winchester hadn't lived there in quite some time.

Olivia was heading to the kitchen when she heard the door-bell ring. Glancing around, she realized there was no one to answer it and turned back to do so herself. She opened the door, and there stood a dark-haired woman who looked middle-aged. The woman looked startled a moment, then composed herself.

"Good afternoon," the woman said, stepping inside the entryway. "I'm afraid I forgot my key when I hurried out earlier." She studied Olivia for a moment. "You must be Aunt Sallie's new secretary."

Olivia stepped aside and then shut the door. This was obviously Mrs. Winchester's niece. "Yes. I'm Olivia Collins."

"It's nice to meet you, Miss Collins," the woman said. "I'm Mrs. Marriott. But Aunt Sallie calls me Daisy."

"It's nice to meet you," Olivia said. She didn't bother to correct Mrs. Marriott on the fact that she was Mrs. Collins. Olivia had no idea who knew her story, and she didn't want to draw attention to herself.

"Is my aunt in the dining room or upstairs?" Mrs. Marriott asked. She seemed a bit stressed and rushed. Or maybe she was normally short in the way she spoke.

"She just went upstairs to her room with Miss Sivera," Olivia told her.

"Wonderful. Thank you. I'll deliver these to the kitchen before I go up," Mrs. Marriott said, pointing to the canvas bag slung over her shoulder. "The berries are already growing quite nicely at the ranch, and one of the men delivered them to me this morning."

"I was just going to lunch. I can take them to the kitchen for you," Olivia offered.

"That's very nice of you. But I'm happy to do it." The two women walked down the hallway toward the kitchen. "So, what is this project my aunt hired you for? She said you were doing dictation and typing for her."

Olivia was surprised that Mrs. Winchester hadn't told her she was writing her biography. Perhaps Mrs. Winchester hadn't wanted anyone to know. "She's writing her family's history. Something for the family to enjoy, I suppose."

Mrs. Marriott seemed to consider this. "Yes. That's a good idea. Once my aunt is gone, there will be no one to tell it. All her sisters and her brother have passed, except my mother, you know."

"I didn't know that," Olivia said. "I'm sorry to hear it."

"Yes," Mrs. Marriott said with a sigh. "And my mother, Isabelle Merriman, isn't doing very well. Has my aunt mentioned that?"

"No, she hasn't. Of course, I haven't been here very long, and we are still in the early stages of her history," Olivia said.

"Oh, yes. Of course." They'd reached the kitchen by then, and the staff greeted Daisy more like an old friend than as Mrs. Winchester's niece. After a quick chat with Alice and Mr. Nakmo, Mrs. Marriot said goodbye and headed up the back staircase.

"Ah, fresh strawberries," Alice said, already getting a strainer to wash them in. "We must add some to Mrs. Winchester's tray. She'll love these."

Instead of going to the dining room, Olivia perched on one of the stools. "Mrs. Marriott seems like a nice woman," she said casually. She didn't want to pry, but she knew the cook would have her own opinions.

"Ah, yes. She is," Alice said as she cut up the fruit. "She used to work as Mrs. Winchester's secretary and companion until she married. Mrs. Winchester adores her and treats her as her own daughter. She's bought Daisy and her husband three different homes, all in different areas, just to please them."

"That's quite generous," Olivia said. She thought of how the elder Winchesters had opened their home to siblings and cousins. Perhaps Mrs. Winchester had learned to give back from their example.

After lunch, at which Olivia had also enjoyed the fresh strawberries, she went to her room to type up that day's work. It was warmer today, so she opened the windows again and left her door open for a cross breeze. As she loaded the paper into the typewriter, she thought about Daisy and Mrs. Winchester. There was a family resemblance. Mrs. Winchester had said she'd had curly hair as a young woman, and even into middle age, Daisy's hair was quite thick and curly. She also had the same distinctive dark eyebrows and brown eyes. But where Mrs. Winchester's face was round and petite, Daisy's was longer and angular. Still, one could see that they were related.

Olivia worked for two hours typing the story as Mrs. Winchester had told it. She held back tears again as she wrote about Annie's death and the loss of her children. She stopped working a moment and placed a hand on her stomach, praying her child would be born healthy. And she was again thankful that Mrs. Winchester would ensure she'd have the best care when the baby came. It was so much more than she would have ever asked for.

After delivering the manuscript to Mrs. Winchester later that evening, Olivia joined the staff for dinner. She loved these easy mealtimes where everyone was friendly and chatty. Olivia had a permanent spot next to Alice, and as they ate, she drew up the courage to ask about Daisy's mother, Belle.

"Ah, yes. Mrs. Merriman," Alice said softly, not wanting the others to think she was gossiping. "She hasn't been well, from what I've heard. She was always confrontational, speaking her mind and becoming involved in causes. Good causes, though, like child welfare and the humane treatment of animals. She's taken in many abused children and helped them find homes. I admire her for that. Daisy and her husband adopted one of the young girls who had been pulled from her home and was living with Mrs. Merriman. That would be Margaret. But over the last couple of years, Mrs. Merriman's behavior became a bit irrational. Daisy sent her to a sanitarium for treatment, and it seems she's been in and out of hospitals ever since."

"Oh, I'm so sorry to hear that," Olivia said. From Mrs. Winchester's notes, she knew that Belle had always been an outspoken person. But to hear she'd had problems with her mental health was sad.

"It can happen to the best of us." Alice sighed. "And here the newspapers are always maligning Mrs. Winchester, calling her crazy when she's as sane as you and me. It would be awful if they got ahold of the information that Belle had a breakdown of sorts."

Olivia agreed. The newspapers would use that information to prove that Mrs. Winchester was crazy, too.

The next day, Miss Sivera left a note under Olivia's door stating that Mrs. Winchester wasn't feeling well and would spend the day in bed so she could take the day off. But Olivia wasn't one to sit idly by. At breakfast, she asked Alice if there was anything she could do to help in the kitchen, and reluctantly, Alice allowed her to help cut up vegetables and fruit for lunch and make some baked goods.

"I really feel you should rest when you get the chance," Alice said. "Instead of working in this hot kitchen."

Olivia glanced over at her, wondering again if the cook knew she was expecting. She still wasn't showing, but maybe the news had spread throughout the household. "I don't mind," she said cheerfully. "I used to work in the kitchen with my mother all the time at our farm. We did a lot of canning every fall, too. And believe me when I say it would get awfully hot in the old farmhouse compared to this nice kitchen with so many windows."

"I didn't know you grew up on a farm," Alice said, looking stunned. "I figured you were a city girl because you're educated."

"I did. An orchard, actually. My parents made a fairly good living, but I wanted more," Olivia said. And wanting more had been her undoing, unfortunately. Olivia often wondered what she'd be doing now if she'd stayed near her parents instead of moving to San Jose. She'd probably be married to a farmer's son and doing this same work every day—the very thing she hadn't wanted to do.

"Well, be careful who you tell this to," Alice said with a chuckle. "Or they'll have you picking fruit over at the ranch come harvest time."

Olivia laughed. Actually, she wouldn't mind doing that.

A bell rang in the kitchen, startling Olivia. "What's that?"

"The front doorbell rings in here so we can hear it. Would you mind answering it? Henrietta is up with Mrs. Winchester, and my hands are sticky with dough."

"I don't mind at all," Olivia said, hurrying out of the kitchen and down the hallway. She wiped her hands on the full white apron she wore over her dress, then opened the door.

"Have you been demoted to the kitchen?" a cheerful male voice asked.

Olivia smiled when she saw it was Mr. Stanley, Frank Lieb's assistant. He was dressed smartly in a suit with a stylish Fedora covering his chestnut hair and was carrying his leather briefcase. "I have demoted myself for the day," she said, stepping aside to let him in.

Mr. Stanley took off his hat and smiled down at her. "You are as rosy-cheeked as a schoolgirl. Working in the kitchen must do you good."

Her face grew even warmer at his compliment. Nervously, she offered to take his hat and set it on the table in the entryway. "Mrs. Winchester isn't feeling well today and is in her room," Olivia said, trying hard not to stare into his expressive brown eyes. "Is she expecting you?"

"I'm sorry to hear she's feeling poorly," Mr. Stanley said, turning serious. "She may have forgotten I was coming here today. Perhaps I should set up another time with Miss Sivera."

Olivia wasn't sure what she was supposed to do, so she invited Mr. Stanley into the living room. "I'll go up and ask what they'd like to do. Meanwhile, would you care for a cold drink? Mrs. Murphy has some delicious iced tea made."

"Oh, yes. That would be nice. Thank you." His smile returned.

"Excuse me a moment." Olivia hurried back to the kitchen.

"Alice. Would you mind taking a tray with iced tea and some of your wonderful cookies to Mr. Stanley in the living area? I have to go upstairs and let Miss Sivera know he's here."

"Oh, that handsome young lawyer is here," Alice said with a wink. "I'll bring him a tray immediately."

Olivia ran up the back staircase and down the hall, then knocked softly on Mrs. Winchester's door. Miss Sivera answered seconds later. "Mr. Stanley is here," Olivia told the secretary. "He said he has an appointment."

"Oh, dear," Miss Sivera said quietly, glancing back toward Mrs. Winchester's bed. "She's sleeping so well right now." She moved them out into the hallway and closed the door softly. "She'll hate missing a meeting with him, but I think it would be best if he returns another day. I'll go down with you and talk to him."

"Should I sit with Mrs. Winchester in case she needs something?" Olivia offered.

"Miss Merrell is in there with her in case she wakes up. Let's go downstairs."

As they walked down the front stairs, Miss Sivera gave Olivia an odd look. "Why are you wearing an apron?"

"Oh." Olivia had forgotten she had it on. "I didn't want to do nothing today, so I was helping in the kitchen." She quickly untied it and pulled it off over her head.

"That was very nice of you," Miss Sivera said. "I'm sure the staff liked having your help."

"I like to keep busy," Olivia told her.

Miss Sivera nodded her approval. Olivia felt she'd earned a little more respect from her for being willing to find work to do.

At the bottom of the stairs, Olivia turned to return to the

kitchen, but Miss Sivera stopped her. "Please join us. Mr. Stanley seems to have taken a shine to you, and it'll help ease the blow that he came all this way for nothing," she told Olivia. "Perhaps we can invite him to lunch before his long trip back to San Jose."

Olivia didn't know what to say. She was still comprehending that Miss Sivera said Mr. Stanley had taken a shine to her.

Miss Sivera smiled. "Just follow my lead." She hurried into the living area with Olivia right behind her.

"Ah, Mr. Stanley. I'm so sorry we didn't contact you this morning," Miss Sivera said as she entered the room. "Mrs. Winchester took ill this morning, and all my attention was on her and her health."

Mr. Stanley had stood as the women entered the room. "I hope it isn't serious."

"Oh, no. Sometimes Mrs. Winchester overextends herself and then pays the price for it. Her arthritis is bothering her more than usual, and that causes her to be extremely tired. But after a day or two of rest, I'm sure she'll be ready to work again."

Mr. Stanley nodded. "Well, I certainly understand. And it's no bother at all coming out here. I love visiting this area whenever I can."

"You are a true gentleman," Miss Sivera said.

"I'll leave the paperwork that Mr. Lieb wants her to go over, and we can meet another day for signatures," Mr. Stanley said. The ladies sat, and he did also and began pulling folders from his briefcase.

"Thank you for understanding," Miss Sivera said. "I'll make sure she looks these over soon and then call you when she's ready."

He handed her the file folders with the paperwork inside.

"Since you're here," Miss Sivera said, "And it's so close to lunchtime, would you like to join Mrs. Collins for a bite to eat in the dining room?"

Mr. Stanley looked over at Olivia, his face lighting up. "If Mrs. Collins wouldn't mind my boring company, I'd love to have lunch. I'd never pass up a meal made by Mr. Nakmo."

"Wonderful," Miss Sivera said. "I'd join you myself, but Mrs. Winchester likes me to be near her when she doesn't feel well. I'll tell Alice so she can serve you in the dining room at noon." After apologizing again and saying goodbye, Miss Sivera left the two alone in the living area.

Olivia was at a loss as to what to do. She'd felt much more comfortable working in the kitchen than she did conversing with the young lawyer. "Did you enjoy the iced tea?" she asked, searching for a way to start the conversation.

"Yes, thank you," he said. "It was quite refreshing." He glanced at the big clock on the wall. "It's still a while before lunch begins, and it's such a nice day out today. Would you like to take a short walk around the house?"

"Yes, that would be lovely," Olivia said, stopping herself at the last minute from sighing with relief. She always felt more comfortable if she was keeping herself busy.

Mr. Stanley led the way to the front door and opened it, allowing Olivia to step out first. A sleek-looking automobile sat in the driveway.

"Is that your motorcar?" Olivia asked, uncertain if it was his or Mrs. Winchester's. She knew her employer owned several automobiles and had a driver to take her places, but she'd never seen this one before.

"Oh, no. I'm afraid not. It's much pricier than what I could afford," Mr. Stanley said. "It's one of Mr. Lieb's automobiles. He lets me use it when I drive out here."

"Oh, so you do know how to drive?"

"Yes. I wanted to learn. I hope someday to buy a motor-car of my own. I truly believe that everyone will own autos someday."

Olivia chuckled as they rounded the corner toward the side of the house. "I doubt I'd ever own one," she said. "It's much too expensive for someone like me."

"I must politely disagree. At some point, we will all need one to get around. And I'll bet I could even teach you to drive," Mr. Stanley said.

"Don't bet too much on that," she told him.

As they walked along, he asked, "How is your work going with Mrs. Winchester?"

"Very well, thank you," she said. "She's had a very interesting life, and having the chance to type it up for her has been intriguing."

"That's good to hear." They continued their walk around the back of the house, admiring the flowers that grew everywhere and the beautiful oak trees that shaded the house.

"Does Mr. Collins also work for Mrs. Winchester?" Mr. Stanley asked. "I know she has a habit of hiring couples to work for her."

Olivia turned her eyes up to his. She didn't want to lie to him because she thought of him as an honest man. But it was the story they'd made up to cover her indiscretion, and she had to follow through, or it would look bad for Mrs. Winchester. "My husband died after coming home from the war," she said softly.

His expression turned serious. "Oh, I'm so sorry. I was

unaware that he'd passed," he said quickly.

Olivia glanced down, hating that she had to lie. But what else could she do? He must have taken her quietness as sadness because Mr. Stanley suddenly became apologetic.

"I really am truly sorry," he said. "I didn't mean to bring up an unhappy memory for you."

"There's no need to apologize, please," Olivia said. They had stopped under one of the many shade trees. "It was as if he'd died right after going abroad. He came home a different man, and we never really reconnected before he passed. I'm getting used to being on my own again." It was as true as she could manage because that was what had happened to her with the man who'd dishonored her. He'd declared his love and then tossed her away after he'd taken what he'd wanted.

"Again, though, I am sorry. I'm glad you ended up here with Mrs. Winchester. She is wonderful to the people who work for her," Mr. Stanley said.

When Olivia dared to look up into his eyes again, she saw him smile.

"And a beautiful, intelligent woman like you will definitely not be alone for long, I assure you."

Olivia's heart pounded in her chest. Was he flirting? Did she dare even believe he was? And what would he think if he knew she was with child?

"That's very kind of you," she said.

"I'm starving. Let's go have that delicious lunch I was promised," Mr. Stanley said, grinning boyishly. He offered her his arm, and she linked hers through his as they walked around to the front of the house and inside to the dining room.

CHAPTER TEN

1865

By the time the elder Winchesters had settled back into their routine at the Court Street house and Oliver had founded his new rifle business, Sarah and William had good news for them—they were expecting their first child. Oliver and Jane were thrilled, as were Sarah's father and mother. When Sarah and William went to the house to tell them, there were hugs all around. But Sarah was worried about her father. Leonard had been suffering from back pain and arthritis over the past few months, and the damp winters didn't help. Often, he didn't go to work, and the running of the woodworking factory had fallen to Sarah's brother-in-law, William Converse, who was the bookkeeper.

"I'm thinking of selling the factory," Leonard confided in Sarah and William after they'd celebrated the upcoming baby. It was a cold November evening, and the family sat around the fire in the study with tea and cakes the maid had brought in.

Sarah's heart sank. She loved her father's factory and all the craftsmen who worked there. "Won't Leo reconsider taking over the business?" she asked. If she'd been a male, she certainly would have continued with the family business.

"I'm afraid it doesn't interest him," her father said sadly. "Believe me, I've tried to talk him into it. And William is very good at handling the finances, but he's not interested in running the business, either."

Sarah glanced over at her husband, and from the look in his eyes, she could tell he knew what she was thinking. He gave her a wan smile and a slight shake of his head. If she'd insisted, William would have bought the factory for her, but she wasn't one to press. And with the baby on the way, there would be no way for her to run it. She knew William didn't have the time or energy right now either. Between his father's gun business and running the shirt business, William was already strained.

"I'm sorry, Papa," Sarah said, truly sad. Belle, Estelle, and Sarah's mother sat silently as they sipped their tea. This wasn't news to them, so they'd already had time to digest it. Of course, the two younger girls were never as interested in the business as Sarah had been.

Leonard smiled at his daughter. "I think it'll work out fine," he said. "This neighborhood is no longer the elite area it once was, with all the homes being turned into boarding houses. If I sell the factory and house, your mother and I can buy a nicer place and retire. To tell the truth, I'm looking forward to it."

Sarah thought about that. Her father had been working hard his whole life to give his wife and children everything he could—and he'd done well. Perhaps it would be for the better that he gave it all up and spent his later years relaxing.

At home that evening, in their bedroom, William hugged Sarah tightly. "I know you would love to own your father's business, dear. And I'm sorry I can't commit to that right now.

If we absorbed it into our businesses, it would be too much. My father is putting so much time and money into his gun company, and I'm already working long hours at the shirt factory."

Sarah looked up into her husband's blue eyes. He did look tired. Winter hadn't been good for his health either, and he coughed at times in a way that scared her. William claimed he was fine, it was just a winter cold, but he was so thin despite eating well. She understood he didn't have the strength right now to take on any more projects.

"I understand," she said softly. "And we both know I couldn't run the business either and raise our children. But I'll miss the days when I used to run down to the factory and see all the beautiful things the craftsmen made."

William knew how much she loved building and creating, and his understanding of that only made her love him more.

The months flew by quickly as William worked long hours and Sarah helped Jane around the house as much as she was allowed to. She visited her parents often and also her father's factory while she still could. Sarah would miss being around the freshly cut wood and watching as the men created beautiful designs for clients' homes. The factory had been a part of her life since she was eight years old, and she couldn't imagine her life without it. But she was also realistic enough to know that once the baby was born, her time would be consumed with being a mother, and she wouldn't have time to visit the factory anymore.

Sarah and William felt lucky that she had an easy pregnancy. Sarah began sewing clothes for the baby—not because she couldn't afford to buy new clothing, but because she loved being busy, creating the little garments herself. Her older sisters also contributed to the baby's layette. By now, Nettie had given birth to three children, but unfortunately, Mary had not yet been blessed with a child. Still, they wanted to contribute to their younger sister's upcoming baby.

As Sarah waited patiently for the birth of her baby, Estelle announced that she was getting married that summer also. Everyone was thrilled, except Belle, who'd yet to become engaged. The Pardee family had much to celebrate that year and felt blessed.

On a warm day in June, William was messaged to come home from the factory because Sarah had gone into labor. When he arrived, Sarah was already indisposed, and he waited anxiously in the study, along with his father, as the doctor went into the room to follow the birth's progression. By that evening, Sarah had given birth to a beautiful little girl.

"I can't believe how tiny she is," William said, holding his daughter for the first time. He looked like a man cradling a glass doll; he was being so careful with her.

Sarah chuckled from her bed. The birth had been tiring, but she felt elated and couldn't sleep. She wanted to stare at her lovely little girl forever. "She won't break. You can hold her close."

"I know," he said, grinning. "But she's so precious. I couldn't bear to do anything that would hurt her." He handed the swaddled baby back to Sarah. "I can't believe you were able to tear my mother away from her."

"She was as tired as I after the birth. Poor Jane. She wanted to be with me, and she was, but she needed sleep. I know your parents are thrilled to have a new little girl in the family," Sarah said.

"What shall we call her?" William asked, looking into his

wife's eyes. "Another Sarah?"

Sarah shook her head slowly. "I want to call her Annie, after your sister."

William smiled. "My mother will be so happy about that." He leaned over Sarah and kissed her sweetly on the cheek. "You are an incredible woman, you know that?"

She turned her face up to his. "For giving birth?"

"No. For always thinking of everyone else."

They decided on the name Annie Pardee Winchester for their little girl, and the entire family was pleased. But as Sarah grew stronger and healed, the little baby grew weaker. Doctor after doctor was called in.

"Your baby isn't getting sufficient nutrients," the doctor said. Sarah hired a different wetnurse, but still, the baby struggled to eat and, despite having a full belly, would wail constantly. Sarah was at her wit's end as her little girl continued to lose weight despite their best efforts.

Sarah held her little baby constantly, and William stayed home from work to do whatever he could. He couldn't bear seeing the strain on Sarah's face as she tried to comfort little Annie.

"Are we just supposed to let her die of starvation?" Sarah asked the doctor tersely one day. "Is there nothing we can do to save her?"

The doctor only shook his head. "I'm sorry, Mrs. Winchester. There's nothing we can do. The baby isn't absorbing any of the food she's eating. It would take a miracle to save her."

Angry and frustrated, Sarah refused to believe the good lord would give her an angel only to take her away. She tried every remedy suggested. The Pardees and Winchesters held prayer meetings at the house, and the minister at their church asked everyone to pray for little Annie. Sarah sat night and day with her little girl but to no avail. A month after her birth, the little infant died in Sarah's arms.

Sarah's heart was broken.

They buried their baby in Evergreen Cemetery, near where William's sister Annie and her children were laid to rest. The site of the tiny casket was too much for Sarah to take. After the burial, she took to her room and refused to come out for days. William joined her to comfort her and to grieve also. These two kindhearted people who'd wanted nothing more than a child to love had lost their greatest joy, and it seemed almost too much for them to bear.

Sarah's mother came to see her daily and tried to coax her out of her dark mood, but the younger Sarah didn't have the energy to care. "It will take time, Sallie," her mother told her. "I know how you feel. I lost my first baby a year after she was born, and it broke my heart."

Sarah took her mother's hand and squeezed it. "I know you understand, but it feels as if we are the only ones on earth who have ever felt this way."

Her mother nodded. "You have every right to feel the way you do. But please don't let it take you away from me and your family. We all love you so much."

Sarah understood what her mother was saying because, in her darkest moments, Sarah wished she could join little Annie and not have to bear the pain of the last month. Hearing her baby wail from hunger and not being able to do anything haunted Sarah's nightmares. She wondered what else she could have done and felt she'd failed to protect her baby. Despite what the doctor said, the guilt of not keeping Annie alive was nearly impossible for Sarah to bear.

"I will try to be strong, Mother," Sarah said. "But it's so difficult."

"We've decided to move Estelle and George's wedding to Manhattan, so you won't feel obligated to attend," the elder Sarah told her gently. "You and William need this time together to mourn."

"Thank you, Mother," Sarah said gratefully. "I just couldn't bear to be around a group of people right now."

"We understand, dear," her mother said.

For months, Sarah and William stayed to themselves, other than William eventually going back to the shirt factory to work.

* * *

"I have a project for you," William said cheerfully to Sarah one day, months after the death of their beloved daughter. Sarah had kept to herself much of the time, although everyone had tried to bring her out of her grief. William, despite his grief over his little girl, hadn't the choice to hide away for long. Too much was happening in his work life between selling his investment in the Winchester and Davies's shirt company to Cornelius and taking over the running of the Winchester Repeating Arms Company factory in Bridgeport. It had meant he was away several days each week, which had also added to Sarah's depressed mood.

Sarah had been sitting in the study, reading a book, although not comprehending it. She glanced up at her husband, surprised he was home in the middle of the week. "Project? What project?" she asked, only moderately interested.

William sat on the window seat next to her. "Father and

Mother want you to help with the building and decorating of the Prospect Hill home," he said excitedly.

"But it's already been designed and is being built," Sarah said, losing interest. "Your parents' home and John Davies' home are the talk of the town, I'm told. What could I possibly do to help?"

"You can help quite a bit, dear," William told her. "Father has no patience for the problems that have arisen during construction, so I've been the one to work with the architects and builders these past few months. And mother needs help decorating. We also need someone who can direct the builders for the outbuildings that will be needed—like the carriage house, a barn for the horses, a gardener's shack, and even living space for the workers. Father thinks your attention to detail would be perfect for that. And Mother also wants a plant conservatory, and she believes you'd be the perfect person to help design that."

Sarah set her book down and sat up straighter. "Really? They want me to help?"

William smiled warmly. "Yes. They do. It'll be a lot of work, but I know how much you love the building process. You said yourself once that you love the smell of freshly cut wood and the details that make a house a home. Now is your chance to show what you know."

The thought of helping with the building and decorating her in-laws' mansion made Sarah's heart beat faster. After all, it would be her home, too. A home that she and William would someday inherit.

"Oh, William," she said, growing excited. "I would so love to help with the house. Do you really believe I would do a good job?"

William hugged Sarah closely. "I think you'll do a wonderful job of it," he said tenderly.

Sarah loved how William was never afraid to show how he felt. He'd been so attentive and loving throughout the loss of their little Annie, and he'd never once pressed her to move past her grief despite all the months she'd mourned. Sarah knew she'd always mourn the loss of their baby no matter how many years went by, but perhaps it was time to move forward and work through her grief.

"When do we start?" she asked, her eyes lighting up.

William chuckled. "Let's start by bringing you up to the house so you can see what's been done. You haven't even been there yet."

Sarah nodded vigorously. "Yes. Let's go right now. And we can walk the grounds and decide what will be needed." She smiled up at William. "I can't wait to get started."

Once she and William walked around the mansion at the top of the hill, Sarah realized how big a job this was going to be. Both Oliver and John Davies were building huge mansions, side by side, each over 20,000 square feet and in a similar style. The Winchester mansion had two main floors plus upper floors for the servant quarters. Large windows were used to bring in plenty of sunlight, and only the best interior finishes would be used. While many of the main items, like marble floors and chandeliers, had already been chosen, there was much more decorating to do once the interior was finished. And Sarah was definitely up to the task of helping Jane choose all their grand furniture and finishes.

Working together with William on the house details was a joy for Sarah. She was adept at speaking with the craftsmen, conferring on design choices. She chose the locations for the necessary outbuildings and, in some instances, drew up rudimentary designs to show the workers what she was thinking. She also made smart choices when it came to money and design so as not to overspend when it wasn't necessary. Oliver often complimented Sarah on her choices and decisions. He bragged proudly to whoever would listen that he couldn't have made better choices for the building of his home than his son and daughter-in-law had.

It was the happiest two years of Sarah's life, and by 1868, the house was finished, and Sarah and William both felt it was one of their greatest accomplishments.

CHAPTER ELEVEN

Today

Morgan held back tears as she read about the loss of Sarah Winchester's baby girl. How heartbreaking it must have been for her to hold her crying baby, knowing there was nothing she could do to keep her alive. Morgan had never read much about Sarah before, so she'd had no idea Sarah and William had lost a baby. Did many people know this about her? If they had, would they have been a little more compassionate toward poor Sarah?

The next day at work, Morgan couldn't get Sarah Winchester out of her mind. She went to work on Luella Perkins' novel, making notes for the phone conversation she was going to set up with her. Where Are The Children? was a good story, and with a little tweaking, it could be a great story. If the author was willing to make a few changes, then Morgan would try to get Amanda's approval so they could set up a contract.

A shadow fell over Morgan's desk, and when she looked up, she saw Amanda standing there, staring at her.

"Your project is a go," Amanda said. "The main company approved it."

Morgan was confused. "Which project?"

"That one by Andrew Marcus. Voices in the Hallway."

"Oh. But you approved that one last month. We already have a contract with him and are starting developmental editing."

Amanda sighed. "Yeah. I know. But now the head brass is reviewing all new acquisitions even after the contracts are signed. They've given you the go-ahead, though, so kudos."

Morgan could tell that Amanda was frustrated but not angry. She supposed it was just another cutback the publisher was pushing to save money. "Well, okay. I'm glad to hear that. I hope they didn't ax anyone's contracts," Morgan said.

Amanda's gaze turned toward Lila's desk and then back to Morgan. "They haven't approved any of Lila's acquisitions so far, and I know it's frustrating for her. She's good at what she does, but it all comes down to how much money her authors can make." She sighed. "I hope Lila doesn't cry again when I tell her. I hate that."

Morgan was surprised by how much Amanda was sharing. She'd never been this vulnerable before. "Want to grab a coffee in the conference room before you tell her?"

This made Amanda smile. Years before when Morgan was first hired, she and Amanda had been almost like friends. But then publishing became tougher, and Amanda became fiercer.

"Yes. Let's do that."

Morgan followed Amanda into the conference room, and they each made a cup of coffee. A plate of bakery cookies was on the side table, so they each took one and sat at the big glass table.

"It sounds like the publishing company is being tight with their budget again," Morgan said to break the ice. She never knew how far she could go with Amanda before her boss thought she was overstepping.

Amanda nodded. She seemed pensive today, something Morgan rarely saw. "I used to have complete control over what we published here. Now, they question my every move. They want their hand in everything."

"I'm sorry to hear that," Morgan said. "It must be stressful."

Amanda stared at Morgan for a minute as if trying to read into what she'd said. Then she let her guard down and sighed. "It is stressful. Not because I can't handle it but because it affects all of you, too. I hire editors I trust to bring in amazing books. But with them second-guessing me, I have to do the same." She shook her head. "And it's not going to get any easier. All the publishers are losing money and dropping authors and editors. If we don't play our cards right, this whole division could be wiped out."

Morgan was shocked. She knew their books did well and made a profit. "Are they threatening that?"

"Not in so many words. But I've seen this before. They panic and get rid of the smaller imprints to have more money for the larger ones." Amanda shrugged. "I guess we've had a good run. I'm just hoping that we pull in a blockbuster novel that will keep us solvent for at least another year."

For a moment, Morgan thought about telling Amanda about her biography about Sarah Winchester. It could be a best seller with the right push behind it.

"What are you thinking?" Amanda asked, cocking her head. "I can tell you have something to say."

Morgan took a deep breath and jumped in. "What if I told you I might have an autobiography that was dictated directly to a typist by Sarah Winchester?"

Amanda's thick black brows rose. "You might? Or you do?"

"I do have it," Morgan said. "But I haven't finished reading it yet, and I want to research the typist a little more to make sure it's legit."

Amanda sat back in her chair and took a sip of coffee. "So, what you're telling me is Sarah Lockwood Winchester told her story to a person who then typed it up for her. It's an actual autobiography."

"Yes," Morgan said. She watched Amanda closely for any sign of interest. She couldn't tell what her boss was thinking.

"How did you come upon this manuscript?"

"My Great-Great-Grandmother, Olivia Collins, worked for Mrs. Winchester sometime around 1918 as a secretary. After Sarah died, she kept a copy of the manuscript. It's been passed down for decades through my family. I just learned about it when my mother and I went through my grandmother's belongings."

"Interesting," Amanda said. She took another drink from her mug and then set it down carefully. "I'm not sure of the validity of it or if we'd have the right to publish it. But there are a lot of people out there who'd love to hear Sarah's side of her story."

Morgan's heart skipped. "It's been interesting to read so far," she said, trying to keep her excitement in check. "I'm sure there are facts about her life that no one knows. I plan on doing more research into my Grandmother Olivia's background to make sure I can prove she worked for her during that time." She hesitated a moment. "If we can prove it was dictated to her directly by Sarah Winchester, do you think it's a book you'd be interested in publishing?"

"That's a lot of ifs," Amanda said. "But why don't you finish reading it and do your research, and we'll see where it lands." She stood, took her mug to the sink at the side counter, and rinsed it out. "But it's worth looking into," Amanda said, turning back to Morgan.

"I'll do that," Morgan said. She smiled. "Thanks for listening."

"I trust your judgment, Morgan," Amanda said. "You're good at your job." She started walking toward the door, then stopped and turned. "Let's keep everything we said in here between us, okay? What I said about the company is just speculation. I wouldn't want everyone running out looking for a new job because I had one bad day."

"Just between us," Morgan agreed.

Amanda nodded, then headed out the door, walking toward Lila's cubicle.

Morgan hoped she hadn't jumped the gun telling Amanda about the manuscript. Maybe it was a good thing to give Amanda time to think about it while Morgan did the research. Still, Morgan was excited. Her mother was already working on their family history and trying to learn more about her Grandmother Olivia. And Morgan couldn't wait to read more of the manuscript.

Chapter Twelve

1918

Olivia's heart broke for Mrs. Winchester as she typed that day's dictation. She'd had no idea her employer had lost a baby in such a heartbreaking way. It would be easy to become hardened by such a loss, especially since they were never blessed with another child. But from what Olivia had seen of Mrs. Winchester's behavior, she had a kind and open heart for all those around her. She'd certainly been more than generous to Olivia.

As she typed, Olivia's thoughts kept returning to her lunch last week with Daniel Stanley. He was always the perfect gentleman around her, but he enjoyed teasing and complimenting her, too. He had a wonderful sense of humor to go along with his devilishly handsome looks. It would be very easy to get lost in his warm brown eyes and kind smile. He was just the type of man she'd hoped to one day meet—professional, mannered, yet funny and endearing. He'd make the perfect husband for some lucky woman.

Just as that thought came to her, the baby flipped in her belly, causing Olivia to stop typing. She placed her hand over the baby and sighed. What would Mr. Stanley think if he knew she was carrying another man's baby?

Olivia's heart sank at that thought. She had no right to think of Mr. Stanley in any other way except professionally. It didn't matter that he believed she'd been married and would also think her child was legitimate. It was all a lie, and she didn't deserve a man as dignified as Daniel.

But oh, how he made her heart soar every time he dropped by.

Straightening her back, Olivia returned to her typing. This is what she was hired to do, and she must keep her mind on her work. Poor Mrs. Winchester had missed several days of their meetings because she'd been under the weather, and today had been the first day they'd been able to continue working on her project. She'd looked much better today, but Olivia was sure talking about losing her little Annie had worn her out. Olivia was happy that today's story ended on a positive note as Mrs. Winchester described working alongside her husband on her beloved "house on the hill," as she called it. It had been a cathartic project for her after such a great loss.

Rolling the last sheet of paper out of the typewriter, Olivia couldn't help but think that building Oliver Winchester's mansion had cemented Mrs. Winchester's love of building and designing. With her seemingly endless supply of money from the Winchester Repeating Arms Company, she'd been able to do whatever she wanted with her San Jose house. Olivia wondered if every time Mrs. Winchester built a home, it gave her a sense of peace—just as building the house on Prospect Street had. There was much more to Mrs. Winchester than any newspaper in the country that had made up stories about her could understand.

That evening, Olivia stopped by Mrs. Winchester's room to drop off that day's work for her to read. Miss Sivera let her in, and the elderly lady smiled up at her from her cushy chair at the small dining table.

"You're always so prompt," Mrs. Winchester said, taking the sheets of paper from her and setting them on the table. She had a shawl around her shoulders and a blanket over her legs despite the warmth of the room.

"That is only because you make my work so easy and enjoyable," Olivia said.

"I do appreciate it," Mrs. Winchester told her. "Would you like to join us for dinner in here tonight?"

Olivia was surprised to be invited to eat with her employer. "Why, yes. That would be lovely."

Miss Sivera's brows had risen ever so slightly but not enough to bring attention to her. "I'll bring up a tray for each of us," she said.

"Oh, I can help you," Olivia offered, feeling awkward about Miss Sivera waiting on her.

"One of the kitchen staff can help Henrietta carry up the food," Mrs. Winchester said. "Please stay so we can chat."

Olivia nodded and sent an apologetic look toward Miss Sivera, who only smiled back. "I'll be back in a few minutes," the secretary said, then quietly left the room.

Olivia sat at the table on Mrs. Winchester's left side. "How are you feeling tonight?"

Mrs. Winchester grinned. "I was going to ask you that very same question. I'm feeling a bit tired from today's work, but otherwise, I'm fine. How are you feeling?"

"I'm feeling well," Olivia said. "I no longer feel sick in the morning, and having a place where I can get outside in the fresh air and take walks has been refreshing. I can't thank you enough for all you've done to ensure I'm healthy."

Mrs. Winchester raised one gnarled hand to brush off her appreciation. "I appreciate your words, but you needn't thank me. I'm happy to take care of you just as I do for all of my staff. Everyone who works here is highly valued by me."

"You're too kind," Olivia said.

"Henrietta tells me you helped in the kitchen when I was under the weather," the older lady said. "You know you have no obligation to work if I can't work, don't you?"

"Oh, I'm sorry if I shouldn't have. I'm just not one to sit around and do nothing," Olivia said quickly. "To be fair, Alice told me not to help, but I begged her to let me. I hope you're not angry with them for letting me."

"Oh, no, dear. I'm not upset at all. In fact, I admire someone who takes it upon herself to chip in and help. Often, in a house with staff, people are very protective of their status and won't do anything they deem beneath them. So, I was pleased that you took it upon yourself to pitch in." A small smile played on Mrs. Winchester's lips. "As you know from hearing my own story so far, I've never been one to shirk work. So, I quite admire you for taking the initiative."

"Oh, thank you," Olivia said. "Being raised on a farm, I was always busy, so I wouldn't know how not to be."

"Precisely. And I think that was why I liked you immediately. I could see you were a woman who could take care of herself." Mrs. Winchester paused. "Having said that, I also hope you will be thoughtful about the baby you're carrying. You're not obligated to do any work that will put a strain on you."

"Yes, ma'am," Olivia said. "I will be careful."

"Wonderful."

Miss Sivera entered carrying a tray, and the young man who washed dishes in the kitchen followed behind with two more. The ladies sat and ate the delicious dinner that included more early strawberries from the San Jose ranch.

"I love the first berries of the season," Mrs. Winchester said, taking small bites and chewing carefully. Her food had already been cut into tiny bites by the staff so it was easier for her to eat.

"They're delicious," Olivia said.

"What do you ladies think of this Spanish Flu that's affecting so many of our soldiers?" Mrs. Winchester asked, changing the subject. "It's been detected in Boston and in Kansas. Do you think it'll spread this far west?"

Olivia knew that Mrs. Winchester received several newspapers and magazines in the daily post and kept up on the latest news. "I didn't know it had come over here yet," Olivia said, suddenly wondering if she should be worried.

"Yes," Miss Sivera said. "But it's not on this coast yet. Let's pray it doesn't come, but if it does, we'll have to be careful where we go and who we're in contact with."

Mrs. Winchester nodded. "Yes. My thoughts exactly." She looked over at Olivia. "I doubt my frail body could fight off such a flu, and it wouldn't be good for your baby, either."

Olivia nodded. She was thankful that her employer kept up with the latest news.

"Daisy said she met you for the first time the other day," Mrs. Winchester said, directing her conversation to Olivia. "She told me she was impressed by your professionalism and even said you are quite pretty." This made Mrs. Winchester smile. "Daisy isn't one for compliments, so you must have truly impressed her."

"Oh, that was very kind of her," Olivia said, stunned that Daisy had said anything at all. They had hardly spoken on their short walk to the kitchen.

"Daisy lived with Madame for thirteen years as her personal secretary and companion," Miss Sivera said. "Luckily, I was able to fill her shoes after that."

Mrs. Winchester reached over and patted Henrietta's arm. "You've more than filled her shoes—you've done a wonderful job taking care of my every whim. And that's not easy."

Miss Sivera smiled. "It's not so difficult."

"Poor Daisy has had a bad time of it lately," Mrs. Winchester said, shaking her head and returning to eating her small bites of food. "Her mother, my sister Belle, hasn't been well, and Daisy has recently gone through a divorce with her husband, Fred. She's been left to care for and support her daughter, Margaret, all on her own. Fred is in Europe now, fighting alongside men half his age. I give him credit for being willing to fight, but I feel he left just to shirk his duties here."

"I'm sorry to hear that," Olivia said. She'd noted how strained Daisy had looked when they'd met but had no idea what had caused her distress. "She seems like a very nice woman."

"She is," Mrs. Winchester said. "She's having quite a time with Margaret as well. The teen years can be brutal. Of course, I help with whatever I can."

Olivia felt bad that so much was happening in her employer's family. She knew Mrs. Winchester's concern was genuine because the older lady seemed to take on everyone else's problems along with her own.

They talked a little about a newspaper article that had reported Mrs. Winchester was having nightly sèances at the

San Jose house, which made the elderly lady laugh. "I haven't even been living there, but I guess the sèances are continuing without me."

Olivia laughed along. She liked that Mrs. Winchester had a good sense of humor.

That night, as she lay in bed, Olivia thought about Mrs. Winchester and everything she knew about her so far. The older lady had seen so much tragedy when she was younger and probably more than Olivia was even aware of. But she'd moved forward despite it all. She couldn't help but admire this supposedly mysterious woman. There was nothing mysterious about her—she was a kind woman who helped her family and lived her life as she pleased. Olivia guessed that the jealousy of others had more to do with the malicious stories in the press than anything else. It was just an awful shame.

* * *

The next day, Olivia met Mrs. Winchester in the office exactly at ten. Olivia was happy to see she was looking well and eager to continue working on the manuscript.

"Ah, dear. There you are. Always on time," Mrs. Winchester said from behind her desk. There were papers and letters strewn in front of her as if she'd been working all morning.

Olivia sat in the chair in front of the desk and placed her notepad in her lap. She'd noticed for the first time that her skirt's waistband was snug this morning, which had brought the reality of her condition back to her. She'd have to try to let out the waistbands on her skirts or only wear straight dresses for a while, although she didn't have many. Olivia wasn't a skilled seamstress, so she wasn't sure how she'd manage to make her clothing fit.

"I would never want to keep you waiting," she told Mrs. Winchester. Olivia gestured toward the older lady's desk. "It looks like you have more than enough work without having to wait for me."

Mrs. Winchester nodded and sighed. "Yes. It feels like I'm always going through paperwork." She looked up at Olivia. "These papers just came from my brother-in-law, Thomas Bennett. Because of the war in Europe, the Winchester Repeating Arms Company is having a banner year, although because we are at war, no dividends can be distributed to stockholders. That doesn't disturb me as much as his personal letter to me. He's hinting at retiring soon and is waiting for his son, Win, to come home from the war and take over the company. That would be fine, but I'm worried about what will happen to the company if Win doesn't return. Who would run it then?"

"Oh, I hope for his sake and yours that he comes home safely," Olivia said. She suddenly felt guilty that the war in Europe hadn't affected her since she'd moved into Sarah's lovely home so far removed from everything. She didn't have to worry about relatives fighting in the war or supply shortages or anything else. Her brothers hadn't gone to war because they were older or heads of households and were needed at home. Only her story of a fake dead husband made it seem like the war had touched her.

"I do so hope Win returns safely," Mrs. Winchester said. "Thomas has been a good caretaker of the Winchester business, and I don't blame him for wanting to finally retire. I just hope he makes the appropriate decisions for us all."

Olivia nodded, not sure how to respond. She hadn't realized Mrs. Winchester kept such close tabs on the business, but since it was the main source of her income, it only made sense.

Mrs. Winchester gathered the papers and letter as best she could with her arthritic fingers and set them aside. "I shouldn't bother you with my personal business when you're all ready to work," she said apologetically. "You're too kind to listen to an old lady complain."

Olivia smiled. "It's not a bother at all. You can bend my ear anytime about anything."

This made the older woman laugh. "Be careful what you wish for," she said merrily.

Miss Sivera came in with a tray of tea and cookies and set it on the table between the two settees. "I thought you might like something to drink," she said. "And perhaps come sit over here where it's more comfortable."

Olivia found it interesting that Miss Sivera always had the perfect timing when it came to Mrs. Winchester's needs. She was either lurking in the hallway or very intuitive. The thought of the proper secretary lurking in the hallway made Olivia want to laugh.

"I think sitting on the settee is a fine idea," Mrs. Winchester said. "This chair can get uncomfortable." She reached for a cane to pull herself up, and Miss Sivera was at her side immediately. "I'm fine, dear," the elderly lady said. "Pour the tea, please, while I hobble over there."

Miss Sivera nodded and returned to the table to pour the tea. "Would you like tea also?" she asked Olivia.

"Yes, please," Olivia said, moving over to the settee, too. "It was so kind of you to bring it in for us."

The secretary poured the tea and set the cups near each woman. "Ring if you need anything else," she said, then vanished again.

"Well, then," Mrs. Winchester said after she'd settled onto the settee. "Where did we end last time?"

"You had finished building the Prospect Hill house for your in-laws," Olivia reminded her.

"Ah, yes. That beautiful home," Mrs. Winchester said. "You know, my husband's sister, Jennie, and her husband, Thomas Bennett, now reside in that very house and have since it was built. Isn't it funny how all this continues to tie together?"

"Your story is much like a complicated tapestry that weaves together to create a colorful story," Olivia said. "I find it all interesting."

The elderly lady's eyes shone brightly. "What a beautiful way to put it. And it's so true. You do have a way with words, Olivia. I've seen it in the way you type the story up each day. There's a writer inside of you."

"Thank you." Olivia felt a flush rise to her cheeks. A compliment like that from such an accomplished woman meant a great deal to her.

"Even though I found joy in helping to build and decorate the house on the hill, so much else was happening around us," Mrs. Winchester said. "A year after Estelle married, Belle married Louis Merriman in 1867. By then, my father and mother had sold the business and moved to a different house in a nicer neighborhood on Orange Street. My father's health was failing quickly—his back pain was intolerable, as was the arthritis that crippled his hands." She glanced down at her own gnarled fingers. "I can now appreciate how much pain he suffered in those last years."

Olivia's heart went out to Mrs. Winchester, but she remained silent and continued to take shorthand. She knew that once Mrs. Winchester began reminiscing, it was best to let her go on without interruption.

Mrs. Winchester continued, her tone changing to pure joy. "And then, in March of 1869, Belle and Louis had their first child—a baby girl. And for the first time in three years, my heart was full again."

CHAPTER THIRTEEN

1869

"Oh, Belle!" Sarah exclaimed when she first laid eyes on her sister's newborn baby girl. "She's beautiful!" Sarah stared down into the dark eyes of the tiny child and could see her own reflection staring back. The little girl had a small crown of black hair, a button nose, and rosebud lips.

"She is beautiful, isn't she?" Belle said proudly. She was resting in her bed per the doctor's orders after having given birth two days earlier. "And perfect in every way."

Sarah's mother was there too, admiring her new grandchild. "She is sure to bring joy to your life." The elder Sarah smiled over at Sallie. "And I think she'll bring joy to your life as well, dear."

Sarah knew that was true. She'd immediately fallen in love with the little baby. "What have you named her?"

"We've decided on Maria Isabel," Belle said. "Although, I love the name Marion also. We can always change it if we decide to."

Sarah held the tiny child close and gazed into her little

face. She was swaddled in a white blanket, and her eyes stared inquisitively up at her. "She's a perfect little flower. Like a breath of fresh air after the long winter," Sarah said. "She's like the first daisy of the season."

Sarah's mother smiled. "Daisy. Yes. She's the perfect little spring flower. We should call her Daisy."

Belle frowned, but then slowly, her face changed into a smile. "That is a cute nickname. Daisy. What do you think, Sallie?"

Sarah smiled down at the bundle that had captured her heart. "I think Daisy is perfect."

From that moment on, Daisy became Sarah's favorite niece. Whenever possible, Sarah offered to babysit the child for Belle, and the little girl spent a lot of time at the Winchester's house on Prospect Hill. Even William fell in love with her, and she was a favorite of his as well. She filled the empty spot in their lives that Annie had left when she'd died. And since Sarah hadn't yet conceived again, having little Daisy around lifted her spirits.

Three months after Daisy's birth, Sarah's beloved father passed. The entire family was devastated, but Sarah and her mother were the most affected. Sarah had always adored her father, and they'd shared a closeness that her other siblings hadn't with Leonard. She knew it was because she'd been the only one of his children who'd understood his love of woodworking and dedication to creating beautiful things. Now, he was gone.

The entire family came together in their parents' Orange Street house after the funeral service. Sarah Pardee had been left a wealthy woman with a large, beautiful home and an even larger, loving family.

"Your father was very proud of all he'd accomplished in his life," the elder Sarah said to her family as they sat in the study—a favorite room of Leonard's. "We came from absolutely nothing, but look at where we are now. He was a good, hardworking man."

Young Sarah nodded, trying hard not to break down in tears. She'd missed her father's factory when he'd sold it, but she missed him much, much more. She was happy, though, that her mother would want for nothing for the rest of her life. But there would be another empty spot in Sarah's heart now that her father was gone.

* * *

Months later, in early 1870, William came to Sarah with exciting news. "Father wants us to take a trip out west to San Francisco to check on the new office he's set up there."

"Really?" Sarah was surprised that they had been chosen to go alone. Oliver Winchester generally wanted to be in the thick of things and went on these trips with Jane or sometimes with William. To send them on this mission was a tremendous act of trust. "That is exciting!"

William smiled at his wife. "I knew you'd be up for it. It'll be a long trip by train across the country, and I'm sure the accommodations will be a bit rough out there, but think of the adventure we'll have."

Sarah loved hearing the excitement in her husband's voice and seeing the sparkle in his eyes. His health had been in decline all winter, but now, with the onset of spring and this trip west, she thought it might be just the thing to boost his spirits. "When do we go?"

They boarded the train not long after William announced their trip and traveled across the United States. Over the years, Sarah had listened carefully when her husband and father-in-law discussed the rifle business and absorbed as much as she could. Oliver was dedicated to making his repeating arms company the very best, and he'd traveled the world to sell contracts to as many countries as possible. He'd modeled himself after Samuel Colt and set his ambitions to outsell Colt. After building the Prospect Hill mansion, Oliver then built a large factory just down the hill from the house where he could manufacture more guns faster than any other company. Since many of his contracts were overseas, setting up an office in the shipping city of San Francisco seemed like the next best idea.

The trip across country was indeed exciting for Sarah. She marveled at the varying landscapes as their train rolled through Nebraska, Wyoming, Utah, and the Sierra Nevada. Each day, there was a new vista to experience. And being able to share this incredible adventure with William made it all the more enjoyable.

Once they reached San Francisco, they stayed at the Palace Hotel on Market Street—the finest hotel in the still rough and tumble city. Sarah stared up in amazement as their carriage took them inside the hotel to the Grand Court, where they were helped down by waiting staff so they could check into their room. Seven floors of rooms rose above them up to the skylight that lit the court up with sunshine. The hotel, the size of a city block, boasted the best rooms in the city, with hydraulic elevators and a conservatory on the seventh floor.

"Have you ever seen anything like this before?" Sarah whispered to William as they were escorted to the front desk.

"It's quite impressive, I must say," he agreed.

Their room was even more exquisite than Sarah had hoped for. They stayed in a large suite with a bedroom, a sitting area, and their own private bathroom with running water.

"I thought we'd be roughing it on this trip," Sarah said with a grin.

William laughed. "It's extraordinary, isn't it? Not quite what I'd anticipated, but I'm thankful we can stay here."

Sarah fell in love with San Francisco. The coastal weather reminded her of New Haven, and even though the streets were still made of dirt and the people outside the hotel were somewhat questionable, she still found it charming. The gold rush was over, leaving people to find new ways to earn their living. Shipping had become an important industry, and buildings were going up all over the town as a new type of prospector found ways to get rich. Bankers and businessmen who'd made money off the thousands of men who'd tried to prospect for gold now built beautiful Victorian houses across the city. Parks, schools, and other signs of civilized life were being erected as well. Sarah could see the beginnings of a great city with beautiful views of the bay being built all around.

They visited the small, wooden building down by the docks that held the offices of the Winchester Repeating Arms Company. William was impressed by the sales the business was already generating. Aside from being the go-between for foreign markets, the little shop sold repeaters and ammunition in great quantities.

"Father was smart to open an outlet here," William confided to Sarah one evening as they ate dinner in an upscale restaurant near the hotel. "It is already making a considerable profit on sales, and they can ensure shipments go out on time. I'm quite impressed."

Sarah smiled at her husband. He looked so happy in this new environment. She knew he enjoyed seeing the many new sights just as much as she did. "Your father is a smart business-man. It doesn't surprise me that he thought of setting up an office here."

On their return to New Haven, William happily reported to his father how successful the office in San Francisco was. Pleased with this information, Oliver took many trips around the world to find new places to sell his prized rifles. His wife, Jane, would sometimes accompany him, but often, William and Sarah were invited to be his partners in traveling as well. Sarah loved traveling, and as she accompanied the men, she learned more about the business, which intrigued her. Just as she'd loved being in her father's woodworking factory, she also enjoyed talking business with Oliver and William and being taken seriously by them. Both men appreciated her intelligence and thoughts on the business.

Since her father's death, Sarah's mother had lived a quiet life in her lovely home with servants to help her. Sarah visited her mother often, taking time also to see her nieces and neph-ews, especially Daisy.

"Do you think it's silly of me to have built homes for Belle and Estelle so they could live nearby?" Sarah's mother asked her one day as they sat enjoying tea in the study. She'd recently used a piece of property she owned not far from the house and had built homes for the two youngest daughters despite them being married and having families. "I felt they should be close to each other, especially with their young children."

"I think it was a generous gesture, Mama," Sarah told her. "They each have a stable place to live, and you can be close to your grandchildren." Sarah knew her mother worried about

Belle and Estelle. They'd each had two children—a girl and a boy—all close in age. And their husbands didn't earn the kind of money that would keep a decent roof over their heads. So, the elder Sarah had used the excuse of wanting them close to give them homes.

"I know you are well-taken care of, Sallie, and I am so thankful for that. The Winchesters have been a wonderful family for you," her mother said.

"You don't have to worry about me," Sarah said. "William takes good care of me, and Oliver and Jane treat me like a daughter."

"You don't know what a relief that is for me," her mother said. "I know Mary is well taken care of by her husband, William, and they seem to be doing fine in Manhattan since their move after your father sold his business. I'm not sure how Nettie and Homer are faring, but she doesn't complain. Belle and Estelle, however, have always needed a helping hand."

Sarah smiled. "Unlike my brother, Leonard. He's as self-sufficient as they come." Leonard had finally married a few months after their father had passed, and he and his wife, also named Sarah, had two young children. They had a little girl named Sarah, although they called her Sadie, and a baby boy named Louis. "Does he ever bring the children around to visit?"

"Not as much as I'd like to see them, but he works hard and makes a good home for his wife and children," her mother said. "And I appreciate that he's a good provider. He's a good man."

Sarah agreed. Her brother was a good father and husband. He kept to himself mostly, but he provided well.

With the new factory now open just down the hill from the Prospect Street mansion, William was home each evening instead of being gone for a week at a time as he'd done before. Sarah was thankful for that. She enjoyed hearing about his day and the work at the factory. Her husband had been given the title of vice-president of the rifle division, and although William didn't share his father's enthusiasm over building guns, he did enjoy working with the gunsmiths and coming up with ideas to make the rifles and the loading of ammunition safer.

William's old position as secretary of the company was filled by a recent Yale graduate, Thomas G. Bennett. Bennett had a mechanical engineering degree but took the position with the hope of rising quickly in the company. Two years later, to everyone's surprise, Thomas married William's little sister, Jennie, and the couple seemed to be a perfect match.

"Seems a bit convenient," Belle said under her breath to Sarah as they sat in the church pews during the wedding ceremony. "How lucky for him the boss's daughter was unattached."

"Shh!" Sarah nodded toward the elder Winchesters sitting in the pew in front of them. "I think they are truly compatible," she whispered.

Belle rolled her eyes, making Sarah sigh. Her sister always spoke her mind and didn't care what anyone thought, but it could be so embarrassing. Sarah had reservations about Thomas and Jennie marrying, too, but kept them to herself. He was a rather stiff and proper person, but that didn't mean he didn't love her sister-in-law.

The newly married couple moved into a suite of rooms in the lavish Winchester mansion on Prospect Street, and a year later, Jennie gave birth to a beautiful little girl they named Hope. While Sarah continued to pray to have another child of her own, she forced herself not to dwell on it. As nieces and nephews were born on both the Pardee and Winchester sides of the family, she celebrated each birth and was thankful her family had healthy children. Sarah used her time instead to learn everything she could about running a large house and managing finances. She also paid close attention to what was happening with the Winchester rifle business. Keeping her mind busy enabled Sarah not to become depressed about her and William not having a family of their own.

In 1874, a great sadness fell over the Winchester family when Oliver's closest friend and trusted partner, John Davies, suddenly died. John had been more than a business partner—he'd been Oliver's closest confidant in all aspects of his life, and the elder Winchester had trusted him completely. It was a great blow to the entire family.

Worse yet, while grieving the loss of his friend, Oliver had to see to the daily running of his business now that Davies was gone. While both Oliver and Davies acted as treasurers for the company, Oliver had placed his complete trust in Davies to take care of the financial aspect of the business and investments. Now, he needed someone else who could do the job with the expertise of his beloved friend.

One evening, Oliver took Sarah aside to ask her about her brother-in-law, William Converse.

"He took care of your father's finances, did he not?" Oliver asked Sarah quietly in the study as the other family members amused themselves with other activities. Jennie was playing the piano in the far corner as William and Thomas were involved in an intense chess game nearby, and Jane worked on needlepoint in a corner chair.

Sarah studied Oliver for a moment. He never asked casual questions. Oliver was a forthright man who always had a reason for what he did and said. "Yes. My father trusted him completely with the financial end of the business. He was quite adept at investing money also and helped to build my father's portfolio after they'd sold the business."

Oliver nodded, taking in everything she said. "Would you trust him with your money?"

Sarah laughed at this. "If I had my own money, then yes, I would trust him," she said.

Later that evening, as Sarah and William prepared for bed, William asked, "What was my father talking so seriously about with you tonight?"

"He was asking about William Converse," she told him. "And whether or not I'd trust him to handle my money."

William frowned. "Odd. Why would he ask about him?"

"I don't know," Sarah said. "But with John now gone, I suppose he's looking ahead and trying to decide who will be the new treasurer. John's death left a big hole in the company, from what I can tell."

William nodded as he sat on the edge of the bed. "Yes, it did. But I assumed Father would move me to treasurer or even Thomas, although finances are neither of our strong suits."

Sarah sat down beside her husband and gazed up at him. His blue eyes had dark circles underneath, and he'd grown thinner these past few months. She knew he had coughing fits at times, but he always brushed her concern aside. Despite his soft-hearted nature, William never liked being coddled or made to look weak. She supposed it was because he needed to be strong for his father, who was always the picture of robust health.

"Well, we both know that nothing is ever as it seems with your father," she said. "He always goes his own way despite his loyalty to his family." Sarah had a deep love and great respect for Oliver, but he could be a stubborn, determined man.

William sighed and kissed her sweetly on the lips. "Yes. He does go his own way. And as always, I won't fight him on it when he does."

Not long afterward, Oliver asked William Converse to join the board of directors of the Winchester Repeating Arms Company, then hired him as the treasurer. William Converse and Mary moved back to New Haven and made their home in Sarah Pardee's house on Orange Street. While William and Thomas both felt put out for being passed over to be chosen as the treasurer, William stood by his father's decision in the end. Converse was a congenial man without airs, and he did know how to manage money in the style that suited Oliver. Once the business was safely on track again, Oliver could continue to promote his rifles around the country and the world without worry. And although Sarah felt hurt that her father-in-law did not choose her husband for the higher position in the business, she understood that Oliver did what he thought was best for all. It was a good lesson she kept in the back of her mind as the years went on.

CHAPTER FOURTEEN

1918

"I learned so much from Oliver about running a business using your mind instead of your heart," Sarah said to Olivia. "You can't always make decisions based on not hurting a family member's feelings. Sometimes, you have to choose what will be best for everyone."

Olivia knew that they were finished for the day by the way Mrs. Winchester addressed her as she spoke. For the past two hours, she had told her story as if reading a book to Olivia. But when Mrs. Winchester addressed her by name, that usually signaled they were finished.

"I'm sure it's difficult to make decisions that will change another person's life," Olivia said. Although from what she'd seen since moving into this house, Mrs. Winchester kept the welfare of her staff and family in the forefront at all times.

"I've had to make a few tough decisions with my family," the elderly lady said. "During this delicate time with Belle, I've had to discontinue her allowance so that she doesn't do anything rash with it. Of course, I still pay for her needs, but

Daisy and I make the decisions for her. It hasn't been easy. Belle is an independent soul and hates to be reined in."

Olivia knew from the story Mrs. Winchester had told so far that Belle had always been difficult. "I'm sure that was a hard thing to do. But you've been so generous with her and all your family. You shouldn't feel guilty about it."

She smiled at Olivia. "You are a dear. Well, look at the clock. It's nearly lunchtime," Mrs. Winchester said. "We should stop for the day. I'm sure you have more than enough to type up in that little notebook of yours already."

"The time flies by," Olivia said, standing to take her leave. When she did, her skirt tightened around her belly, and she tried to straighten it without success.

"It seems you are starting to outgrow your clothing," Mrs. Winchester said. "The baby is getting bigger."

Olivia's cheeks grew warm. "I'm afraid so. I have a few loose dresses I can wear. I guess I hadn't thought that far ahead until this skirt was too tight this morning."

"That's easily fixed," Mrs. Winchester told her. "I'll have my dresser, Misa, drop by your room this afternoon and gather up your skirts. She can add a panel in each one that can grow along with the baby."

"Oh, that is so kind of you," Olivia said, stunned she would offer up her own dresser to help her. "I'd be happy to pay her for her time."

"Oh, my dear," Mrs. Winchester said. "I pay her enough to do it for both of us. And she likes to keep busy. If my hands weren't so sore, I'd love to get out my sewing machine and help her. I used to sew all the time as a young woman."

Olivia couldn't even imagine the grand lady of the house helping her, a secretary, make her skirts bigger for her pregnancy.

She'd have died of embarrassment if Mrs. Winchester did so. "Thank you for offering Misa's help. I hope she won't mind."

"She won't mind at all," Mrs. Winchester said. As she spoke, Miss Sivera entered the room. "Shall we go upstairs, and I'll get your lunch?" she asked her employer.

"Yes. It's been a long morning."

"I'll take the tea tray into the kitchen on my way to lunch," Olivia offered, and Miss Sivera thanked her. She watched as the two women left the living area and walked slowly to the elevator. As always, Mrs. Winchester had surprised Olivia with her seemingly unending kindness.

Olivia carried the tray to the kitchen, and Alice practically ran up to her to retrieve it.

"You shouldn't be carrying heavy things," Alice admonished her, then turned away quickly as if she'd said something wrong.

Olivia watched the cook as she gave the tray to the dishwasher. She was stunned she'd spoken so harshly to her.

Alice returned, a bright smile on her face. "Are you ready for lunch? I'm starved."

"You know, don't you?" Olivia asked. "Have you known all along?"

Alice frowned and looked like she would deny it, but then sighed. "No. Not the entire time. But yes, I guessed you were carrying a wee one soon enough. But I haven't told a soul, I swear. That is your business."

"I wish you had just come out and told me you knew," Olivia said angrily. Seeing the downcast look on Alice's face, she suddenly felt guilty. "I'm sorry. I didn't mean to sound angry. I guess my emotions are all over the place. The baby is getting larger, and soon everyone will know, so I don't know why I'm upset."

"It's all right," Alice said. "I'm sure it can't be easy, being a widow and carrying a baby. But there's nothing to be ashamed of. You were married. Everyone will be very understanding and helpful."

They wouldn't be if they knew the truth, Olivia thought to herself. But as long as they believed she was a widow, she guessed everyone would be sympathetic to her situation.

"Thank you, Alice. For understanding and being so kind these past few weeks. But please, from now on, just say what's on your mind. I think we've developed a true enough friendship to be honest with one another."

Alice beamed. "I think so, too. I'm so glad you feel that way." She linked arms with Olivia, and they walked to the servant's dining room. "Let's eat!"

Olivia greeted the other workers as she and Alice sat down. Misa smiled over at her but said nothing about sewing her skirts. Olivia thought she must have already heard from Mrs. Winchester or Miss Sivera, though, from the way the petite woman had acknowledged her.

"How is your work with Mrs. Winchester coming along?" Alice asked, her green eyes sparkling with curiosity. "How I wish I could read that story, but I know I can't."

"It's coming along quite nicely," Olivia said. "She has had such an interesting life. And so many losses. But I suppose it's the tragedies that shape our personalities throughout life."

"Ah, yes," Alice said. "And we all have tragedies in one way or another. But the good experiences shape us as well. Look at all the missus has accomplished since moving here decades ago. I think that helped to make her a generous person as well."

"I agree," Olivia said. She hoped she wasn't saying too

much about Mrs. Winchester because she'd hate to have her think she'd share personal information.

The group spoke among themselves as they ate their delicious meal of tender roast beef, garden-fresh green beans, and fresh fruit, along with delicious bread Alice had made just that morning. Everything always tasted so good here at the house. It reminded Olivia of living on the farm and all the work she, her mother, and her sisters had put into each meal.

"Let me send up some fresh cookies and a glass of milk with you so you won't go hungry while you're typing," Alice offered after they'd eaten.

Olivia laughed. "That's so sweet of you, but I couldn't eat another bite. If I get hungry, I'll sneak down and steal a few of your cookies."

"Okay. But remember, you need to fatten up for that little child," Alice said, grinning.

Olivia walked upstairs to her room, and like before, she left the door open so the breeze through the windows would pass through her room. It wasn't too hot outside today, but the cool air felt good, especially since Olivia had felt warmer lately. She supposed the baby was causing her body temperature to rise. She couldn't even imagine what it was going to be like when her belly grew large.

Just as she sat at her typewriter, a brisk knock came on her door, and Olivia turned to see who it was. There stood Misa, a measuring tape in her hand, waiting to be invited in.

"Come in, please, Miss Hirata," Olivia said, standing to greet her.

"Call me Misa, please," the woman told her kindly. "I've just come to gather your skirts and measure you. It will only take a moment."

"Yes. Thank you," Olivia said.

The tiny woman buzzed around her quickly, measuring her waist and the length to her ankles. She stopped momentarily and studied Olivia's belly as if she were seeing something that wasn't there. "May I?" she asked, looking up at Olivia. The woman's hand was hovering around her mid-section like she was expressing she wanted to touch Olivia's belly.

"Of course," Olivia said, wondering why but figuring it had something to do with getting the correct measurements.

Misa laid her hand over Olivia's small baby bump and held it there for a moment. "You'll carry low," she announced. "I can make the panels on the skirts low so it will be more comfortable."

Olivia was stunned by her prediction. "How do you know that already?"

Misa smiled. "The baby is already low. You're going to have a girl."

A girl? Olivia had dreamt of having a baby girl, but how could Misa know that this early? "Are you sure?"

Misa laughed. "I've always been right before. Let's gather your skirts."

The two women went to the wardrobe, and Olivia pulled out three of her skirts and draped them over Misa's outstretched arm. "This should be enough," she told her.

Misa shook her head. "Give them all to me. You'll be big for several months, and you'll need more than this."

Olivia hadn't wanted to make Misa work so hard, but she did as she asked and handed her the other three skirts. "My dresses are loose now, so they will be fine," she told Misa.

"We can fix those too when the time comes," Misa said matter-of-factly. "And once the baby comes, I can take the panels out of your skirts, and they will be as good as new again."

"Thank you so much for doing this," Olivia said. "I'm terrible at sewing and wouldn't even know how to fix these."

"That's why you type, and I sew," Misa said, a mischievous grin on her face. She nodded goodbye and headed out of the room.

As Olivia watched Misa leave, she decided she liked the little woman very much.

Walking back to her desk, Olivia sat and prepared the paper and carbon paper to make the two copies as she typed. Olivia didn't know what she'd do with the second copy other than it being a backup in case something happened to the originals, but she liked being careful.

As she typed, Olivia couldn't help but think of what Misa had said. A baby girl. Maybe one could tell the sex of the child this early by where the small bump was. She placed her hand on her belly, and the tiny baby inside her flipped. It was a slight, fluttery feeling. While Olivia knew that she should only hope for a healthy baby of either sex, she couldn't help but be elated at the prospect of having a little girl.

* * *

The weeks went by quickly, and summer grew warmer at the Atherton home. Mrs. Winchester had experienced several bad health days, leaving Olivia to find other ways to occupy her time. A couple of times, she'd sat in the elderly lady's bedroom and took dictation from her bedside so that they might continue with the project. But because it seemed to tire Mrs. Winchester, Miss Sivera and Maud both discouraged their employer from working from bed.

"I'm so afraid I'll expire soon and never finish this project," Mrs. Winchester confided to Olivia one day as they tried to work in her bedroom. "But I should listen to Henrietta and Maud, I suppose. They are just trying to help."

"We will finish, I promise you," Olivia said, even though she had no idea how Mrs. Winchester's health was progressing. "I feel you'll rally at any time."

"You are kind to say that," the older lady told her. "And I'll believe what you've said."

The skirts that Misa had fixed worked perfectly for Olivia. The panels were hidden underneath but allowed Olivia to expand the skirts as her stomach grew larger. And over the weeks, she had grown much bigger than she'd imagined she would so quickly. It was like the baby had suddenly decided to make its presence known. Olivia assumed by now that the entire staff knew she was expecting, although no one said a word to her out of politeness. But it was becoming more obvious by the day that there would be a little baby in the house soon.

On days she didn't work with Mrs. Winchester, Olivia went to the kitchen and was allowed to help with small jobs like baking.

"But not when it's too hot in here," Alice told her. "We don't need you fainting in the bread." That made Olivia laugh. She didn't want to fall face-first into the bread either.

One morning in early July, Miss Sivera came to Olivia's room to tell her that Mrs. Winchester would be at her desk that day. "She's expecting Mr. Lieb and Mr. Stanley later in the morning," the secretary told her. "But would like to work a little with you first."

"Wonderful," Olivia said. "I miss our days of work."

Miss Sivera stood quietly at the door a moment, looking like she meant to continue speaking.

"Is there something else?" Olivia asked.

"Oh, I'm sorry," she told her, looking embarrassed. "I've just been so caught up in Mrs. Winchester's health that I hadn't noticed how your pregnancy is coming along until now."

Olivia looked down at her increasing waistline. "Yes. It's becoming quite obvious."

"Oh, dear. I hadn't meant to make it sound like that. I'm so sorry. But the baby is growing. Are you feeling well? Is there anything you need to make yourself comfortable?"

Olivia was touched that Miss Sivera cared enough to ask her that. "I'm doing fine, thank you. I don't need anything. Living in this fine house with the delicious meals and easy work is more than I could have ever asked for."

Miss Sivera smiled. "I'm glad you're feeling well. Let me know if you do need anything. And please feel free to use the elevator instead of the stairs."

"Thank you. I may get so big I might need it."

Once the secretary had left, Olivia gathered her notepad and pencils and made the trip down the hallway to the front stairs. The doorbell chimed as she reached the last step. Since no one else was around to answer it, Olivia opened the door. There stood Mr. Lieb and Mr. Stanley.

"Ah, Mrs. Collins. It's so nice to see you," Mr. Lieb said, reaching for her hand. "You look the picture of health."

"Thank you, Mr. Lieb," Olivia said, surprised they were there so early. In fact, his being there at all was uncommon. Frank Lieb was a very busy man who handled work for several illustrious clients. The fact that he was there told Olivia that the matter was of the utmost importance. "Please, do come in.

You, too, Mr. Stanley. It's nice seeing you again."

Daniel Stanley stood and stared at Olivia. It took him a few moments to reply. "Why, yes. It's nice seeing you again, too, Mrs. Collins."

Olivia noticed how formal he sounded and wondered why. Perhaps it was because his employer was with him.

"We're earlier than expected," Mr. Lieb said apologetically. "Do you know if Mrs. Winchester is ready to receive us?"

"I believe she is coming down very soon," Olivia said. "I was just going to wait for her in the office. Why don't you wait in the living area, and I'll have the kitchen bring a tray of tea and coffee."

"That would be most welcomed," Mr. Lieb said, smiling. "Thank you."

Olivia smiled back. She liked Mr. Lieb immensely. He'd been kind to her over the last couple of years and conveyed a warm, fatherly-like feeling toward her. He was a tall, handsome man with his hair graying at the temples, and he was very down-to-earth despite the money he made and the extravagant way he lived. Of course, Olivia knew the extravagance had more to do with his wife, Lida, than with him.

Olivia glanced over at Daniel before leaving but noticed he was outwardly staring at her. The look in his eyes seemed to be one of shock. "I'll be back momentarily," she said, feeling off-kilter by Daniel's stare. She hurried down the hallway to the kitchen, and as she turned around a corner, she caught her reflection in a large mirror. Olivia stopped short. Over the weeks, she'd become used to how much her belly had grown. But Daniel hadn't seen her in all that time. She realized he'd been stunned by the fact that she was with child.

CHAPTER FIFTEEN

Today

Morgan drove to her parents' house, excited to hear what her mother had learned about Olivia Collins. It was a beautiful July day, cooler in the city, where the breeze came off the bay. As she drew closer to San Jose, it grew warmer, but she didn't mind. It was Saturday, and she could step away from her work for a while and focus on her Sarah Winchester project instead.

Morgan parked in her parents' driveway and entered the air-conditioned house. It felt refreshing compared to the heat outside. She headed directly to the kitchen because she knew her mother would be working at the counter as usual.

"Hi, Mom," Morgan said as she entered. Her mother was right where she'd expected and had her laptop out and papers strewn all over the counter. The printer beside her was shooting out paper.

"Hi, dear," her mother said, smiling at her. "I'm printing out my notes about what I've found so far. It's easier for me if I keep notes and records instead of just trying to remember it all."

Morgan nodded. She was also a note-taker. Sticky notes lined her desk all the time. She went to the cupboard for a glass and put ice water in it from the fridge dispenser, then sat down across the counter from her mom. "Did you find anything interesting?"

"Oh, yes. I found so much on our family digging through the censuses and other records. I started with my mother and worked my way back. Of course, I knew names and birth dates for everyone up until Olivia. They were the easy ones. Now, I'm trying to make sense of Olivia's family."

"Make sense?" Morgan asked.

"It's a little more confusing than I'd thought it would be," Annie said.

"What's been confusing?" Morgan asked.

Annie picked up her paperwork and sorted through it, then placed it all in a nice, neat pile. "I haven't gotten too far, but this is what I have. Olivia Anne Collins was born on January 16, 1896, the second-youngest child in a family of eleven children. Her parents lived on property north of San Francisco. They had moved out to California from Ohio long before Olivia was born. In the 1910 census, I found her parents and the children all listed, and her father's occupation was orchard farm owner. So, I suppose he had his own farm that they all worked on. Olivia was listed as age fourteen. Then, I searched for her in the 1920 census. She no longer lived at home but instead was living in a house in the affluent neighborhood of Atherton, California. The head of the household was Sarah L. Winchester."

Morgan grew excited. "So, you found proof that she actually worked for Mrs. Winchester? That's wonderful!"

"It is," her mother said, smiling widely. "She's listed as a secretary. In fact, almost all the other people who lived in the house at the time were servants. One was a maid, one was a nurse, and two women were secretaries. Olivia was one of them. But there's more."

"What?" Morgan asked, totally intrigued.

"I know that my grandmother, Rose Sarah Collins, was born in 1918. The 1920 census shows a Rose Sarah Collins born in 1918, and it states she's Olivia's daughter. I couldn't find any marriage records for Olivia prior to 1920. That means that Olivia had a daughter two years before she was married."

"Hmm. That's interesting," Morgan said. "Do you think your grandmother was illegitimate, and that's been kept a secret all these years?"

"She would have bristled at being called illegitimate, that's for sure. The man Olivia married in 1920 adopted her because Rose always used that surname. Olivia could have been married, and her husband died in the war, but there's no record that I can find. Plus, she used her maiden name for her child, so that's suspect." Annie stopped for a moment and studied her notes. "By today's standards, no one would even blink at Olivia being a single mother. But back then, it would have been a scandal. Do you think Mrs. Winchester would have hired a pregnant single woman to work in her home?"

"I don't know," Morgan said. "From what I've read in the manuscript so far, she seemed like a very generous person. She was also independent and didn't hold to other people's standards. Do we know exactly when Olivia went to work for her?"

Annie shook her head. "No, unfortunately, there are no records between 1910 and 1920. I'm assuming at some point, Olivia went to business or secretarial school and then went to work for Mrs. Winchester. That could be anywhere from 1914 to 1920."

"Maybe by the time she went to work for Sarah, she had already had the baby. Maybe Mrs. Winchester assumed she was a widow and didn't ask questions. Wasn't the Spanish Flu pandemic around 1918? Maybe Olivia married, and her husband died of that."

"All of those are possibilities," Annie said. "But would she have returned to using her maiden name for her and her daughter?"

Morgan shrugged. "Yeah. That's a little confusing. But the good thing is I now have proof Olivia lived in Mrs. Winchester's house as a secretary, so the manuscript must be legit. That's the information I needed."

Her mother nodded. "Yes. We have the proof. I'll give you a copy of the census so you can put it with the manuscript."

"Great. Thanks, Mom."

"But I'm going to continue digging into this history. I need to find out more about Olivia and Rose and what happened. I may not find anything, but it's been fun digging up little tidbits like this."

"Family secrets, you mean?" Morgan teased her. "Everyone was so secretive in those days. But I guess they were too embarrassed to tell the truth that they were all just as human as we are today."

"That's for sure." Annie closed her computer and set the paperwork aside. "How is your job going?"

"Better now that I have this information," Morgan said. "I've been working hard on a few acquisitions, and I have a couple of really good books we're going forward with. I know I should have waited, but I spoke with Amanda about the Sarah Winchester biography and asked if she'd be interested in publishing it."

"Really? What did she say?"

"She said I'd need proof that my relative typed up Sarah Winchester's actual words. But I think now we have the proof we need." Morgan was excited again. "But I'm not finished reading it yet since I've been so busy. Once I've read the entire manuscript, I'll take it to Amanda, and we can discuss it seriously."

Annie shook her head. "Wouldn't that be something after all these decades? Publishing Sarah Winchester's autobiography as written by Olivia Collins. Our relative. I'm not sure if she'd be thrilled or would be rolling over in her grave."

Morgan laughed. "Let's hope she's resting peacefully in her grave."

Annie stood. "Let's go out for dinner. I know your dad is starving by now."

* * *

Monday at work, Morgan was too excited to keep the new information her mother had learned to herself. But she knew better than to go to Amanda just yet, so she invited Jonathan out for lunch. They walked to a small pub that served the best hamburgers around and sat in a corner booth where they would have privacy.

"You must have something exciting to tell me if you invited me to lunch," Jonathan said with a grin after they each had ordered a burger and fries. "So, spill."

Morgan liked how well Jonathan knew her. She didn't have to pretend or make small talk with him to slowly bring up the real reason for inviting him here. "Remember the Winchester biography I found?"

"How could I forget it? It's the find of the century," he said.

"Well, my mother has done some digging into the family history, and we can prove that our relative Olivia, who typed up the manuscript, actually did work for Mrs. Winchester as her secretary around 1920. She's listed on the census report for Mrs. Winchester's house. I'm so excited, I could burst!"

Jonathan chuckled. "I'd like to see that. I don't think you've ever been more than just a little amused. Excited is way up there."

"Well, it's true," Morgan said. "I've never been this excited over a project in my life. This is big, Jon. If I can convince Amanda to publish this biography, it would be big. Especially with me as the editor and the person who found it. Finally, after all these years, I have something to be excited about."

"I'm happy for you," Jonathan said. "This is the type of thing that could put you on the map, as well as raise up Generation Publishing. Have you read the whole manuscript yet? Are you ready to tell Amanda about it?"

Their food came, and they waited until the waiter left before speaking. Morgan took a bite of her burger and washed it down with her Coke. "Actually, I told her about it a few weeks ago."

Jonathan raised his brows. "Really? I thought you were going to wait until you read it all and could prove your great-great-grandmother was legit."

"I was going to wait. But do you remember that day Amanda had that meeting where she was knocking down everything we pitched? The next day, she was in a contrite mood, and I almost felt sorry for her. We had a long talk in the conference room, and she confided in me about a few things happening with the business. I felt like I was in a safe zone and told her about it."

"So, what did she say?" he asked.

"Basically, what I'd thought she'd say. I'd have to prove it was real, and then we could look into publishing it. She believed, like you and I do, that it would be big for the publisher."

"That's good." Jonathan took a bite out of his burger and ate a few fries.

Morgan watched him a moment. She could feel his mood changing. "Is something wrong?"

He shook his head. "No. I mean, not really. It's your manuscript to do with as you wish. I'm just surprised you jumped the gun and told her about it right after we'd both agreed it might be better to wait."

This surprised Morgan. "I didn't think it would matter. It wasn't like she was going to drop everything and buy the manuscript anyway. And I'm not going to run to her with it right away now. I have to finish reading it and write up an evaluation just as I would any manuscript I pitch. I figure that will give me a better chance of talking her into it."

"That's a good idea," Jonathan said.

His voice sounded distant, something Morgan wasn't used to. "Are you mad at me? And why?" she asked.

"I'm not mad at all," he said. "But sometimes, I feel like you bounce things off me and then ignore my advice. I don't care if you don't take my advice, but when you agree with me and then do the opposite, sometimes it's a little annoying."

Morgan frowned as she tried to remember their conversation about the manuscript. He'd only agreed with her that waiting was the right thing to do. Why was he so offended she hadn't waited after all? "I'm sorry if I do that," she finally said. "I guess I didn't think it mattered. We give each other advice all the time, but I don't get mad if you don't listen to me."

Jonathan sighed. "Ignore me, okay? I didn't mean to make

a big deal about it. It's just been a bad Monday for me, that's all. You have the right to do whatever you want."

Their walk back to the office wasn't as comfortable as it had been on the way to lunch. Jonathan went straight to his cubicle and started working while Morgan sat wondering what she'd done to upset him. They'd always been casual friends, but he'd acted like she'd somehow hurt his feelings. It was true, they both bounced ideas off each other all the time, and often, she followed Jonathan's advice. But this manuscript had nothing to do with him, so why would he take it personally?

By the time her day was over, Morgan was tired of thinking about Jonathan and his sudden change of attitude. She hoped by tomorrow, he'd be back to his same old carefree self. Tonight, she didn't bring any work home with her. Instead, she couldn't wait to get back to the Winchester manuscript, curl up on her bed, and read.

CHAPTER SIXTEEN

1880

Spring couldn't come soon enough for Sarah. William had been ill all winter but still went to work each day despite looking drawn and pale. His cough was the worst it had been in months, and although the doctor did what he could, William continued to weaken. The family knew that William had been diagnosed with consumption, and although he seemed to rally each spring, Sarah worried he'd wear himself out by not resting as the doctor ordered.

Sarah's mother hadn't felt well over the winter either, and Sarah hoped both William and her mother would grow stronger as the days grew warmer. With so many others to worry about, it was a shock to everyone when the strongest, most robust family member of all, Oliver Winchester, was suddenly struck down in the early weeks of spring.

At the age of seventy, Oliver worked as hard as he ever had, constantly on the go and running his factory and worldwide business. And suddenly, it all stopped. Jane rushed to Sarah and William's bedroom one spring morning, calling out frantically for help.

"It's your father," Jane told William, who'd just finished dressing for work. "Hurry. He fell to the floor, and I can't help him up."

William rushed to his father's side and saw immediately that he needed medical attention. "Send for the doctor," he told Sarah, who'd followed him down the hallway. She hurried downstairs and told one of the maids to run and get the doctor. By the time Sarah was back upstairs, Thomas and William had been able to lift Oliver into bed. The older man was unconscious but still breathing.

Everyone in the house was in a panic by the time the doctor arrived. No one had anticipated that Oliver could possibly become ill. He'd always been in such good health.

"It seems Mr. Winchester has suffered a stroke that's incapacitated his ability to move," the doctor told the family after he'd examined Oliver. Jennie, Thomas, Sarah, William, and Jane were all in the hallway outside the bedroom. They'd kept the grandchildren out of that wing of the house so as not to scare them.

"Is he conscious yet?" Thomas asked. He was the only family member who'd stayed calm during the ordeal.

"Yes. He is conscious but unable to speak and move," the doctor said. "We need to keep him calm so he doesn't experience another episode. He'll need full-time care over the next few weeks, and hopefully, he'll be able to regain his ability to speak and move."

"I must go in and see him," Jane said, twisting a handkerchief in her hands. "He must be confused and scared." She hurried toward the room, then turned and beckoned for William. "Come with me."

Sarah watched as William turned paler than he already was. She knew seeing his father as an invalid was difficult for him. Patting his arm gently, she whispered, "He needs you now more than ever. It'll be all right."

William swallowed hard and followed his mother into the room.

Later, as the family waited downstairs, barely eating their breakfast, the doctor, William, and Jane came down. Sarah's heart went out to Jane. She looked broken.

"The doctor gave Oliver something to help him sleep," Jane said, sitting heavily in a dining room chair. The maid quickly brought her tea and a plate of food. Jane pushed the food aside but gratefully sipped the warm drink. "He's confused right now. The doctor explained what had happened to him, but I think it's too much for him to grasp at the moment." Tears filled Jane's eyes. "I've never known your father to look so helpless."

The doctor gently patted Jane's back. "Once he's rested, he'll be able to understand what is happening. Your husband is a strong man—I've no doubt he'll be determined to get better again." The doctor left a few minutes later, promising to send the best nurses he knew to start taking shifts at Oliver's bedside.

Sarah noticed that William looked drained. She tried to get him to eat something, and when he refused, she encouraged him to go up to their room with her to rest. This William agreed to do. He turned to Thomas. "Will you inform William Converse of what's happened? And then we'll have to bring the board together and discuss the running of the company during this time."

Thomas nodded, and William followed Sarah up to their room. Once inside, William broke down. They had lost a child together and had experienced losses of close family members in the years they'd been together. But never had Sarah seen William this distraught.

"What will I do if Father doesn't come through this?" William said, sitting on the bed and dropping his head in his hands. "I will be the acting president if Father dies. I just can't do it right now. I don't have the strength or the stamina to fill his shoes."

"Oh, my dear Will." Sarah sat beside him and wrapped her arms around him. "Your father will get better; I just know it. We all know what a strong disposition he has. He won't let this keep him down."

William shook his head. "Even so, it will be a long time before he'll be able to work, let alone run the business. Everyone will look to me to continue running the business. And also make all the financial decisions for the family. I haven't the strength. I can barely get up and go to work as it is."

Sarah knew it was fear that was making William speak this way. Yes, he'd been ill, but seeing his father incapacitated had scared him. William had never been one to shirk his duties, and she knew she had to help him find the strength to continue his father's work.

"Darling," she said gently, reaching for his hand and making him look her in the eyes. "You are not alone in this. I'm here for you in any way possible to help you through this terrible time. And you have both William Converse and Thomas Bennett to help you make intelligent decisions. William is a fine treasurer and will continue to handle the money responsibly, and Thomas knows how to keep everything running smoothly. Both men are trustworthy and only want the best for the company because they are family, too. You don't have to put everything on yourself, dear. You can let others help you."

Her words seemed to help because the panic in William's eyes abated, and his heavy breathing calmed. "Yes, of course. You're right, dear." He lifted her hand up to his lips and kissed it gently. "I'm not alone in this. Seeing Father unable to speak or move was difficult. I think it paralyzed me for a moment. You know I've always found my strength in trying to please him. But my source of strength will now have to come from within."

She smiled. "Why don't you rest a bit? It's been a difficult morning."

"I'm better now," he said, standing. "And I should make an appearance at the factory to buoy everyone's spirits and also bring the board together this afternoon." He reached for her and hugged her tightly. "You, my dear, give me strength too. You always have. How can such a tiny person be such a powerful source?"

Sarah laughed. "I'm not so sure I'm that powerful, but we get our strength from being together."

The first few weeks after Oliver's stroke were difficult ones, especially for Jane and William. Oliver had a nurse with him twenty-four hours a day, and Jane was at his bedside every day, encouraging him in his recovery. Sarah, too, sat with her father-in-law at times, reading the newspaper to him or a book in the evenings. She knew he hated having to be cared for in every way, but his progress in movement was returning very slowly. Sarah wouldn't give up on Oliver. She knew he was headstrong enough to eventually move and speak, and she told him so. She'd even made him smile crookedly when she told him he was too ornery to give up. They both knew it was true.

In May, Sarah was summoned by Belle and Estelle to her mother's house. She'd been keeping close tabs on her mother's health and had thought she'd been getting better. Sarah hurried to the house on Orange Street to find her mother bedridden and breathing laboriously.

"Mama was up and talking just yesterday," Estelle told Sarah. "She'd eaten well, and we thought she was doing fine."

"She was having tea in the study the other day when I came to visit her," Sarah said, still stunned to see her mother so ill. "What happened?"

"Nothing happened," Belle said sharply. "She took a turn for the worst. But I'm sure Mama will be up again in a few days." She looked at her sisters, suddenly sounding worried. "Should we call the doctor?"

As Sarah watched her mother, she knew deep in her heart that the elder Sarah would not be getting up on her own again. Her mother had aged in just two days and looked so pale and thin under the coverlet. Had they ignored the signs of her wasting away? Her mother was seventy-two years old and had worked hard nearly her entire life. The early years with her father had been demanding ones, and her mother had given birth to several children. Of course, she was tired. Why hadn't they seen she was near death? Her mother had done her best to make them think she was going to be fine.

"Yes," Sarah finally said. "Ask a maid to summon the doctor. I don't think Mama has much time left."

The doctor, as well as all the children and grandchildren, were summoned to the house to say their last goodbyes. William Converse and Mary lived in the house and were there already. Sarah's William also came immediately to be with his wife. He'd always been warmly accepted in the Pardee family and thought of Sarah's mother as his second mother.

After examining their mother, the doctor pronounced there

was nothing more he could do except give her medicine in case she suffered any pain. They all knew now that their mother was dying.

The next day, Sarah Pardee passed quietly in her bed with Sarah, Belle, and Estelle by her side. The others had left for the night except for Mary, who'd grown tired and had gone to bed. But the three sisters had stayed beside their mother, not wanting her to take her last breath alone.

Sarah was heartbroken to lose yet another beloved family member. She was at loose ends with worry over Oliver and her husband's faltering health. When Belle began planning their mother's funeral, Sarah didn't object. She didn't have the strength or heart to do the planning herself.

Days later, Sarah Burns Pardee was laid to rest beside her husband Leonard in Evergreen Cemetery after a funeral service at Belle's home. All the children and grandchildren attended, as well as friends and neighbors of the family. Jane Winchester came, escorted by Thomas and Jennie Bennett, to give her condolences. These two prominent families who had lived near each other for decades as they grew their businesses and wealth were now both dealing with tragedy.

"Please know that I'm always here for you, dear," Jane told Sarah the evening after the funeral. "You're like my own daughter. I know I can't take the place of your mother, but I hope it gives you some solace to know you are loved by us all."

Sarah appreciated the sentiment, and she did think of Jane as a second mother. But Sarah's free-spirited, liberal-thinking mother could never be replaced by anyone. Her mother had not only raised her children with love, dignity, and respect but had also given them each the ability to be free thinkers themselves, and to question old ideas and search out new concepts or beliefs. While Belle was the most outspoken and liberal one of them all, Sarah had also tried to keep an open mind to all things new and different. That was Sarah's mother's legacy to her children, and Sarah would be forever grateful for it.

As spring turned to summer, the Winchesters enjoyed a reprieve from personal tragedy. With pure grit and determination, Oliver regained some movement in his arms and legs and was able to speak a little. William's cough had subsided, and he had gained some weight and color to his face. Sarah was thankful that he'd made it through another rough winter and was once again healthy for the summer. With his renewed energy, William was better able to cope with the pressure of running the business in his father's absence. Only occasionally did Sarah see him tire quickly or breathe heavily as he walked up the stairs to bed at night.

"Don't worry so much about me," William told her one evening after a bad coughing fit. They had retired to their room for the evening. "I'm feeling much better now, and between me, Thomas, and William, we're running the business well. I'm thankful to have two family members I can trust and work well with."

"I'm glad you're feeling better," Sarah told him. "Maybe if you're careful and rest when you're tired, you won't be as sick once the cold weather returns. The doctor said you should have plenty of rest and fresh air to heal your lungs."

William chuckled, which then made him cough. "I wouldn't put much stock in what the doctor says. We haven't had much luck with doctors healing anyone lately."

Sarah gasped. "Don't say that," she chided him. "You will get better. Many people with the same illness as you have rallied and felt better. I know you can, too."

"My dear." William hugged her closely. "Don't worry, please. I'll do everything I can to stay well. And now that Father is working so hard to get better, the pressure of the business will soon be off my shoulders. I know Father will be as good as new once he's recovered."

Sarah, however, wasn't so sure. Oliver worked daily on his movement and walking, and he also did his best to speak. But she had trouble believing Oliver would make a full recovery—especially one that would allow him to go to work every day again.

Miraculously, Oliver was walking near the end of summer with the use of a cane and had also regained much of his vocabulary. Friends came to visit him, and although he wasn't the powerhouse he'd always been, Oliver could hold short conversations with those around him. William talked business with his father at dinner as he used to, and this seemed to please Oliver. Although, no mention was made of Oliver returning to the business or the board room.

Sarah and her siblings were busy settling their mother's estate during this time as well. Sarah Pardee had invested in several properties, including the houses she'd built for her two daughters, which went directly to them. She had also invested in stocks, which included Winchester rifle company stock. William and Mary continued to live in the house on Orange Street and took it over as their own. While working on the other details of the will, Belle mentioned to Sarah that Estelle and her husband, George Gerard, were on the verge of divorcing.

"No," Sarah said, sorry to hear their marriage was falling apart. Sarah had never been close with George since he was always on the road as a traveling Singer Sewing Machine salesman, but she had thought their marriage was fine. They had two children, Saidee and George Jr., who were now ages twelve and eleven.

"It's true," Belle said, lifting her chin with pride that she knew something Sarah didn't. "Estelle confided in me that she told him not to come back to the New Haven house. She hasn't seen him in quite a while."

"Did she give a reason?" Sarah asked.

"No, but I'm not surprised." Belle lifted her brows knowingly. "He is a *traveling* salesman, after all. Men tend to stray when they aren't home with their wives."

"Oh, Belle. I do believe you think the worst of everyone," Sarah said, shaking her head. "Well, I'm sorry to hear it. I'm only thankful that Estelle has the home Mama gave her and some money once we settle the estate."

As fall approached, William's health once again declined. Sarah refused to believe it was anything more than the usual winter troubles that he generally had. Unfortunately, just before the Thanksgiving celebration, Oliver's progress deteriorated, and he was bedridden again. The doctor thought he'd had another stroke and proclaimed it didn't look good. Two weeks later, he died, leaving behind a stunned and devastated family. No one had thought a man as strong and willful as Oliver Winchester, who'd come from nothing and amassed a fortune from his business prowess, could be knocked down so quickly.

After Oliver's grand funeral, in which he was eulogized by many as a great man, William took to his bed. He'd been automatically proclaimed by the board as the president of the Winchester Repeating Arms Company, with William Converse as his vice-president and Thomas Bennett remaining as secretary. But William wasn't well enough to take on his duties.

He tried, but his poor health fought him. Even though Sarah refused to believe William was terminally sick, it seemed he knew he was.

"I need you to accompany me to New York tomorrow so I can sign my revised will," William told Sarah one evening in February. "I want to make sure you're there to see and sign it."

Sarah's heart pumped furiously. "Why now?" she asked, not wanting to discuss such a thing. She felt it was bad luck for them to even think of it when he felt so badly. "You should stay in bed and recuperate. It's the only way you'll get well."

"My dear," William said gently. "It's something that must be done. With Father gone, it's even more important that our affairs are in order. If anything happened to me and I didn't have your interests taken care of, I couldn't bear it. The lawyers have it ready; all we need to do is sign it. But I need you to go with me. I can't make the trip alone."

Sarah understood he was being practical, so she agreed. The next day, they took the train into Manhattan and signed the paperwork that would make her the sole heir to William's inheritance. She knew it was his only way to protect her interests, but somehow, Sarah felt that by signing his will, she was also signing his death warrant.

"Now I can rest easy," William said on the train ride home. He seemed more relaxed than he had in months, and Sarah thought this might have been the right thing to do to help appease his worrying. He'd get better soon, she told herself. He always did once spring came and summer bloomed. This time would be no different.

But as February changed to March, William's health grew worse. Although friends and neighbors had no idea how sick William was, the Winchester Repeating Arms Company's Board of Directors did, and they voted to make William Converse acting president of the company. Once again, Thomas Bennett was overlooked and remained as secretary. Doctors were called in as William faded, but there was nothing more they could do. On March 7, 1881, William took his last breath as Sarah sat by his side. At the age of forty-two, Sarah Lockwood Pardee Winchester became a widow.

CHAPTER SEVENTEEN

1918

Olivia paused her pencil over the notepad when Mrs. Winchester uttered those last words. The story was so sad she felt like crying, but she tried to remain professional for the older lady's sake.

"My beloved William's death was more than I could bear," Mrs. Winchester said from where she sat on the settee across from Olivia. "I was completely lost. I let Jane plan his funeral, and my only request was that he, our daughter Annie, and I have our own family headstone and not be attached to the main family headstone." She looked up at Olivia, her glazed expression clearing. "It sounds odd now that I was worried about such a menial thing. But I felt we'd been tied too closely to the family name in life and never had our own identity. At least in death, our little family of three would have our own spot together."

Olivia watched the woman who still wore dark colors and Victorian-style dresses despite them having gone out of style. She still mourned her baby girl and her husband. And despite all that she'd accomplished, Mrs. Winchester would never get past those losses.

"I don't think it sounds odd at all," Olivia said. "Your little family deserved its own identity."

Mrs. Winchester smiled at her. She was no longer self-conscious about her failing teeth around Olivia or her gnarled hands and twisted arms. Olivia took that as a compliment that Mrs. Winchester felt comfortable around her. But then, Olivia knew the older lady's secrets just as Mrs. Winchester knew hers. They didn't have to fool each other as to who they really were.

"I disappeared to the seashore for a while after William's funeral," Mrs. Winchester said. "I couldn't bear to be in the house where he'd died or the town where I'd lost three people in one short year. The sound of the ocean waves helped soothe me, but I still felt the pain of William's loss deeply.

When I returned to New Haven in June, I knew I needed to get away. Far away. So, I set out on a trip to Europe. Everyone thought I was crazy, going across the ocean alone. But I'd traveled there several times with William and Oliver, and we had so many connections and friends over there that I didn't feel alone. In fact, I stayed away for a long time."

"Did it help you?" Olivia asked, immersed in her story. She was still taking shorthand as Mrs. Winchester spoke.

"It helped a little for me to be in different locations and around other people. Although, I've never been much for socializing." She grinned mischievously.

Olivia laughed lightly. "No. I suppose you haven't."

"You know, dear. If I had ever had an inclination to delve into spiritualism or talk to a medium or even join in on a séance, it would have been then. It was all the rage, and the upper class even thought it was respectable. But I didn't search out any of those things. My faith told me that when we die, we die. And even though my dear mother may have been open-minded to those types of ideas, I never really was. But I suppose the way I've lived my life made me a good target for newspaper reporters to think that I would turn to such fanciful ideas."

"No one would have blamed you for doing so," Olivia said. "Especially since so many people believe in those ideas."

"Yes. I guess if I'd told the world openly that I believed in spiritualism, they may have left me alone. But it wouldn't have been the truth. There was a woman who lived not far from my San Jose ranch who'd built a huge mansion and started her own church on the property. Her name was Mary Hayes-Chynoweth, and she believed herself to be a healer, and people came to her self-made church to be healed. No one ever called her crazy for either building a huge house or believing in her healing powers." Mrs. Winchester chuckled. "But then, when your sons own two of the newspapers in town, I suppose no one is going to print that you're crazy."

"I guess you should have invested in your own newspaper," Olivia said.

Her words seemed to tickle Mrs. Winchester because she laughed. "Yes, I should have."

Miss Sivera entered the room asking if Mrs. Winchester was ready for lunch, thus ending their conversation. Olivia had been enjoying her employer's frank discussion. The more she got to know the real Mrs. Winchester, the more she admired her.

Olivia exited the room and went to have lunch with the rest of the household staff. The longer she'd been there, the more open the staff was with her. They all chatted as they ate, and Mae, the housekeeper, even ventured to quietly ask Olivia how her pregnancy was coming along. Olivia wasn't shocked by the question since it was obvious that she was with child.

"I'm feeling quite well, thank you," she told Mae. "And I fear I'm eating like a horse and will look as big as one soon."

The women at the table chuckled.

"You eat as much as you need," Alice said seriously. "At your age, you'll spring right back to that tiny waist once the baby is born. But for now, you both need your nourishment."

As Olivia walked upstairs to her room, she felt relieved that everyone knew she was having a child and had easily accepted it. She could no longer hide how she looked, so it was for the best that everyone knew. But it still felt strange to her that she was actually growing a small life inside her. She'd always been the good girl and the good daughter, and yet here she was, unmarried and with a child on the way. Of course, everyone thought she was a widow, so that kept the tongues from wagging, but she knew the truth, and she still had trouble understanding how she'd let this happen.

Despite it all, as she felt the baby move inside her, she couldn't help but love the little one already.

Sitting at her typewriter, Olivia prepared the paper and began to type that day's dictation. Her mind always wandered as she typed, and today was no different. Despite trying to forget the memory, she could still see Daniel Stanley's shocked expression when he realized that Olivia was carrying a baby. It had been a week since that day, but it was still crystal clear in her mind.

"It was for the best," she whispered to herself as she stopped typing and placed her hand gently on her belly. "I had no right to believe for even a second that Mr. Stanley had any interest in me. It was a fool's dream."

Concentrating on her work, Olivia typed up that day's pages and carefully put the copy away in the box in the bottom drawer. Not wanting to disturb Mrs. Winchester in case she was napping, Olivia left the other copy on her desk and went down the back stairs to the kitchen. As usual, there was activity as Mr. Nakmo prepared dinner and Alice worked on making dessert. Despite the breeze coming through the large windows, the ovens made the kitchen unusually hot today. Olivia waved to Alice as she made her way through and left out the back door to take a leisurely walk around the grounds.

It was another warm day, but the breeze off the distant bay helped cool the air. Olivia turned out the back door and headed to the path that led around to the gardens at the back of the house. The trees and grass were as lush and green as always despite the weather having turned warmer. And the flower gardens were in constant bloom. Olivia wasn't sure how Mr. Yen did it, but he kept the landscape in the most beautiful shape she'd ever seen. She wished Mrs. Winchester was able to come out and walk the grounds so she could enjoy the beauty she paid to maintain.

Breathing in the fresh air, Olivia understood exactly why Mrs. Winchester loved living here. It was close enough to the bay for the gentle breezes and yet far enough from the ocean so as not to be damp and cold. The moisture from the ocean would aggravate the older lady's crippling arthritis, but the warmth here would help her feel better. Of course, Mrs. Winchester had bought this house to be near her beloved Daisy, but it was also the perfect spot for her to reside.

As Olivia turned past a gardener's shack, she saw Mr. Yen hunched over a bush of gorgeous pink roses. He turned and smiled at her, and she waved and smiled back. Then he waved her over, something he'd never done before. Curious, Olivia walked over to him.

"I have something for you," he said, smiling widely. He picked up a woven basket filled with pink and red roses and handed it to her. "Please take some for your room and some for Madame." He bowed his head slightly and crouched down again to work.

Olivia lifted one of the pink roses and drew in a breath. It was the perfect scent of sweet yet musky, a combination that blended well together. "Thank you, Mr. Yen. I know Mrs. Winchester will love them."

He turned and nodded again before returning to his work.

Olivia continued on her walk, carrying the basket. The scent of the roses surrounded her as the smell of freshly cut grass also emanated into the air. In the few weeks that Olivia had lived there, she'd fallen in love with the land, the house, and the people who resided inside. She wished she could live here forever, completely encapsulated by the beauty of everything around her. But, of course, she knew that was just a dream. Someday, she'd have to leave. She only hoped it wouldn't be too soon. With a sigh, she turned again and returned to the kitchen door and inside the house.

"Oh, my. What beautiful flowers you have," Alice said, rushing over to Olivia as she entered. "Charlie has outdone himself again. I'll find a vase."

"Do you have two vases?" Olivia asked, setting the flowers on the counter and sitting down, too. She hadn't realized just how tired her short walk had made her feel. "He said they were for me and for Mrs. Winchester."

"Of course," Alice said, bustling to a cupboard across the kitchen. She selected two crystal vases, poured water in them from the oversized sink, and then brought them back to Olivia. "It's quite an honor when Charlie offers you his flowers. Of course, he always makes sure Mrs. Winchester has fresh flowers, but it was kind of him to include you."

Olivia smiled at this. It was nice being accepted into the fold by those who'd worked here so long. "There's enough for you to take some, too, if you'd like," she told Alice.

"Ah, dear. I'd love to, but they'd be dead by the time I get them home tonight. Would you like me to arrange them?"

"I can do it," Olivia said. "I used to enjoy picking wildflowers for my mother and arranging them for her table. Of course, they weren't as lovely as these, but I had a bit of a knack for it."

Alice nodded and went back to her work.

Later that evening, before heading down to dinner, Olivia brought the crystal vase of roses and the manuscript to Mrs. Winchester's room. Miss Sivera answered the door, and her face lit up when she saw the flowers.

"Come in, dear," she said, moving aside. "Are those from the garden?"

"Yes. Mr. Yen asked me to give them to Mrs. Winchester."

Mrs. Winchester was sitting at the table and beamed when she saw the roses. "Ah, Charlie has outdone himself again," she gushed. Her face looked twenty years younger. Impish and happy. "Did you arrange them so beautifully, dear?"

"It was easy to do with such gorgeous blooms," Olivia said, setting the vase in the middle of the table. It was then that she saw Daisy sitting in a padded chair over by the window. "Oh, good evening, Mrs. Marriott. I didn't know you were here."

Daisy stood and walked over to the table. "Please. Call me Daisy. I actually just arrived a few minutes ago."

Mrs. Winchester was still admiring the flowers. "I wish I

could stroll around the yard as I used to," she said dreamily. "I loved watching Charlie and his assistants working in the yard. They are so skillful at what they do."

"The yard is beautiful," Olivia said. "It looks like everything is in bloom all the time. I was walking around today when Charlie offered me the flowers. You have such a beautiful place, inside and out."

"Thank you, dear. I hope you don't wear yourself out in this heat. You must be careful," Mrs. Winchester said.

"I admit I was tired afterward and snuck in a nap this afternoon," Olivia said. "I've never had a job before where I could nap mid-day."

Daisy laughed. "The perks of working for my dear aunt."

Olivia left after giving Mrs. Winchester the typed sheets and followed Miss Sivera down the back stairs to the kitchen.

"I'm sorry you weren't invited to join us for dinner tonight," Miss Sivera said. "Madame had meant to invite you, then Daisy arrived. I assume they will be talking about family matters."

"Oh, I don't mind," Olivia said. "I wouldn't want to intrude. And I enjoy eating with the staff. Everyone is so kind."

"That's good to hear. I know we have a wonderful staff, and they all adore Mrs. Winchester. I'm glad you feel at home here."

They parted ways in the kitchen, with Olivia going to the staff dining room and Miss Sivera going to collect their trays. Olivia thought dining with Daisy and Mrs. Winchester might be nice. Now that she was typing her employer's life story, it would be interesting to see how the two interacted. It would have helped Olivia understand their relationship better so she could give it a more personal point of view when she typed up more notes later on. Even though her job was to just type what Mrs. Winchester said, the elderly lady had told her she could type it like a story and add a little flair. Olivia liked adding those personal touches, and so far, Mrs. Winchester had liked what she'd done.

The next morning, Olivia arrived in the office precisely at ten o'clock. Mrs. Winchester was already there, sitting at her desk. They'd had to cancel their meetings so often over the past weeks that she was happy to see her there a second day in a row. It meant that Mrs. Winchester felt well enough to continue.

"Good morning, dear," Mrs. Winchester said. "How are you feeling today?"

Olivia had felt tired that morning, extremely tired, but she wasn't going to worry her employer with her minor pregnancy woes. She'd also had to change dresses twice. The first dress had become tight overnight, and the one she wore now would definitely need Misa's sewing magic if Olivia planned on wearing it again.

"I'm fine, thank you," Olivia said. How could she complain when her job was so easy and her living conditions so exquisite?

"I'm happy to hear it," Mrs. Winchester said. She pushed a scrapbook from the corner of her desk closer to Olivia. "Would you like to look at these photos of Llanada Villa? Some are from when it was just a farmhouse, and others are from when I began adding on."

Olivia set the scrapbook in her lap and looked at the many photos. The first photo showed a sturdy farmhouse with a long, covered front porch and double gable roof. It could have been any farmhouse, anywhere in the country.

"The farmhouse looks lovely," Olivia said, admiring some of the Victorian-style decorations. "Did it need a lot of updating?"

"Need?" Mrs. Winchester asked, chuckling. "No. But I wanted to make it larger so my family could join me there. It originally had only eight rooms, and that wouldn't have been enough. Of course, by the time I was finished adding on, one could say it was quite sprawling."

Olivia smiled because she knew it had become an enormous mansion. She flipped the pages and studied the photos that showed the mansion growing with each month. "It looks like you added rooms quickly that first few months," Olivia said.

"I did," Mrs. Winchester told her. "At first, I hired an architect to design the additions and added twenty-six rooms in the first few months. But after that, I started to design the rooms myself. I found great joy in designing new rooms and decorating."

Olivia set the scrapbook aside and opened her notepad. "What made you decide to come here, to California? You could have built a home anywhere."

"Ah, yes. I could have stayed in New Haven, built a home, and lived out my life there. But I wanted more. As I'd said, I went to Europe on an extended tour after my husband died. I went to all the places we'd visited together and new places as well. I found solace in all the beautiful architecture from Paris to Rome to castles in Scotland, Germany, and Bavaria. After a time, I grew excited about possibly building my own home somewhere warm, where I could start a new life. Then, my sister, Mary, grew ill, and that was the catalyst that brought me home. But I was ready for a change, and I was already forming a plan in my mind."

CHAPTER EIGHTEEN

1884

Sarah returned to New Haven with renewed energy after her extended trip to Europe. Unfortunately, her return was due to her eldest sister's illness, but she realized she'd been ready to return home anyway. As she sat at Mary's bedside in the final stages of her sister's cancer, Sarah entertained her with stories of Europe and all the beautiful places she'd visited and the castles she'd toured. Mary, the practical sister, enjoyed her descriptions and stories.

"Imagine having a tower in your house," Sarah said excitedly. "Six or seven stories high so you could climb up and see all the land and homes below you."

Mary chuckled, even though it hurt. "Sallie, you are quite the dreamer. Who would want such a thing in their house?"

Sarah smiled. "I would. And turret rooms and beautiful stained glass all around. And the most intricate woodwork in the ballroom and chandeliers glittering high above. I want beauty all around me."

Mary sighed. "I hope you have your beauty, little sister. You deserve it after all you've been through."

Sarah thought they all deserved it—she, her sisters, her nieces and nephews. They'd all lost people in their lives and had also suffered hardships. But Sarah now knew she could afford to create the life she wanted. She'd recently paid attention to her financial situation, and William had left her a very wealthy woman. Since his death, she'd let William Converse handle her money, but now, as she looked over her own interests, she realized she could live anywhere and do anything she pleased. And that was exactly what she was going to do.

Mary Converse died in mid-October as the fall leaves scattered across the ground and winter approached. They laid her to rest in Evergreen Cemetery, near the other Pardee family members. While the family was devastated over the loss of Mary, her sister Nettie was the most affected. Nettie and Mary had been constant companions since childhood, sharing a double wedding and living near each other for years. With her beloved sister now gone, Nettie was at a loss.

Mary's death also made Sarah face her own mortality. Sarah was only six years younger than Mary, and she was already suffering from the same painful rheumatoid arthritis that had crippled her father. None of the sisters were young anymore. If Sarah was going to change her life, she needed to do it sooner rather than later.

While traveling, Sarah remembered how much she and William had loved taking the train west to California and spending time in San Francisco. She knew the weather there was warmer and had read a great deal about the valley below the bay where the air was cool but not damp, and fog didn't roll in every morning as it often did in New Haven. As another dreaded winter settled over New Haven, Sarah gathered her sisters together to propose a plan.

"I want to move to California where we'll enjoy nicer weather, and we can build a big house that all of us can live in," Sarah announced one snowy afternoon. They were sitting in the Winchester study with tea and cakes, and everyone in the room stared up at her, stunned.

"So far away?" Belle asked, staring wide-eyed at Sarah. "What would we do in California?"

Belle's husband, Louis, was there, as was Nettie's husband, Homer Sprague. Estelle also stared at her sister in surprise. Now divorced from her husband, Gerard, she had also been floundering. Her seventeen-year-old daughter, Saidee, sat beside her, looking interested in the idea of moving.

"We can do whatever we please there," Sarah said cheerfully. "Start a ranch or farm or find jobs. I'm sure there would be plenty of opportunities in an ever-expanding place like San Francisco."

The room was quiet for a time as everyone considered Sarah's idea. Homer finally spoke up. "It's interesting that you brought this up," he said in his stiff, authoritative way. "I have recently applied for the position of president at a women's college near San Francisco. I agree with you that maybe it's time for a change."

Nettie looked at her husband, alarmed. "Why haven't you mentioned this before?"

Homer went to stand behind her chair and gently placed his hand on her shoulder. "I didn't want to upset you until I received a reply. I know how sad you are about losing Mary, and I just thought a change of scenery would do us good."

"As do I," Sarah said, encouraged that the Spragues might be moving to California too. "It will be a marvelous adventure for us all."

"I'm not completely against the idea," Estelle said, glancing around the group.

"I think it sounds exciting," her daughter, Saidee, said.

"But how will we manage?" Estelle asked. "I haven't the funds to travel there and buy a house. And I would want my children with me. What if my son wouldn't want to come along?"

"Oh, Mother," Saidee said. "George would most certainly want to come. Besides, he's sixteen, he has no other choice."

"And I'll take care of the cost of moving there," Sarah said. "Once I secure a home for us all, you won't have to worry about buying a house of your own."

"It does sound intriguing," Belle said, glancing at her husband. "I've always wanted a place where I could have a big garden and animals. Wouldn't that be nice?"

Louis looked uncertain. "I'm not a farmer, dear. I've worked at my father's carriage business my entire life. At my age, I'm not sure that type of change makes sense."

Belle sighed heavily. "It's something to think about, though. We can discuss it."

"That's an excellent idea," Sarah said. "We don't have to make a decision today. All of you can think it over and decide. I've already made up my mind to leave by spring. Whoever wants to accompany me is welcome to come."

Sarah felt emboldened as she said the words. She'd made her decision, and she was going to stick to it. Now, she had to tell her mother-in-law that she was leaving. That was going to be the most difficult discussion of all.

* * *

"You're going where?" Jane Winchester asked that evening after dinner. Sarah, Jennie, Thomas, and Jane were sitting in the study where, hours earlier, Sarah had proposed her plan to her siblings.

"California," Sarah said. "The San Francisco area, to be exact. The weather is warmer, and I feel it would be better for my health and well-being than the damp winters here."

"But it's so far away," Jennie said, looking stunned. "Why would you leave New Haven? You've lived here all your life."

"Yes, I have. And I love this town. But when William and I visited San Francisco, I felt a connection there, too. It is much like New Haven, except with a milder climate. There's a valley south of the city that is warm and not damp like it is near the ocean. It would be better for my arthritis there."

"That makes sense," Thomas said, nodding his head. "But won't you miss your family? Everyone you know lives here."

Sarah smiled. "I've spoken to my sisters, and they are considering moving out there with me. If I purchase or build a large enough house, we can all live together, much like I've done here with all of you."

Jane frowned as she wrung her hands. "What would William think of this? Would he really want you to move so far away from everyone who cares about you?"

Sarah watched her mother-in-law as she grew more nervous about the conversation. She knew that Jane wanted to have familiar people around her and didn't take change well. Hadn't she and William stayed there all these years because Jane couldn't cope with the loss of Annie? But as much as Sarah cared about Jane, she needed to do this for herself. Walking over to sit beside Jane, Sarah gently took her hands in hers.

"William would be the first person to tell me to go on an

adventure," Sarah said soothingly. "He loved to travel, and he fell in love with California just as I had. I'm sure he'd approve."

This seemed to calm the older woman a little, so Sarah added, "Plus, you have Jennie living here with you, and Thomas. And, of course, I'll come back and visit whenever I can."

"What if you absolutely hate it there?" Jane asked, looking hopeful.

"Then I'll come back here," Sarah told her. "But I need to try something different for a while. I hope you understand."

Jane nodded but didn't look convinced. Sarah could tell she thought she'd be home within the year.

"If you do decide to go," Thomas said. "I think you'd benefit from contacting the agent in charge of our offices in San Francisco. Edward Rambo has been living there for about three years and should know the area well. He's doing an excellent job of running the company there, and sales are extraordinary. I'm sure he'd be a great help to you."

Sarah hadn't thought about that connection and was thrilled by Thomas's suggestion. "That's a wonderful idea."

"Don't encourage her," Jennie said, shooting her husband a scathing look. "We don't want her to leave."

Thomas shrugged. "I'd rather our Sallie have a connection there that we can trust instead of depending on strangers helping her. Rambo is a good man. He'll look out for her."

At forty-six years old, Sarah felt she would be fine looking out for herself, but she didn't contest Thomas' words. In fact, she thought it was an excellent idea that she had a contact in California she could trust.

Homer was hired for the position of President of Mills College, and he, Nettie, and their twenty-five-year-old son, William, moved to the San Francisco area in the fall of 1885.

William was studying medicine at the time and thought he'd have greater opportunities in the growing city. They settled in a house near the ladies' college in Oakland Hills.

Excited to be on her way, Sarah joined them that winter but soon learned that living with the Spragues wouldn't work well for her. She needed her own place soon. Homer, with his strong opinions, was already making enemies at the college, especially with the founder, Susan Mills. His strict ideas did not go over well with the board, the young ladies attending, or with the founder. Sarah had seen Homer lose jobs before because of his inability to compromise, and she could tell he'd be asked to leave Mills College soon enough.

Added to that, Nettie was very unhappy in California. She was not as adventurous as her sister and missed her daughter and grandchildren. Despite that, Sarah knew she still wanted to try living in California, even if the Spragues ended up leaving.

Sarah contacted Edward "Ned" Rambo when she arrived in San Francisco and met with him at the Winchester Repeating Rifle Company offices to discuss finding the right location for her. Ned Rambo was a short, stocky man with a good, firm handshake, and Sarah liked him immediately. He seemed to know his way around the area well despite having moved there from Chicago just three years earlier.

"I know the perfect spot for you," Ned told her the day she visited him. "I recently purchased land in the valley where I planted fruit trees, and we have a small house. My wife and family and I like to go there to be away from the city. I'm sure you'll like it there, too."

So, on a spring day in 1886, Ned took Sarah for a long carriage ride out of the city toward the town of San Jose to show her his property in the Santa Clara Valley and let her assess the land for herself.

For Sarah, it was love at first sight. Set thirty miles south of the city and twenty miles east of the ocean, the valley lay wide open, fringed with foothills all around. She saw Rambo's thirty-acre orchard and was intrigued by the idea of growing fruit trees herself. Then, he took her to a forty-five-acre ranch that was near his property. It was for sale and also had an eight-room farmhouse that sat right in the middle of the property.

"It's perfect," Sarah said, scanning the land and house. "I have plenty of space to add onto the house and could possibly buy more land over time."

Ned agreed it would make a nice home for her and her sisters. "And I'd encourage you to plant an orchard. There is good money in fruit, and this is the perfect land and climate for growing it."

Sarah couldn't have agreed more. She especially loved the privacy of the place, and it would be close enough to San Jose for any needed supplies.

Sarah immediately bought the ranch and couldn't wait to start adding onto the house. For the first time in her life, Sarah owned a place where she could do whatever she wanted with. She was home.

* * *

Within six months, Sarah was living at her secluded ranch that she'd named Llanada Villa after a beautiful valley in Switzerland she and William had seen on their travels ten years before. She'd hired a contractor and had added twenty-six new rooms to accommodate her sisters and their families. She'd also hired Ned Rambo as her foreman to handle the planting of her orchard. Even though he still worked as the agent at the Winchester offices, he was also happy to help her begin her new orchard farm.

Sarah had also invited her New Haven coachman, Frank Carroll, and his wife, Mary, to come out and work for her at the ranch. She generously provided a house on the property for them to live in.

With all the building going on around her, Sarah was in her element. After the initial remodel, she began designing rooms herself, then worked with the contractors to build them her way. Sarah had been around woodworkers and factory employees since childhood and felt comfortable working alongside the men. She loved the noise of the saws and hammers and the smell of freshly cut wood and was thrilled every time one of her new rooms was completed. It reminded her of how accomplished she'd felt all those years ago while helping with the Prospect Hill house for her in-laws.

By the time Sarah had added more space to her ranch house, Homer had already lost his job at Mills College and had accepted another one as president of the recently formed University of North Dakota in Grand Forks. Nettie reluctantly followed him there, but their son, William, remained in California.

When Belle, Estelle, and their families arrived in 1887, they were all shocked to learn how far away from the city the ranch was.

"What are we to do here?" Louis Merriman asked. His son Willie and Estelle's son George were also surprised. "I didn't come here to be a farmer," Louis said.

Sarah was equally surprised by their reaction. Belle had told her that Louis hadn't been satisfied working for his father's carriage company and had agreed he needed a change. But now that they were there, it was clear the men in the family weren't pleased with the situation.

While Sarah was happily adding on to her house, the rest of the family found it noisy and tedious. It was soon decided by the sisters that each family needed a home of their own, so Sarah obliged.

Estelle felt her children, Saidee and George, needed to live in the city where there were more opportunities for them. A house was found in San Francisco for them to rent, and Sarah gave them $150 a month to live on.

Belle also wanted a place of her own, at least until Sarah finished adding onto her house. Excited to embrace the country lifestyle, Belle and Sarah found a house on twenty-five acres near the tiny town of Mountain View. Once a place where stagecoaches stopped, Mountain View sat between San Francisco and San Jose. Sarah bought the property and house for her sister's family and then paid to renovate it from a four-room home to a twelve-room house. They added Victorian-style charm that they were both fond of, with lovely windows, intricate woodwork, and a large front porch. Belle named her new home El Sueño, meaning "The Daydream."

The women also had a plan for Belle's property. Sarah purchased an additional one-hundred and forty acres next to the ranch so they could breed large carriage horses. When Ned heard of their plan, he fully approved and wrote to William Converse, who was still managing Sarah's money, to assure him that it was a fine idea. Although Belle and Sarah were complete opposites in temperament and personality, they were in tandem when it came to business. They both had new homes and new lives and were excited about the future.

CHAPTER NINETEEN

Today

Morgan ran a hand through her short hair as she lay on her bed with the Winchester manuscript in her lap. She'd finally finished reading it and was still astonished at what a remarkable story it was. Sarah Winchester had not been the crazy spiritualist who feared death as the legend would have everyone believe. She was a strong, independent woman who enjoyed building her house, and she had also been a generous person. Her only flaw was that she liked her privacy—and Morgan didn't see that as being a negative personality trait.

Morgan wished she'd learned more about her distant grandmother, Olivia, but the manuscript didn't reflect her story. It was mentioned near the end of the book which members of the staff received an inheritance from Mrs. Winchester, and Olivia's name was among them. But otherwise, there was nothing. Morgan would have to rely on her mother to learn more about Olivia from other sources.

Morgan wanted more than anything to share what she'd learned about Sarah Winchester with someone. She'd talked incessantly to her mother about everything in the manuscript, but she wanted to share it with someone else. But who? Her instincts told her to not say anything yet to her boss, Amanda. She wasn't ready to hand over a copy to her to see if she wanted to publish it. First, she wanted someone else's advice. What surprised her was she really wanted to share all this with Jonathan. She knew he'd appreciate the historical value of this story. Yet, since their lunch two weeks ago, he'd kept to himself at work. He wasn't rude to her because they did talk, but only if she initiated it. Morgan missed bouncing ideas off him and joking around.

The next day was Saturday, and Morgan decided she'd give it a chance and call Jonathan to see if he wanted to do some sightseeing. There were two places she wanted to visit that were connected to Sarah Winchester, but she didn't want to go alone.

Clicking his number on her phone, she waited, holding her breath. Would he even answer?

"Well, this is a surprise," Jonathan said when he answered. "What's up?"

"Hi." Morgan suddenly felt strange about calling him. What if he already had plans? What if he was dating someone, and she didn't know about it?

"Hello?" Jonathan said, then chuckled.

"Oh, sorry." Morgan felt so ridiculous. "I finished reading the Winchester manuscript last night."

"Really? Was it good?" he asked.

"It was really good. It's actually amazing. Sarah Winchester was not the crazy woman everyone painted her to be. She was truly an incredible person," Morgan said quickly, then stopped. She sounded like she was gushing.

"That's great," Jonathan said.

"Yeah." Morgan hesitated, then said in a rush, "Do you want to go sightseeing with me today? I mean, if you don't already have plans."

"Sightseeing?" Jonathan sounded amused. "As in the Winchester Mansion?"

Morgan smiled. Jonathan knew her too well. "Yes. To start with. Shall we take a tour?"

"Sure. Why not? I've never been there before, so it might be fun," he said.

"Great. I'll pick you up in about an hour, okay?"

"Works for me," Jonathan said. "See you then."

An hour later, Morgan pulled up to the sidewalk next to Jonathan's apartment building in her Jeep Wrangler, and he slipped inside.

"Nice car. I guess I never pictured you driving a Jeep," he said as she pulled out of the parking space. "It's weird that after all these years, I've never seen it before."

"Thanks," Morgan said. "It's not new, but it gets me around. I usually walk to work, and you ride your bike. I guess since we live near work, we never drive."

"True," he said. "But this beats out my old Honda Civic any day."

Morgan laughed and glanced over at Jonathan. Today, he wasn't wearing his typical button-down shirt like he did at work. He wore a graphic t-shirt with loose jeans and black, high-top Converse sneakers. He looked relaxed and comfortable, words she would never typically use to describe Jonathan.

"Tell me about Sarah," Jonathan said as she approached the I-280 South onramp that would take her to San Jose.

"She was smart," Morgan said. "She'd experienced so much loss, but she didn't let it stop her from moving forward. Sarah was eccentric in personal things. She chose to wear mourning black for the rest of her life after the death of her husband, and she didn't step out of the Victorian age for style in most cases. Although, she did eventually have cars, and her Atherton house wasn't decorated in the Victorian style she loved. And most of all, she knew how to invest her money. The properties she owned back then would be worth a fortune today."

"Such as?" Jonathan asked.

"By the time she was done adding land to the San Jose mansion, she had 160 acres. Can you imagine what that would be worth today? It was the same in Atherton. She bought one house, then the one next door. She bought property in Burlingame, too. That's where she kept her houseboat. She knew the value of high-end property."

"She had a houseboat?" Jonathan stared at her, wide-eyed. "The tiny widow wearing black actually lived on a houseboat?"

Morgan laughed. "Yes. The tiny widow in black used it for a vacation house. She was an extraordinary woman. But we're getting ahead of ourselves. The mansion came first. I can't wait to tour it."

It was an hour's drive to the mansion, and they talked easily about Sarah, work, and the places they'd traveled to over the years. Morgan had no idea that Jonathan had grown up in Minneapolis and had moved to San Francisco when he was sixteen.

"How could I not have known that after all these years?" Morgan asked. "I thought you grew up around here."

He shrugged. "We only talk about work. We don't talk about personal things."

She suddenly felt terrible. Why hadn't she ever bothered to ask him about his life? She'd shared parts of her life when they'd have lunch or meet up for coffee. "I'm sorry I never asked," she said.

"No need to be sorry. If I'd thought it was important, I would have brought it up. It's just my life."

"Yeah, but it's part of what makes you interesting. You have a background that I don't," she said. "What else don't I know about you?"

Jonathan laughed. "A lot, I'm sure. Just like I don't know much about you." He sat quietly for a moment. "Maybe we can fill in the gaps sometime."

Morgan smiled over at him. She'd never thought of Jonathan as anything other than a co-worker—just someone to bounce work-related items off of, and that was it. But today, she saw him in a whole new light. "Yes. We'll have to do that," she agreed.

They arrived at the Winchester Mansion and followed the signs to park in back. As they walked around to the front garden, Jonathan whistled softly. "Wow. It's beautiful. Do you think the front entrance looked like this when Sarah lived here?"

"I hope so," Morgan said, admiring the landscaping. Carefully manicured shrubs and flower gardens filled the landscape with a circular driveway coming from the front gate. "Her head gardener, Tommie Nishihara, and his son, Ryoichi, worked on the gardens here, and Charlie Yen supervised the gardens in Atherton. Tommie cried the day Sarah died; he was so devoted to her."

"Wow, that's sad," Jonathan said. "Yet what an amazing tribute to the kind of employer she was to have such a reaction from one of her staff."

Morgan nodded. "From what I can tell, the staff adored

Sarah and took great care of her. She trusted them, too, despite the rumors that she thought they were trying to poison her. Why would they? They loved working for her."

"Well, let's buy our tickets and take the tour," Jonathan said. "You might have to bite your tongue during the tour, though, when they say outrageous things about Sarah."

Morgan grinned. "You mean you don't want me embarrassing you by blurting out true facts over their scripted ones?"

"Let's just say that I might sneak out the back door if that happens," he said, chuckling.

They bought their tickets and waited outside the main entrance for the tour group to form. A woman appeared in period clothing and said she'd be their guide. After talking briefly about the house, she led them inside the front door.

"It's believed that the main entrance is part of the original eight-room farmhouse Sarah bought," Morgan whispered to Jonathan. "The rest she added on."

The woman spoke about details of the house, pointing out the beautiful and the strange. Morgan, who had never paid much attention to house styles, found she loved the fireplaces in nearly every room and the intricate wood floor patterns that Sarah had chosen. There was so much detail, from the stained and leaded glass windows everywhere to the flooring, wallcoverings, spindle accents, and lighting; it was all too much to take in at once. Morgan was mesmerized by it all.

"This furniture did not belong to Mrs. Winchester," the tour guide told them. "Her niece, Mrs. Marriott, sold most of it. But all the furniture is from the correct time period."

"Interesting," Morgan said softly to Jonathan. "So, they are guessing what each room was used for. Without the original furniture, how would you know if there were dual dining rooms, as they think, or if a room was used as a parlor?"

He nodded as they wandered from room to room. "Did you notice how there are windows that look into other rooms?" he asked. "Do you think that was on purpose, or she just kept adding new rooms and didn't want to replace the windows with walls?"

"Maybe she thought the windows between rooms would increase the lighting throughout the house," Morgan said. "Plus, it's kind of a neat feature. She wasn't spying on anyone; it just kept the flow of the house going."

As the tour continued upstairs, they finally entered the area they were told was Sarah Winchester's bedroom. Morgan looked around the room, which was much smaller than she had imagined. There was a little sitting area near the fireplace and an outer area where Sarah could visit with guests. But the best part of Sarah's space was just outside the door. There was a walkway filled with windows letting in natural light for plants to grow. From here, Sarah could see all over her property and enjoy a sunny day without ever going outside.

"What a great spot to have off your bedroom," Morgan said to Jonathan. "It's beautiful."

"It is cool," he agreed. "Especially so high up. She had a great imagination when it came to building."

The guide said the room down the hallway from Sarah's was Daisy's room while she lived with her aunt. The room and area were larger than Sarah's. Morgan knew that Sarah had built a special room for Daisy with stained glass windows that had daisies on them. Morgan doubted this was Daisy's room. More than likely, it had been Henrietta Sivera's room when she worked as Sarah's assistant and companion.

The tour took them to a large area at the front of the house where the 1906 earthquake had done the most damage. Walls were unfinished, ceilings were cracked, and no work had been done to repair most of the damage. It was here that Morgan saw the room with all the daisy-inspired stained glass windows and decorations. This would have been Daisy's room when she lived with her aunt.

Morgan knew from her reading that the strange things about the house—like doors or staircases going to nowhere— were the result of the great earthquake. By then, Sarah was living in the Atherton house and had no energy to repair the mansion in San Jose. She'd had things cleaned up to make the house safe and had never lived full-time in the house again.

Once the tour was over, Morgan and Jonathan walked around the outside of the house, taking in all the many design features Sarah had used.

"That was really interesting," Jonathan said as they wandered the garden. "Imagine all the time and money that went into creating this house. And Sarah just kept adding on, even if it looked like a hodgepodge of rooms clustered together. I can see why some people thought she wasn't in her right mind. But I can also see it was the work of a woman who had a lot of money and time on her hands to spend it."

Morgan glanced over at him. "So, you think she was just spending money frivolously?"

"No, and yes. I get that she had the money to spend, but to order so many stained-glass doors and windows and then not even use them seems wasteful. Or maybe she did use them, then had them taken out to build another room. Who knows?" Jonathan looked thoughtful. "She had to have been a little obsessive to want to keep adding onto the house, don't you think?"

"Maybe," Morgan said. She didn't like thinking of Sarah as obsessive, crazy, or anything other than intelligent. "I think it made her happy. The happiest time in her life was helping her husband build her in-laws' mansion. I think constantly building on this house made Sarah happy."

"Interesting," Jonathan said, smiling at her. "I haven't read the manuscript, so I'll take your word for it."

Morgan stopped walking. "If I make a copy, would you read it? I'd like to know what you think of it before I decide whether or not to give it to Amanda."

"Of course, I'd read it," he said. "But I thought you'd already decided to submit it to Amanda for publication."

"Not yet," Morgan said as they began walking again. "I'm not sure if our publisher is a good fit for this."

Jonathan's brows rose. "Why?"

"I don't know," Morgan said. "I'd really like your opinion first. I trust you'll tell me the truth and have your own ideas on who should publish it."

He studied her for a moment. "Okay. I'll read it and let you know."

"Great."

They started walking to the parking lot at the back of the property. "What other place did you want to visit?" he asked as they reached the car.

She grinned. "I found another house that Sarah remodeled, and it's still standing today. Let's go see if we can take a peek at it. We can't tour it—although there are some great photos of it on Zillow."

"I'm intrigued," Jonathan said. "Let's go."

Morgan drove the short distance to Los Altos, where the house was. She parked across the street from the house, and they stood on the sidewalk in front of it. Although trees blocked part of the view, they could still see the lovely home.

"It was a farmhouse with twenty-five acres when Sarah bought this house for her sister, Belle," Morgan said. "She and Belle went to work and transformed it into a Victorian style, and some of the features are still the same today."

"Wow." Jonathan looked genuinely impressed. "What year did they remodel it?"

"1888," Morgan said. "Belle had decided she and her husband and children couldn't live with Sarah, especially with all the building going on at Sarah's house. So, Sarah bought them this home. Eventually, Sarah purchased one hundred and forty additional acres connected to this property so she and Belle could raise horses. Basically, Sarah Winchester owned most of what is now Los Altos."

"That's incredible," Jonathan said. "I'm deeply impressed. And it's still here after all these years." He turned to Morgan. "I'm beginning to understand why you're so inspired by Sarah Winchester."

Morgan smiled. "She had so much more going for her than anyone gave her credit for."

They got back into the car, and she found the onramp to the freeway that would take them back to San Francisco.

"I can't wait to read this manuscript," Jonathan said as they drove along. "After seeing Sarah's house, then knowing she bought her sister a house, too, I'm looking forward to learning more about her."

"You won't be disappointed, I promise you. And my great-great-grandmother did a good job of writing it. Olivia seemed to have a talent for telling a good story."

"Well, now we know where your talent comes from," he said.

"Talent?" Morgan glanced at him. "I've never written anything."

"You edit," Jonathan told her. "You help writers make their good stories even better. You have an eye for a great story. That's a talent. And I'm sure someday you'll write, too. I know you want to."

"I do. But that's a dream. I still have to work, and you know that we both put in too many hours helping build other writers' dreams to make our own come true."

"Or we use our work as an excuse not to try to build our own dreams," he said.

"Maybe." Morgan couldn't argue with that. Technically, she could use her weekends to write if she wanted to write a novel. She just hadn't come up with a great idea yet. Maybe she never would.

"Would you like to go somewhere for dinner?" Jonathan asked. "My treat. I'm starving. And then you can tell me more about Sarah."

"Sure. Name the place."

He told her about a little off-the-beaten-path restaurant, and they mapped it on his phone so she could find it. Their day of sightseeing couldn't have ended better. Morgan was happy she'd invited Jonathan along. She parked on the street across from the restaurant and shut off her car, then turned and looked over at Jonathan. She'd never had a chance to get to know him before, and she was still a little surprised at how much fun she'd had with him today.

"Something wrong?" he asked.

She chuckled. "No. Nothing is wrong. In fact, everything seems right for a change."

He smiled. "I couldn't agree more. Let's go eat."

CHAPTER TWENTY

1918

Olivia stopped writing in her notepad when she heard Mrs. Winchester sigh. They'd been working much longer than usual, and she was afraid the older woman had overtired herself. But when she glanced up at her, Olivia saw how her eyes shone with excitement.

"It was during the negotiations for the extra property for Belle's ranch that I met Frank Lieb," Mrs. Winchester said. "I'd gone to New Haven to take care of some business, and the property deal didn't go through due to the title not being cleared. I finally hired Mr. Lieb to clean it up, and he worked his magic, as he's done for several of my properties. He's brilliant at what he does."

"He is an intelligent man," Olivia agreed. "And thoughtful and generous, too. I don't know what I would have done if he hadn't helped me." After the words came out of her mouth, Olivia immediately regretted them. She hadn't meant to make a personal remark about herself to Mrs. Winchester.

But the older woman just smiled. "He was a great help to

you, and that's what makes him so special. You lived with him and his wife for a time, didn't you?"

She nodded. "Yes, twice. They were kind enough to let me live with them when I first came to the city, and then they also took me in before I came here."

"What did you think of their home? Or should I say homes?" Mrs. Winchester chuckled. "Mrs. Lieb, Lida, did more than add on rooms; she bought the house next door to make their house larger."

"She did," Olivia said. "And she added on a two-story walkway between the houses to connect them. She used that for their big twenty-fifth wedding anniversary party. The lower area was used for dining, and the upper area had additional guest bedrooms. It's incredible. I stayed in the second house when I was there but went to the main house for meals with them."

"Mr. Lieb has never said a derogatory thing to me about my big, sprawling mansion, and I figured out why a long time ago. He was used to his wife constantly building onto their home. He probably never even thought twice about my house project. It's sort of funny, actually. I've known about other women through the years who have built big homes and keep working on them. But I'm the one who gets the 'crazy' moniker for doing the same thing."

"I can confirm you are definitely not crazy," Olivia said. "And your story proves it."

"You are very sweet, dear."

Miss Sivera entered the room quietly. "Is everyone ready for lunch? You both have had a long morning."

"Yes, I am ready to have lunch," Mrs. Winchester said. "I've kept Olivia from her own lunch long enough." She stood with the use of her cane and turned to Olivia. "I'm looking forward to reading this portion of the manuscript. You do such a nice, neat job of typing it up."

Olivia rose, notepad in hand. "Thank you. I'll have it to you by dinner."

"Wonderful."

Miss Sivera walked beside Mrs. Winchester to the elevator as Olivia headed down the hallway to the staff dining room. Everyone was already seated, but Alice had saved her usual spot next to her.

"You worked longer than usual this morning," Alice said, already passing platters and bowls of food to Olivia. "It must have been an interesting story today."

Olivia began filling her plate. The food smelled so good, and she was suddenly starving. "It was. It's always interesting listening to Mrs. Winchester talk about her life. We're at the part where she came to California and began working on Llanada Villa. She loves that place so much. You can tell by the way she speaks about it."

"It's a beautiful place," Alice said. "Such a shame what happened to it during the big earthquake. The missus lost interest in it after that. But the orchard and gardens are still big earners for her as well as a way to sustain our own supply of food. She's one smart lady, that's for sure."

"I hadn't thought about the earthquake," Olivia said. "I suppose the house had a lot of damage."

Alice nodded as she ate the last of her roasted potatoes. "It did. Many parts of the house are still livable, but the missus rarely goes there. Her other Atherton homes had damage as well. This was the third one she bought in this neighborhood, and it was built after the earthquake."

"I hadn't realized how long she's had this home," Olivia said.

"Oh yes. And she bought much of the property around here, too." Alice chuckled. "In case you haven't noticed, Mrs. Winchester likes her privacy."

"Yes, she does," Olivia said, smiling. "I can't say I blame her. Especially after the way she's been maligned by the newspapers over the years."

Alice shook her head. "It's a shame she's treated so disrespectfully. She's nothing like how they portray her. You wouldn't believe how many times over the years I've had to come to her defense among my friends and others who find out I work here. But no one believes a word I say. They think she has midnight sèances calling on the dead and that the San Jose house is haunted. It's all hogwash."

Olivia believed it was all hogwash, too.

As the summer days flew by, there were many times when Mrs. Winchester didn't feel well enough to work, so Olivia found other ways to occupy her time. Each day, she grew larger, and she felt awkward and cumbersome as she walked around the house. Sarah's physician, Dr. Clyde Wayland, had checked on Olivia a few times and proclaimed she was doing well. Olivia felt relieved after each visit. She was trying her best to take care of herself, but having the doctor's approval helped to ease her mind.

The one thing Olivia missed most was Daniel Stanley's visits. Since the day she knew he'd realized she was carrying a baby, he'd only been to the house twice, and he hadn't spoken to her either time. She knew it was for the best because they could never have a relationship, but she would have loved to have counted him as a friend.

One evening in August, Miss Sivera invited Olivia to have dinner with Mrs. Winchester, and she found herself sitting that evening with Daisy, her employer, and Miss Sivera.

"I'm sorry we haven't worked as much as I'd like to lately," Mrs. Winchester told Olivia as they waited for their food to arrive. "I'm hoping to feel better soon so we can start up again."

"I'm ready to work as soon as you are," Olivia told her.

"But we don't want you to wear yourself out, Aunt Sallie," Daisy said, sounding concerned. "You need your rest."

"Pish," Mrs. Winchester said. "Work is what keeps me alive."

Olivia thought the older lady's retort might offend Daisy, but her niece only smiled.

"Yes, I know work keeps you going," Daisy said. "And I'd never take your work from you. Just pace yourself, please."

When Miss Sivera arrived with a kitchen helper to serve the food, Mrs. Winchester brought up a subject that had been bothering her.

"I'm very worried about what I read in the newspapers about the Spanish Flu. It's spreading all over, and it wouldn't surprise me if it comes to California very soon."

"It is a worry," Daisy said seriously. "Especially since you haven't felt well for some time, Aunt Sallie." Daisy looked over at Olivia. "And it would be detrimental to you and your soon-to-be baby if the flu comes into this household."

Olivia hadn't been keeping up on the progress of the flu, but Daisy's words grasped her attention. "What can we do?"

"I don't want to wait until the flu is at our doorstep to make a plan," Mrs. Winchester said. "I think we should be proactive. Normally, several of the Atherton staff go to Llanada Villa to help with the fruit harvest, but this year, I believe everyone should stay here, away from San Jose. I'd also like to close off the house from guests for a time."

Daisy chuckled. "What guests? Me?"

"True. I don't entertain," Mrs. Winchester said. "But even you should stay closer to home and not venture around town if you'll be coming here. We must be vigilant so we don't bring that dreaded flu inside the house."

Miss Sivera suggested all deliveries to the house should be left on the kitchen doorstep instead of letting the delivery men inside. Mrs. Winchester thought that was a good idea.

"And I should call Mr. Lieb to complete any open business this next week if there is any. That way, he or Mr. Stanley won't be coming to the house over the next few weeks," the elderly lady said. She looked over at Olivia. "Do you mind having a self-imposed exile for the time being? It's not only for your own good but for that of the baby."

"No, I don't mind," Olivia said. "I haven't gone anywhere since I came here anyway. And I believe you're right. We need to be careful."

"Then we have a plan," Daisy said, sounding satisfied. "You'll still can some of the fruit from the ranch here at the kitchen, though, won't you? That's the best part of autumn."

Mrs. Winchester chuckled. "Of course. We can have Mr. Hansen bring boxes of fruit for canning and leave them here. But I do think we need to keep everyone from the ranch away from here for the time being."

"Has Mr. Lieb settled the business of the rifle company yet?" Daisy asked as she buttered one of Alice's flaky biscuits. "Or are they still pressuring you to sell?"

Mrs. Winchester sighed. "He thinks they're trying to pull a fast one on me and has been looking into it. I refuse to sell out until I believe it's the right thing to do. Thomas is only looking at what's best for him so he can retire. I'm not sure he's looking out for my best interests."

Olivia listened as she ate, feeling a little uncomfortable hearing Mrs. Winchester's private business. But Mrs. Winchester didn't seem uncomfortable speaking about it with Olivia and Miss Sivera both there.

"I suppose he's ready to retire," Daisy said. "And he wouldn't want Jennie to lose money on her stocks. Unless he's at the point where he doesn't think it matters."

"Losing money always matters," Mrs. Winchester said. "I must ensure I don't end up on the wrong end of this transaction."

"I'll call Mr. Lieb tomorrow and set up an appointment so you two can finalize anything that needs a signature before we stop admitting guests," Miss Sivera said as she passed around plates of apple crisp for dessert.

"Thank you, Henrietta." Mrs. Winchester turned to Olivia. "Now tell me, dear. What do we need in your room for the baby? It's time we get a cradle for the little one, and diapers, and sleeping gowns. Oh, I wish I could sew again. I'd love to make baby clothes."

"Oh, you are much too kind," Olivia said.

"Nonsense! Who doesn't enjoy buying baby necessities?" Mrs. Winchester said. "I have several catalogs from stores in New York. We can browse through them and pick out the items you need. It won't be long now. Only a couple of months."

"It's coming fast," Olivia said. "I'd appreciate anything that you find."

Daisy laughed. "Then be prepared for your room to be overflowing with baby items because when Aunt Sallie sets herself to shopping, she does it in style."

Miss Sivera grinned at this, too, but Olivia was nothing but grateful. To have an employer who took it upon herself to give much-needed items was a blessing. Olivia appreciated Mrs. Winchester's generosity greatly.

Two days later, Mr. Lieb and Mr. Stanley arrived at the house and were in Mrs. Winchester's office with her for most of the morning. Olivia made herself scarce, first visiting Alice in the kitchen while she worked and then taking a long walk outside. The day was warm, and after a time, Olivia found a bench near a rose garden and sat. It was getting more difficult for her to walk very far these days. She couldn't even imagine what it would be like in two months right before the baby came.

Sitting back against the wooden bench, Olivia closed her eyes and inhaled the sweet scent of roses. She loved living here. Everything was so beautiful, and Mrs. Winchester and everyone else had been very kind. Although she didn't know what her future held after Mrs. Winchester's project was completed, Olivia would make the best of these days while she could.

"Ah, there you are," a male voice said softly.

Olivia's eyelids fluttered open, and there, standing before her in a tan suit and white shirt, was Daniel. "Oh. I thought I was alone," she said, feeling awkward.

"I'm sorry." He took off his hat. "I didn't mean to scare you. You looked so peaceful sitting there."

"I was just relaxing after a short walk," she said, sitting up straighter.

"May I sit?" Daniel asked.

"Yes, of course." She moved over a bit to put space between them.

Daniel sat and set his hat in his lap. He glanced around.

"This is a beautiful spot."

"The whole property is beautiful," Olivia said. "You just have to choose a spot."

He smiled. "Yes. I guess it is. I'm glad I chose this one."

His words made her frown. Again, he sounded like he was flirting with her. Who would flirt with a woman as pregnant as she obviously was? "Are you finished with your business?"

"Oh, yes. Mr. Lieb is having coffee with Mrs. Winchester, and we've been invited to lunch. I was hoping I'd find you out here and invite you to join us," Daniel said. "Miss Sivera told me where you might be."

"Oh, yes. I do this almost every day. Although it's getting more difficult now." She glanced down at her large belly.

Daniel glanced at her belly, too, then quickly looked away, seemingly embarrassed to have been staring. "I wanted to talk to you alone for a moment," he said. "I'm sorry for the way I behaved a few months back. And that I've ignored you all these months. I've felt terrible about it."

Olivia turned her head to look out over the lawn. "I have no idea what you mean."

He smiled. "I think you do, but you're going to make me say it, aren't you? Okay. I was shocked to learn that you were expecting a child. But over the weeks, it occurred to me that it shouldn't have been so surprising. After all, you were married. It's just that the first few weeks I knew you, it wasn't obvious, and then it was." He paused. "I'm sorry. I'm babbling. I don't quite know how to say what I want to say."

She turned toward him. "Just say what you feel."

Daniel looked into her eyes and reached for her hand. "I was, I mean still am, very attracted to you. And it had felt that you may have had feelings for me, too. The fact that you were expecting threw me for a loop, but after much introspection, I don't know why it did. After all, I am still very attracted to you. Maybe even more so now."

Olivia's heart was beating so fast she thought she might faint. Daniel had feelings for her. It was more than she could have ever hoped for. "I'm attracted to you, too," she said in barely a whisper. "But I was sure you wouldn't be interested once you learned I was expecting my husband's baby."

"I'm still interested," he said. "My feelings for you haven't changed." He smiled. "Would it be odd for me to ask a pregnant woman if she would let me court her?"

Olivia couldn't help but laugh. This was what she'd wanted, yet it was all so crazy since she was going to be a new mother in two months. "Only if you don't mind there being a third wheel around," she teased, glancing down at her belly.

Daniel laughed, too. "I know this is unconventional. But I do love children. I helped raise my two younger siblings." His expression sobered. "Can you forgive me for being such a jerk before?"

Olivia nodded. "I didn't blame you for that. It was a natural reaction. But I'm glad you thought it over."

"You know, Mr. Lieb told me I was a complete idiot for letting someone as lovely as you get away," Daniel said with a grin. "And Mrs. Winchester told him to tell me I was acting like a fool. Those two hold you in high regard."

Olivia laughed. "I can't believe they said that to you."

"They did. Mrs. Winchester always speaks her mind." He laughed also.

"I'm lucky to have them both on my side," Olivia said.

Daniel raised her hand and kissed it gently. It was such a sweet gesture that it filled Olivia's heart with even more affection for him.

"May I ask when the baby is due?" he asked.

"Mid-October," Olivia said. "The sooner, the better. I feel like an elephant."

"That is soon," he said. "Mrs. Winchester said you've all decided to self-quarantine for the next few months just in case the Spanish Flu comes this way. Do you think she will make an exception for me to come and see you?"

Olivia had forgotten that. Her heart sank. "I'm not sure. I understand her fear because her health hasn't been very good, and she's worried about me and the baby, too. We'll have to see what she says."

He nodded. "I understand. I don't want to be the one who puts any of you at risk. But I do wish to see more of you over the next few months."

This made Olivia's heart sing. That a man as caring and respectable as Daniel was interested in her—in her condition no less. She felt like the luckiest woman in the world.

Chapter Twenty-One

1890 – 1898

Sarah happily spent her time adding new rooms and other additions to her ranch house. If a room didn't work out, she'd have it torn down and start a new one. She studied architectural magazines and books to learn the craft of design, then tried new concepts. Sometimes, she loved the end results, sometimes, she didn't. But through it all, she enjoyed the process of designing and building.

As the house grew, she'd find new ways to add light in the rooms so it wouldn't be too dark. In some areas, she'd keep the windows between rooms so the light would filter through from one room to the next. She also added skylights in odd places to brighten the areas. Sarah realized that some might call her house a crazy hodgepodge of rooms, but she didn't care. She loved each room once it was completed and decorated them with care in her favorite Victorian style.

Her favorite spot in the house was her own modest second-floor bedroom that had a long walkway off it with large windows where she could grow plants and flowers. Down the hallway near the front of the house was where she'd created a big, beautiful room for her favorite niece, Daisy. That room had several stained-glass windows with a daisy motif on them, along with daisy decorations as well. She had hoped that when the Merrimans moved in, Daisy would live there, but now that they lived on the ranch in Mountain View, Daisy only came to visit. Still, at least she had a beautiful room ready for her when she came.

Sarah hired many local residents as her staff, especially for the yard and gardens. She had beautiful shrubbery, trees, and flower beds put in and ordered water fountains and statues that she loved to decorate the yard. Llanada Villa was a refuge for Sarah, and her only regret was that she couldn't share it with her husband, William. She knew he would have loved this place as much as she did.

While Sarah enjoyed the continuous building of her house, Belle was content with her own lovely ranch and all the animals she kept there. Living off Sarah's generosity of a home and a monthly income, Belle took advantage of her no-worry lifestyle. The sisters' idea of raising carriage horses didn't become the moneymaker they had hoped for, but Belle raised a few anyway. She also had goats, sheep, chickens, and ducks. Belle loved flowers and cultivated an extraordinary garden full of colorful blooms. And unlike her reclusive older sister, Belle made herself known in the neighborhood. She was active in local charities and invited ladies to her house for tea and small dinner parties. Her husband, Louis, became interested in growing grapes to make wine, and their son, Willie, became a teamster, delivering items all over the valley to homes and businesses. This left Daisy, who at the age of twenty-one, saw no prospects of marriage or chance to even socialize with others her own age. One day, she packed her bags and showed up on her aunt's doorstep.

"Daisy! What a surprise," Sarah said, elated to see her niece. "Have you come for a visit?"

Daisy stepped into the house and closed the door to block out the sound of saws and hammers outside. "I was hoping I could stay with you permanently," she said. "Perhaps I could work as your assistant?"

Sarah clapped her hands with joy. "What a marvelous idea. Why hadn't I thought of that? Of course, you can live here, dear. You can be my secretary."

Daisy looked relieved. "Thank you, Aunt Sallie. I can no longer abide being at my parents' house. There is nothing there for me."

Sarah suddenly turned serious. "What about your mother? Does she know you decided to move here permanently?"

"I told her I was going to ask to work for you. She thought it was a good idea, especially since you already pay for all her expenses. I think she thought it was a good trade-off—her daughter for free money for life."

"Oh, my dear," Sarah said. "I would continue to support Belle even if you didn't come to work for me. But this is wonderful. You can earn money working, and we can have so much fun together. Come. Let's get you settled in your room."

With the young woman in her home, things changed for Sarah. She continued building on her home, but Daisy also encouraged her to join community charities and to travel a little. Sarah wanted Daisy to have all the opportunities a young woman should have, so she went along with Daisy's suggestions, and they spent time in San Francisco, Monterey, and other places so Daisy could socialize with people her own age.

Daisy worked hard for her aunt as well. She often was the go-between for Sarah and Frank Lieb and helped with the daily running of the ranch. Because writing and typing were difficult for Sarah with her arthritis, Daisy did most of her communication. Having Daisy there was a godsend for Sarah. It also left her time to create and build new additions to her home.

Sometimes, Sarah's sister Estelle, who resided with her children in a home in San Francisco through Sarah's generosity, came to the ranch for an extended visit. Sarah enjoyed having her there and would halt work on the house so there was a quiet respite while she visited. Sarah worried about Estelle. She had made friends in the city, but her health seemed to be declining each time she saw her. Sarah had inquired of Estelle's daughter and son, Saidee and George, about Estelle's health, but neither of them knew why she was feeling poorly. When Estelle stayed at the ranch, though, Sarah noticed her sister enjoyed wine and other alcoholic beverages a little too much.

"Do you think Estelle may be drinking too much?" Sarah asked Daisy one evening before they retired to bed. Estelle had already gone to her room for the night.

"She does enjoy the wine at dinner," Daisy said seriously. "And a sherry beforehand."

"I'm worried about her," Sarah confided. "She's lost weight, and her memory isn't what it used to be. She seems so sad, too."

Daisy agreed with her aunt. "But what can we do? She doesn't seem to be drinking spirits in excess enough to make her sick."

Sarah shook her head in dismay. "She could be taking something that makes her unwell. As a pharmacist, her son George would have access to many different drugs, but he denies that his mother asks him for any. I guess all we can do is wait and see. I can't possibly ask her outright if she's taking any drugs."

Despite watching Estelle closely during her visits, there was little Sarah or Daisy could do. But Sarah continued to worry about her and invited her to the ranch often to keep an eye on her.

Sarah had other worries on her mind as well. She came to Belle and Louis' aid when Louis' grape crop was ruined by an influx of phylloxera, as many of the local grape growers had experienced. Belle suggested to Sarah that she could open a florist shop in Mountain View—with Sarah's funding—and Louis could manage it. Sarah agreed, knowing her sister grew the most beautiful flowers around. But in 1893, the banking system failed, and many people lost their money. Stocks Sarah had purchased dropped in value, and she also didn't receive dividends from the Winchester Repeating Arms Company for nearly five years after the downturn. Sarah was frugal with her money, despite her excessive building and supporting her family, and had enough savings to support her needs.

Unfortunately, Louis and Belle lost everything. They closed the flower shop and claimed insolvency so they didn't have to pay their past-due bills. Since Sarah owned their home and property, bill collectors couldn't go after them for those assets.

Once again, the townspeople and newspapers attacked Sarah, claiming she should pay her sister's debts. Sarah refused to pay Belle's debts, and companies tried to sue Sarah, but in the end, she was not responsible. This was yet another transgression the people in the area had against Sarah.

"I don't understand why people blame me for everything," an exasperated Sarah told Daisy one evening at dinner. "I'm not responsible for everyone's debts. It's ridiculous."

"Yet my mother and father get off scot-free, and you're the

one shouldering the blame," Daisy said bitterly. "I'm sorry they did this to you, Aunt Sallie."

"It's not your fault, dear," Sarah said, patting her arm affectionately. Sarah sighed. "The locals and the newspapers have had it out for me since the day I moved here. No one seems to understand that some people just enjoy their privacy."

Daisy nodded. "If they all knew how generous you are to your family and employees, maybe they wouldn't be so harsh."

Sarah laughed. "Or maybe they still would be. Who knows?"

Just before Christmas that year, as Sarah and Daisy were planning a holiday gathering at the ranch for the family, Saidee and George showed up with Estelle, who looked dazed and confused.

"We didn't know what to do," Saidee said, looking anxious over how ill her mother was. "George thought your personal physician could see Mother."

Sarah immediately had them take Estelle up to the guest room and then sent a note with her coachman, Frank Carroll, to bring her physician to the house immediately. Dr. Euthanasia Meade, one of the few female doctors in California, came and tended to Estelle. She was used to making house calls for Sarah for her arthritis, but this was a much different case.

"Your sister is very sick," Dr. Meade told Sarah and the other family members after she'd examined Estelle. "She's jaundiced and is retaining water in her ankles, hands, and abdomen. She also seems confused. When I asked her a few simple questions, she answered differently each time, if she answered at all."

They were all sitting in the parlor downstairs, listening carefully to the doctor's words. "What do you think is wrong?" Sarah asked.

"It may be she has liver damage. I've seen these signs before for cirrhosis of the liver. Does anyone know if she's been taking any medication or if she overindulges in alcoholic drinks?" the doctor asked.

Sarah watched as Saidee and George glanced at each other, but neither said a thing. She didn't want to dredge up any family issues, so Sarah asked, "What can we do to help her?"

Dr. Meade took out a pad of paper from her bag and began writing down instructions. "We'll try a healthy diet. No salt, no alcohol. She should eat fruits and vegetables and lean meats. Limit anything too sweet. If she feels better, maybe short walks around the property. We want to stop the buildup of fluids and try to get a little weight on her."

"We can do that," Sarah said determinedly. She knew then that Estelle would be staying with her so Sarah could watch over her.

"Good," Dr. Meade said. "I'll come to see her in a couple of days. Hopefully, a lot of rest, good food, and healthy living will help her feel better."

Daisy saw the doctor out so Sarah could speak with Estelle's children privately.

"Please bring your mother's belongings here," Sarah told them. "I think your mother would do better here with me, and I can ensure that she is taken care of."

The two nodded. "Thank you, Aunt Sallie. We didn't know what to do," Saidee said. "Mom has been so depressed lately, and to tell you the truth, I think she's been drinking too much. I also found a bottle of laudanum in her bedroom before we brought her here. I had no idea she was taking it."

"Ah, now it makes sense why she has seemed confused lately," Sarah said. She turned to George. "Did you know she was taking it?"

"No, I didn't. I've never given her any drugs." He cleared his throat. "But both Saidee and I have seen her drinking excessively. It's gotten worse over the last few months."

"I was afraid of that, too," Sarah said. Determined to help her sister get better, Sarah stood a little straighter. "Well, she won't get alcohol here, nor will she have any laudanum. We'll do our best to help her get well."

Sarah and Daisy tended to Estelle, encouraging her to eat and helping her take short walks inside the sprawling house. Estelle wasn't a very cooperative patient at first, but finally stopped complaining and did as they asked. She said she wanted her medicine, and when Sarah said no, she asked for wine or sherry. Sarah didn't allow her anything with alcohol, which infuriated Estelle, but she was much too sick to fight her older sister.

Estelle felt a little better by Christmas and was able to join the family in the dining room for a delicious holiday meal and presents around the tree in the cozy parlor. Her children were there, along with Belle, Louis, and Willie. Estelle told Sarah that it was one of the best holidays they'd had since moving to California. But despite everything Sarah and Daisy did, and even with the many visits from Dr. Meade, Estelle's health began to decline again. By early January, her condition worsened, and Estelle fell into a coma. She died on January 8, 1894, with her children, Sarah, Daisy, and Belle, around her.

Once again, Sarah had lost a beloved family member.

Sarah arranged for Estelle's cremation and funeral. Her children chose to stay in California after her death. They had already made their lives there, and both continued to live with the financial help from their Aunt Sallie for a time.

Time went on for Sarah as she immersed herself even deeper in building her dream mansion. She decided to create a third and fourth floor to add more living space for her servants. A housekeeper's office and living quarters were added, along with additional rooms for maids. When the idea of a seven-story tower came to her, Sarah excitedly drew the design. It would be the highest point of the house, and from there, she could see views of the San Francisco Bay and Stanford University.

Of course, the newspapers had a heyday over the continued building of the Winchester mansion. In 1895, the articles took a particularly cruel turn. If one paper printed a story about Sarah being unsociable and turning away neighbors, another printed practically the same story but put additional lies in their article. They stated that Sarah was superstitious, and that was why she kept building onto her house. Then, another paper would add that a medium told her she'd die if she didn't keep building. The lies went on and on. And because Sarah wouldn't take interviews from newsmen, she was an easy target. She refused to fight back. Sarah felt she didn't have to defend her reasoning for the way she built her house, so she ignored the rumors and continued with her work.

"It probably doesn't help that you always wear black and still ride in a carriage while others are driving motorcars," Daisy said one morning at breakfast after reading another mean-spirited article about Sarah. "People might consider that a bit odd."

Sarah's brows shot up. "You think I dress oddly?"

"I'm not criticizing you," Daisy said quickly. "But others wouldn't understand why you still dress as if you're in mourning."

"It feels like I am always losing someone I care about," Sarah said, feeling stung by Daisy's words.

"I'm sorry, Aunt Sallie. I didn't mean to upset you. I'm just pointing out that it might be one of the reasons people are so cruel to you. Maybe if you updated your wardrobe and added more color, you won't look so imposing."

This made Sarah laugh. "How can anyone under five feet tall look imposing?"

Daisy grinned. "You manage to, believe me."

"Pish posh! I'll dress as I please, and they can take me or leave me as I am," Sarah said. "But the idea of a motorcar sounds interesting. I may look into that."

"I'd like to see that," Daisy said with a chuckle.

Sarah didn't rush out to buy an automobile but as the century came near a close, she did lose yet another family member. Her mother-in-law, Jane Winchester, passed away in March of 1898 at the age of ninety-one. Even though Sarah hadn't seen Jane in years, she'd continued to write to her and send her gifts for holidays and birthdays. Jane's passing impacted Sarah in more ways than one. While Sarah had spent much time with her in-laws, living in their home, she'd come to respect both Jane and Oliver, and she'd learned so much from them about how to cherish and respect family. Jane and Oliver had opened their home to many of their siblings, nieces, and nephews throughout the years. Sarah had done the same since moving to California. She'd taken care of her sisters by supplying them with homes and monthly incomes and also helped her nieces and nephews in the same way. Jane's passing also increased Sarah's stocks with the Winchester Repeating Arms Company. The stocks that would have been inherited by her husband, William, were now hers, making Sarah even wealthier than she'd ever imagined.

Chapter Twenty-Two

1918

Sarah's fear that the Spanish Flu would come to California proved true just one month later. The *San Jose Mercury Herald* first reported the influenza outbreak on September 24, 1918, with the headline, INFLUENZA RAGES IN CAMPS. Military camps across the country had cases of the flu spreading quickly, and by early October, Camp Fremont near San Jose had new cases every day.

The residents and staff at the Atherton house had been diligent in isolating themselves as much as possible up to that point, and once the flu was reported, they became even more vigilant. Alice moved into one of the servant's rooms on the third floor for the time being and made her husband promise to be careful at the house where he worked. Deliveries were dropped off at the kitchen door, and no one went into San Jose or to the ranch. Those who worked at the ranch were being just as careful. No one wanted to be responsible for bringing the deadly flu to Mrs. Winchester or Olivia, who was due to have her baby at any time.

Olivia was thankful for the precautions everyone was taking, but she was also heartbroken she couldn't see Daniel during this time. After he'd asked if he could court her, she'd confided in Mrs. Winchester about his being able to visit the house occasionally, even though they would be self-isolating.

Mrs. Winchester had been pleased that Daniel had professed his feelings for Olivia, but she was also wary about his coming from San Jose to visit.

"I'm so happy that you and he have found each other," the elderly lady told her. "Daniel is a wonderful young man who will be respectful of you. But if he comes here from the city, the chance of him bringing that awful influenza here is quite high."

Olivia had to agree. She'd been reading the newspapers, too, and the flu was spreading rapidly around the area. Despite that, Mrs. Winchester did allow Daniel to visit twice before the news broke that the influenza was now in their county.

"Maybe it's for the best we can't see each other," Olivia told Daniel over the telephone one evening before dinner in early October. "I'm as big as a house. You don't need to see me this way."

He chuckled. "You were already fairly big the last time I saw you, and it didn't change my feelings in the least."

"I'm glad to hear it," she said, smiling to herself. "The next time I see you, I'll have had the baby. How will you feel then?" Olivia was still afraid that once the baby was born, he'd have second thoughts. Most men wouldn't want to be tied to a woman with another man's baby. But she also knew that Daniel was not like most men.

"I can't wait to meet your baby," he said sweetly. "Maybe you'll have a girl, and she'll look just like you."

"Misa has said from the beginning that she knows it's a girl," Olivia told him. "I guess we'll know soon enough."

As the pandemic spread throughout San Jose, San Francisco, and all the surrounding towns, the staff and residents of the Atherton house went about their daily business feeling safe and secure that they were protected. In the early afternoon of October 12th, Olivia suddenly felt strange. She'd been tired all day but hadn't thought much of it and had just finished lunch. Afraid that she'd eaten something that hadn't agreed with her, Olivia went to her room to lie down. That was when the first pain hit her. Her stomach felt like it had clenched and hardened, then it slowly subsided. When it happened again twenty minutes later, Olivia panicked. She remembered when her mother had her last child and how quickly the baby had come. Maybe her baby would do the same.

Taking deep breaths, Olivia moved as fast as she dared out of her room and down the hallway to Miss Sivera's room and knocked on her door. She'd been in such a hurry she hadn't even bothered to put her shoes on. When there was no answer, she quickly went to Mrs. Winchester's room, but before she could knock, the door opened, and Miss Sivera stood there, looking concerned.

"Olivia. Is something wrong?" the secretary asked.

A pain hit Olivia and brought her to her knees. Miss Sivera grabbed her arm and held her so she wouldn't fall down.

"The baby's coming," Olivia said, breathing heavily. "And I don't think this baby will wait long to join us."

Miss Sivera placed her arm around Olivia and guided her back to her room. "Lie down, and I'll call the doctor. I'll also get Madame's nurse, Miss Merrill. She'll know what to do."

Olivia did as she was told, and again, a pain shook her

body. Maud Merrill bustled into the room just as it subsided
and took in the situation. She ran into the hallway and called
for Mae to bring sheets to protect the bed, then returned with
several towels from the hall cabinet.

"How far apart are your pains?" she asked Olivia.

"I just had one before you came in. They're fairly close
together," Olivia said, already feeling worn out from the few
she'd experienced.

"Well, let's get you into something more comfortable. You
don't want to have a baby wearing your nice dress, now, do
you?" Maud found a nightgown in one of Olivia's drawers and
helped her into it. Mae came in with white sheets, and as Olivia
sat in a chair, the two women changed the bed so the sheets
would protect it.

"Oh, dear!" Olivia grasped the arms of the chair as another
pain gripped her body. The nurse quickly came to her aid and
held her shoulders so she wouldn't fall out of the chair.

"That's seven minutes apart," Maud said. "I don't think the
doctor will get here on time." She helped Olivia onto the bed.
"But don't you worry about that. We women have been assist-
ing in births long before men became doctors, dear."

The nurse told Mae to run and get Alice from the
kitchen, and the housekeeper looked relieved. "Alice will be a
more level-headed helper than Mae, I think," she told Olivia.
"Believe me, you're in good hands."

There was a knock on the door, and Maud hurried to
answer it. Miss Sivera stood in the hallway, looking nervous.
"The doctor didn't answer, but his wife said he's been attending
to influenza patients all day. She said she'd send him over as
soon as he was able." She lowered her voice. "Mrs. Winchester
is wary about him coming after being around the flu patients.

She's afraid he'll bring it into the house, and the baby will get sick."

Olivia cried out as another pain seared through her. Miss Sivera jumped at the sound. "Is she okay?"

"The young miss is fine, but I don't think this baby is going to wait for the doctor. Let's see if the doctor shows up and if we'll need his help by then. Otherwise, we can send him on his way," Maud told her.

"I'll tell Mrs. Winchester," Miss Sivera said. "Please let us know if you need anything at all."

"Yes, ma'am."

"Well, so we're having a baby, are we?" Alice walked down the hallway with a wide smile carrying two freshly laundered full aprons, more clean towels, and a large bowl to put water in.

"I knew you were the perfect choice to help," Maud said, accepting one of the aprons to wear over her dress. She turned to Miss Sivera. "We'll let you know as soon as the baby has arrived."

Miss Sivera nodded and hurried down the hallway, looking relieved not to be invited in.

"Not everyone is suited to help with childbirth," Alice said with a chuckle.

Olivia was no longer paying attention to what was happening around her. The pains were so close together and so intense that she could barely catch her breath in between. Alice kept a cool cloth nearby to pat her face between contractions, and Maud checked at intervals to see how far Olivia had dilated.

"You're doing fine, dear," Alice said soothingly as each pain wracked Olivia's body. "It will be over soon."

Olivia thought it couldn't be over soon enough.

"Your water hasn't broken on its own," Maud said. "I think

it's time we break it. Be prepared for the contractions to get stronger." Maud and Alice placed towels underneath Olivia, and she felt warm water spreading out around her. A minute later, a contraction hit her hard. Olivia grasped Alice's hand tightly as the pain came quickly. Just when she thought she couldn't get through another one, she felt the urgent need to push.

"That's it, dear," Maud said. "The baby's head is crowning. Push with all your strength."

Olivia didn't think she had the strength to push, but with the next contraction, her body did what came naturally. She pushed hard.

"A few more, and we'll have a baby, dear," Maud said calmly. "Push again."

Olivia was breathing heavily, and she tried again to push but didn't have the strength.

"You can do this, dear," Alice told her. "Grab my hand and squeeze as hard as you need to."

Taking a deep breath, Olivia grasped Alice's hand tightly and pushed down as hard as she could. She let out a guttural cry as the baby slipped into the world.

"You did it!" Maud cried out excitedly. "Alice. Take the baby in a towel, and we'll finish this up."

Alice opened a towel, and Maud placed the little baby into her arms. She quickly cleaned out the little one's mouth and nose, and the baby let out a small cry. "Beautiful," Alice said. "Olivia, dear. You have a little girl. Just like Misa predicted."

Tears streamed down Olivia's face. She was so tired her body was shaking, but she wanted to hold her little girl. She reached out her arms for the baby.

"Just a moment, dear. Let me cut the cord," Maud said. She

smiled up at Alice afterward and nodded. Alice brought the child to her mother.

"Here you go, dear. But only for a moment. We need to clean you and the baby up. You have a lifetime of holding this precious baby," Alice said, placing the baby in the circle of Olivia's arms.

Despite her shaking and feeling dizzy, Olivia's heart filled with love when she gazed down at her little girl. She had a slight smattering of light hair and her eyes were closed, but despite it all, she was the most precious baby Olivia had ever seen.

"She's beautiful," Olivia said. "So tiny and perfect."

"Of course she is," Alice said. "Beautiful, just like her mother."

"I don't feel very good," Olivia said slowly, her head falling back to the pillow. "What's wrong?" She tried to hold the baby close, but her arms had no strength in them.

"You're just tired, dear," Alice said. "After what your body just went through, it's only natural." She scooped up the baby. "I'll clean her up, and you can hold her again."

"Alice. I need more towels. A lot more," Maud said seriously.

"I'll get them," Alice said.

Maud looked up at Olivia. "We're just going to try to stop the bleeding, dear. Some people bleed more than others, that's all."

Olivia lay on the bed, her legs and arms shaking uncontrollably. The room was spinning, and she couldn't concentrate on what was happening. Alice and Maud's voices began to sound nervous, and then the door to the room opened, and Olivia saw Miss Sivera standing there but didn't hear what she said. Everything was in a haze—like a dream.

"Yes. Bring him up quickly," Maud said, sounding frazzled.

Those were the last words Olivia heard before passing out.

* * *

Olivia's eyelids fluttered open as her eyes adjusted to the nearly darkened room. She felt so weak. Slowly turning her head, she saw Miss Sivera sitting in a chair by the bed, her head resting on her hand and her eyes closed. Why was the secretary in her room? Had something happened?

All at once, Olivia remembered. She'd had the baby. A girl. But where was her baby? She tried sitting up but fell back again. She didn't have the strength. Her movement awoke Miss Sivera.

"Oh, Olivia." Miss Sivera sat up straighter, looking startled. "You're awake. Thank goodness."

Olivia stared at her, wondering why she was so surprised she was awake. "My baby," Olivia said. "Where is my little girl?"

Miss Sivera leaned toward the bed and smiled. "Your little girl is just fine, dear. She's healthy and doing well. We've hired a wet nurse, and she's feeding right now."

"A wet nurse?" Olivia frowned. "Why?"

"Oh, dear. I'm so sorry, but we had to. You've been sleeping for two days. We almost thought we'd lost you, dear. But the doctor and Maud took great care of you, and you're on the mend."

"What happened?" Olivia asked, still confused.

"Let me go get Maud. She was coming to watch over you next anyway. She can explain it better than I," Miss Sivera said, looking uncomfortable. "Don't try to move. I'll be right back." She hurried from the room as Olivia lay there, trying to remember what had happened. She remembered how tired and shaky she'd felt after giving birth, and how hazy everything looked. After that, she had no memory of anything.

"You're awake, thank goodness!" Maud said, coming into the room. She turned on another light so she could see Olivia better. "And you don't look as pale. That's wonderful."

Miss Sivera came in behind her. Olivia tried to sit up again but couldn't manage it. Maud came to her aid, helping Olivia up and asking Miss Sivera to place another pillow behind her so she could sit up.

"Better?" Maud asked.

Olivia nodded, but she felt a little light-headed. "I'm a little dizzy."

"Well, I don't doubt that," Maud said, lightly touching her forehead with her hand. "You don't have a fever, which is great news." She turned to the secretary. "Would you mind going down to the kitchen and warming up some broth for Olivia? And maybe a slice of bread or a few crackers? Alice kept a pot of chicken broth in the icebox for when Olivia woke up."

"Of course. I'll go do that now," Miss Sivera said, hurrying off.

Maud sat down in the chair that Miss Sivera had vacated. "You gave us quite a scare for a while," she told Olivia. "But you have come out of it fine."

"What happened?" Olivia asked. "The last thing I remember was holding my baby girl, and then everything went black."

"Well, dear. After you gave birth, I was having trouble staunching the bleeding. That's why you were shaking and dizzy. I've never seen anyone lose so much blood before. Luckily, Dr. Wayland had arrived, and he took over. I have to admit, I was relieved. He was able to slow down the bleeding, and your pulse rate increased after that. But you've been sleeping since then, and the doctor felt you needed the rest, so we didn't disturb you."

"Is that why a wet nurse was hired?" Olivia asked.

"Yes, dear. We felt it was for the best. Had you hoped to feed the baby yourself?" Maud asked.

Olivia had thought she would, but she knew it was frowned upon in upper-class households. She hadn't thought it all through, though. "Would I still be able to feed my baby?"

"To tell you the truth, Dr. Wayland felt you'd be too worn down from your ordeal to take on feeding the baby yourself. He wants you to rest and not overdo it. But if you're determined to nurse your own baby, there's no one here to stop you." Maud smiled and winked.

There was a knock on the door, and a young woman came in, holding the baby. She smiled when she saw that Olivia was awake.

"Olivia, this is Emily Carran," Maud said. "She had a wee one of her own recently and was willing to be a wet nurse for your little girl, too."

Emily walked over to Olivia. "It's nice to meet you, ma'am," she said kindly. "Would you like to hold your little girl?"

"Oh, yes," Olivia said.

Maud placed a pillow underneath Olivia's arm to steady it, and Emily set the baby in the crook of her arm.

Olivia stared down at her baby, surprised at how much she'd already changed in only two days. Her face and head were rounder, and her eyes were open. Baby blue eyes stared up into Olivia's, and her heart melted. Her daughter was all hers—she had Olivia's nose and eyes and even her lips. She'd never felt so much love for anyone else as she felt for this little girl.

"Thank you for taking care of her," Olivia said to Emily.

"It's an honor, to be sure. She's an angel, is she not?" Emily said.

"She is." As Olivia stared down at her daughter, she realized how weak she still felt and knew the doctor was right. She'd probably not have the strength to take over feeding her baby on her own. Perhaps having a wet nurse was the right thing to do for her little girl. Olivia could no longer make choices based on her own needs—she now had another life depending on her to make the right choices.

Miss Sivera entered the room with a tray and set it down on the table next to the bed. She smiled at the baby in Olivia's arms. "She is the sweetest thing, isn't she? Your baby has already won the hearts of everyone in the house."

"Everyone has seen her already?" Olivia asked, surprised.

"Alice couldn't help herself, I'm afraid," Maud said. "She showed her off to the staff yesterday morning. And Mrs. Winchester was anxious to see her, too. I hope you don't mind."

Olivia smiled. "No. I don't mind. This little girl is going to have the best family around her as long as we live here."

"Well, let's get you to eat something," Maud said, becoming all business again. "I'll lay the little girl in the bassinet here by your bed. If it doesn't bother you, Emily will come back in a few hours to feed her again. Emily is staying in the small room next door with her own little babe."

"That will be fine," Olivia said, smiling up at Emily. She snuggled her baby a little more and kissed her on the forehead before allowing Maud to place her in the bassinet.

"Have you thought of a name for the child?" Maud asked. "We can't be calling her the little girl or baby forever."

All three women looked at Olivia with interest, hoping to

hear the baby's name. Olivia smiled. "I had thought of a name before she was born, and I think it will suit her just fine."

"What is it?" Miss Sivera asked.

"I'm going to name her Rose Sarah Collins. After the beautiful flowers that grow here on the property and after the woman who gave me and my daughter a home."

All three women smiled warmly.

"Mrs. Winchester is going to be so honored," Miss Sivera said.

Olivia smiled down at her daughter as she lay fast asleep. She felt the happiest she'd ever been in that moment.

CHAPTER TWENTY–THREE

1903

Daisy was getting married. Sarah couldn't believe this day had finally arrived after months of planning the event. Sarah had rented a house in San Francisco to be near all the activities and to help Daisy plan the wedding of her dreams. Despite the damp weather causing her arthritis to flare up, Sarah was happy she could share this time with her niece. Soon enough, she'd be back in San Jose at her beloved ranch, although Sarah would feel the emptiness of not having Daisy by her side any longer.

The man who had won Daisy's heart was a hand-some, blond-haired newspaperman named Frederick Marriott III. His grandfather had come to San Francisco decades before and started the newspaper, *The San Francisco News Letter*, and his father, also named Frederick Marriott, had taken it over after the grandfather's death. The younger Fred had served in the Spanish-American War and felt his true calling was the service, but he returned to working for his father at the *News Letter* after he'd returned home. He also had a passion for the new automobiles filling the streets of cities all across the country.

Daisy and Fred were married on July 3, 1903, in a tasteful ceremony at the Palace Hotel in San Francisco—the same hotel Sarah and William had stayed at years before on their first trip west. It was still an elegant place, having remodeled the carriage entryway into a lovely pavilion where the wedding and reception were held. Sarah did not enjoy large events and crowds of people, but she attended the wedding that she'd helped plan and paid for, thrilled that her favorite niece had finally found happiness.

Once she was back home in San Jose, Sarah missed the company of her niece terribly. While in San Francisco, she'd looked around for a suitable home for herself where she could occasionally stay to visit Daisy but hadn't found one. When Daisy visited a month after her wedding, Sarah asked her to help her find a home closer to the city.

"You? In the city?" Daisy had asked, shocked. "You hate being in crowds."

"Well, dear. Maybe not right in the city. Just closer so you and I can visit more often," Sarah said. "Or possibly in a place where you and Fred might like to live yet close enough so he can commute to work."

By Daisy's silence, Sarah could tell she was thinking this over. Two months later, Daisy stopped by the mansion with exciting news. "I've found the perfect house for you, halfway to the city. But you must come to look at it first."

Sarah was excited but didn't want to venture out to look at someone else's house. "I trust your judgment, dear. Let's just buy it."

"Aunt Sallie," Daisy said, sounding exasperated. "You're

the one who'll be living there. I need you to go and see it."

Sarah agreed, and Daisy took her twenty-three miles north-west to a lovely home in Atherton, an affluent neighborhood where the wealthy made their homes away from the city. Sarah loved it immediately and bought it on the spot. Its craftsman style was completely different from her Victorian-style mansion, but Sarah liked the clean lines and simpler décor.

Sarah had a new project—she furnished the home in Ather-ton in a less cluttered style than her San Jose house. She liked how simple and easy everything was. The house had beautiful touches already, with its gorgeous chandeliers and gleaming hardwood floors. She added practical but elegant furniture and brought her favorite landscaping staff over from the ranch to create beautiful gardens on the six acres of land. Immediately, Sarah felt at home.

Two months later, Sarah bought the house next to hers and asked Daisy and Fred if they'd like to live there. It, too, was a lovely home with acreage, and since Daisy and Fred weren't happy living in the city, they accepted.

It wasn't long before Fred complained that his commute to the train that took him to the city was too far from the Ather-ton house. Again, Sarah came to the rescue and bought the newlyweds a home in Palo Alto near the train station. Sarah was desperate to be near Daisy, so it was worth the price of another house to her. Daisy loved the house, but Fred still felt his commute was too long and ended up staying each week at a hotel in the city and coming home on weekends.

After a time, Daisy grew anxious that she and her husband were missing out on important connections during the social season by living so far from Fred's friends and acquaintances. Sarah wanted Daisy to be able to mingle with the upper class, and Sarah had the money to help her. Scouting out the best possible places, Sarah bought several acres directly on the San Francisco Bay near the small town of Burlingame. Many of the elite had summer homes in this area, and others had houseboats floating on the bay. Sarah saw this as an opportunity to invest in prime land and help Daisy all at once.

By the summer of 1904, Sarah had commissioned a large houseboat to be built as a summer retreat. Compared to her homes, it was small, but it was the perfect getaway for her and for Daisy and Fred to use over the summer season. With three large bedrooms, a bathroom, kitchen, and living room, plus a deck all around it, the houseboat was comfortable enough for them to invite friends to visit. While Sarah was not interested in attending social events, she was pleased to be able to place Daisy in the perfect spot where she could enjoy socializing with the elite.

Just when Sarah thought everyone in her family was settled happily, she had a visit from Belle with bad news.

"The Southern Pacific Railroad has sent us a notice that they're going to run tracks directly across our land," Belle told her sister, clearly agitated by the situation. They were sitting on the settee at the Atherton house, and the maid had just brought in a tray of coffee and cookies. "It'll split the ranch in half, and the animals won't be able to cross over from the grazing land to the creek, which is their only water."

Sarah was incensed. "They told you this? I've heard nothing of the sort. I should have been contacted since I own the land."

Belle smoothed a linen napkin over her lap and began to pour the coffee into pink-flowered China cups. Her hand shook as she poured, which didn't go unnoticed by Sarah. At sixty-six, Sarah's arthritis caused her a great deal of pain, and she was unable to do simple tasks. But Belle, now sixty-two, had never had trouble before. She'd been quite active up to this point. Seeing the creases of concern on her younger sister's face caused Sarah to become even angrier at the railroad company for disturbing the home Belle loved.

"The railroad doesn't care whose land they cross over— they just want the quickest route possible, and they're insisting everyone sell to them," Belle said, tears filling her eyes. "I don't want them to ruin my ranch. I love my home so much. And with Louis' health failing, what am I supposed to do?"

"We'll fight it," Sarah said, patting her sister's arm. "They can't take what isn't theirs. How dare they think people will just roll over and do as they want. I'll contact Frank Lieb immediately, and we'll fight this."

Unfortunately, it was a fight that Sarah couldn't win. She spent the summer of 1905 on the houseboat, procuring property in the Burlingame area and adding it to her ever-increasing portfolio of land. She also used that time on the bay to fight against the railroad. But in the end, she was forced to sell the land to them, which made horse and cattle grazing useless without access to the creek. Belle was heartbroken, as was Sarah, but there was nothing they, nor Frank Lieb, could do.

Whether it was from the stress of fighting to keep her sister's home all in one piece, or her increasing age, Sarah became ill over the next few months. She was under the care of her doctor, and hired a nurse to assist her. Writing to Frank Lieb, she mentioned she'd been housebound with bronchial issues. By April of 1906, Sarah was feeling better and living at her Atherton house, still trying to sort out issues with property lines in Burlingame and also dealing with paperwork for splitting up Belle's property. After talking to Frank Lieb on the telephone and setting a time for them to meet in person, she decided to return to the San Jose mansion since it was closer to Frank's office.

In the early morning hours of April 18th, Sarah was jolted awake from the bed suddenly shaking. She sat up as the movement stopped and heard the sound of glass shattering and walls creaking around her. Her heart pounded with fear. The house shook violently again, but this time, Sarah was wide awake. Before she could jump out of bed, something large and heavy crashed through the roof of her bedroom. Bricks and roofing fell everywhere on the floor around her bed. Sarah covered her head with her arms, afraid she'd be hit. When the shaking stopped and the dust cleared, Sarah saw that both doors leading into her bedroom were blocked by heavy rubble all over the floor. Had she jumped out of bed during the second episode, she would have been crushed by the debris.

Sarah realized that they must have experienced an intense earthquake.

Sitting on her bed, she waited to see if the shaking would return. She was petrified that if she moved, she'd surely be crushed by more debris. But there was a hole in her ceiling, and one wall was open to the elements, and she realized her bed had no protection whatsoever if the world shook again.

"Mrs. Winchester!" A male voice called from the other side of her door. "Are you okay?"

She recognized the voice as her carriage driver, Frank Carroll. "I'm fine," she called out, relieved that he was fine too and that someone had been able to reach the second story. "But there is damage in here, and rubble is blocking both doorways."

"I'll get some tools to take the door off. Please stay safe in there," he called out. His footsteps could be heard running down the hallway.

Sarah felt helpless just sitting on the bed. The cool morning air was pressing in on her through the openings, and she feared she'd catch a chill. Sarah reached for her robe, which was lying at the foot of the bed, and shook off the dust. Carefully climbing out of bed, she pulled on her robe and then searched the floor for her slippers but couldn't find them underneath the roofing. Cautious of the nails that might be in the debris, she walked carefully to her wardrobe and found a pair of hard-soled shoes to protect her feet. As she slipped them on, the house shook again, but only for a second. *Aftershock,* Sarah thought, as she grabbed ahold of the armoire to steady herself. Then she realized the cabinet could fall on her—anything in the room could—and she let go immediately. Taking a deep breath, Sarah made her way over large piles of brick and roofing to the door. If she could only pick up some of the debris, it would make it easier for Frank to help her out of there.

After trying to pick up some of the rubble, however, Sarah knew it was useless. Her arthritic arms and hands couldn't lift the heavy bricks. Sarah hated feeling helpless. She'd always been able to work and take care of herself, but here she was, a crippled old woman who couldn't even push bricks out of the way. Frustrated with herself, she made her way back to the bed and sat, waiting to be rescued.

Frank soon returned, and with the help of the ranch foreman, John Hansen, they were able to take the door off the frame and help Sarah out of the room. Both men were shocked to see how much damage the room had incurred.

"The seven-story tower is what did it," John said, shaking his head. "That's what fell through your room, ma'am."

Sarah turned and looked at the debris with new eyes. She

hadn't thought of which part of the house had fallen. "You're right. My own tower nearly killed me."

The men made sure their employer was safe in the downstairs parlor before excusing themselves. They wanted to check on the other household staff and then on the livestock in the barn before inspecting the rest of the house damage.

While walking downstairs with the men, Sarah had already seen more damage than she'd thought possible. Windows had shattered everywhere, and chandeliers had torn from the ceiling and fallen to the floor—some shattering into pieces. Sarah's housekeeper came into the parlor looking pale, her hair in a braid for nighttime and wearing a robe over her nightgown. She, too, was taking in the damage all around her.

"Can I get you anything?" she asked Sarah at last. "Tea? Breakfast?"

"Maybe we both should go into the kitchen and sit and have a cup of tea," Sarah suggested. If her housekeeper felt as rattled as she did, then they both needed to help each other.

Once morning came and Sarah was able to dress and get the dust and dirt out of her hair, she went outside to inspect the damage. The tower had definitely fallen into her bedroom, and nearly all the fireplace chimneys had cracked or fallen into piles on the ground. Glass was everywhere, and porches and even whole sections of her beloved house lay on the ground in shambles. Twenty years of building her home had been destroyed in a matter of seconds with the shaking of the earth. Sarah's heart was broken.

* * *

March 1919

Mrs. Winchester stopped speaking, and Olivia ceased writing in her notepad. It had been the first morning in months that they had worked since Olivia had given birth to her beloved Rose. The influenza pandemic had finally passed over their area, and everyone could now return to leading a normal life. And the war was over. Soldiers were returning home, and the world once again felt like a safe, happy place.

But for Sarah Winchester, as she described the many problems she'd endured over the years, happy wasn't a word Olivia would use right now.

"What did you do?" Olivia asked, urging the older lady on.

Sarah's eyes sparked back to life after Olivia spoke. "I'm sorry, dear. I was lost back in 1906. I was very downhearted over the damage to my most favorite project—my house. All the pleasure I had building it was gone, and I just didn't have the strength to rebuild. I even thought about razing the whole structure, then decided against it. So, I had workers come in and clean up the mess. They closed off fireplaces where the chimneys had fallen, covered over outside spots where balconies or walls had been destroyed, and basically just patched the whole place up. There was no sense in working on it anymore. The house looked like a crazy lady had built it."

"I'm sorry. I know how much you loved that house," Olivia said.

She nodded slowly. "Yes, I did. But I still had my homes in Atherton and my lovely houseboat. There was damage to the Atherton homes, too, but those could be easily fixed. So, I went off to my houseboat for the summer while all the repairs were being made."

"I'm glad you had a safe place to go," Olivia said.

"I was very fortunate. So many others weren't. So many unfortunate people died at the Agnew Asylum down the road from my house, and I can't even think about all the people who lost their lives in San Francisco. It was all so tragic. Daisy and Fred were safe, but their house was damaged too, so they stayed on the houseboat with me for a couple of months."

"Were you afraid another big quake would hit again?" Olivia asked. She had been only ten years old when the big quake hit, but her family's farmhouse had been spared. It hadn't fazed Olivia like it might have an adult.

"I think we all were afraid of another earthquake for quite some time. Every aftershock made your blood run cold," Mrs. Winchester said. "Well, dear. I've taken up enough of your time already. And don't you have company coming for dinner tonight?"

Olivia smiled. "Yes. Daniel is coming for dinner. Thank you for allowing me to invite him here."

"This is your home, too. And Rose's as well. You should be able to entertain your beau here." Mrs. Winchester grinned.

Olivia chuckled at the word beau. She supposed that was what Daniel was. They'd been seeing each other regularly since the end of the pandemic, and he'd been so wonderful with Rose. At five months old, Rose was a chubby, sweet baby with the face of an angel and a wonderful temperament. Everyone in the house was under the little girl's spell. Olivia was afraid she'd become spoiled from all the attention given to her.

Miss Sivera entered the room. "Are you ready for lunch yet?" she asked.

"Yes," Mrs. Winchester said. She pulled her silver-tipped cane toward her and slowly raised herself up to stand. The folds of her long black skirt rustled as they fell into place. "Don't worry about finishing your typing this afternoon, Olivia. I can read it another day. Just focus on looking pretty for Daniel tonight."

Olivia felt the heat of a blush rise to her cheeks. "I'm sure I can type it up and get ready in plenty of time," she told her employer. "But thank you."

They went their separate ways, and Olivia joined the staff for lunch. Elaina Carson, the new maid Mrs. Winchester had hired who also watched baby Rose when Olivia worked, had brought the baby to the table. Rose sat in her wooden highchair, banging a spoon on the tray, gaining everyone's attention.

"There's my baby girl," Olivia cooed, sitting down beside Rose. The little girl smiled up at her mother, her blue eyes bright.

"Here's a bit of mashed carrots," Alice said, handing a small bowl and tiny spoon to Olivia. "She seems to like them. We'll mash up some peas tonight and see what she thinks."

After Rose was born, they'd kept the wet nurse on for the first few months and then transitioned Rose to bottle feeding. Now that she was a bit older, they were trying new foods in her diet. Even though Alice had never had a baby of her own, she'd had many nephews and nieces, and she was a great help to Olivia.

After lunch, Olivia asked Elaina if she would watch Rose for an hour while she typed the latest section of Mrs. Winchester's story. The young girl nodded and took the baby to the small room next door to Olivia's that Mrs. Winchester had insisted on making into a playroom/nursery. Even though baby Rose still slept in her crib in Olivia's room, it was nice to have a separate room where Elaina could watch over Rose.

Once she finished typing the manuscript, Olivia went next door to the nursery to get Rose. Elaina was on the floor with the baby, playing. Seeing them there warmed Olivia's heart. Elaina was nearly as old as she was, but she seemed so much younger. She was short and slender, and her long red hair was always braided and coiled on her head. Her porcelain skin was lightly freckled, and her light blue eyes shined. She was such a sweet girl, and Olivia felt lucky to have someone she could trust with her baby.

"I can take Rose now for a while," Olivia said. "Thank you for watching her."

"Of course," Elaina said. "She's a joy to watch. Much more fun than dusting or sweeping." She grinned.

"I'm glad to hear that," Olivia said. She bent down and lifted Rose in the air, twirling her around. The baby giggled with delight.

Olivia put on Rose's coat and bonnet and took her outside. She carried her as she walked around the property, stopping occasionally to let Rose smell a flower or touch a leaf. Rose smiled widely when she saw Charlie, and he handed her a white rosebud that he'd cut the thorns off of. Olivia loved how everyone treated her and Rose like family. She'd never been happier in her life.

That evening, Daniel showed up around six, and Olivia opened the door carrying Rose. He kissed her sweetly on the cheek and then took Rose into his arms and twirled her around in the entryway. Rose giggled, which was the sweetest sound Olivia had ever heard.

"I knew she would want to see you before she went to bed," Olivia said.

"I'm glad she waited for me." Daniel smiled over Rose's blond head at Olivia. "And I'm glad you waited for me too."

Her heart melted. Olivia knew he meant that she'd waited for him to come to his senses and realize that her having a baby hadn't changed anything. He was smitten by her, and now he adored Rose as well. They would make the perfect family if, hopefully someday, that was what Daniel wanted. For now, Olivia would just enjoy their time together and not pressure Daniel or herself into anything more.

Elaina took Rose upstairs to bed, and Olivia and Daniel went into the formal dining room for dinner. One of the kitchen helpers had brought their dinner in on trays, and the two enjoyed their delicious meal as they talked about everything and yet nothing in particular. It didn't matter what they talked about—Olivia only wanted to be around Daniel.

"How is Mrs. Winchester's biography project coming along?" Daniel asked as he sliced a piece of tender roast beef and dipped it in the rich gravy.

"We worked today," Olivia said. "I'm glad we're finally working again. I felt like I was taking advantage of Mrs. Winchester by living here all those months and not working."

"She wasn't feeling well most of the time, though, so you shouldn't have felt guilty," Daniel said.

"I know. But I also think she was giving me time to heal and adjust to motherhood. She was so afraid that either I or the baby would get ill or something bad would happen. Now that she knows Rose is thriving, I think she feels better about me working with her again."

"I'm sure it does her good to have a little one around," Daniel said.

"Oh, yes, she loves it. When Rose was tiny, Mrs. Winchester

would ask to hold her every evening after dinner for just a little while. When she did, her face lit up with joy. I suppose she was remembering her own little girl," Olivia said. Seeing Mrs. Winchester with Rose had warmed her heart.

Daniel reached for her hand and squeezed it. "I think you're doing more good for Mrs. Winchester by being here than she is for you."

Olivia thought back to the first day she came for her interview and how nervous she'd been that Mrs. Winchester would tell her she had no place being in her home. Hiring her that day, despite knowing her circumstances, was the kindest thing anyone had ever done for her. Daniel would never know that Mrs. Winchester had basically saved her life.

"I'll forever be grateful to Mrs. Winchester for all she's done for me," Olivia said softly. "And for leading me to you."

Daniel grinned, looking wickedly handsome and sweet all at once. "Shall we go for a car ride and watch the sunset after dinner?"

Olivia most certainly wanted to.

CHAPTER TWENTY–FOUR

Today

"I loved that manuscript!" Jonathan told Morgan just seconds after arriving at work Monday morning. He was looking over the partition, and his eyes were alight with excitement. "I couldn't put it down."

Morgan had made copies of the manuscript for him and her mother and one for herself the week after she and Jonathan had gone sightseeing. She'd made sure he had it for the weekend so he'd have time to read it. "It really is good, isn't it?"

"Absolutely. I don't want to talk about it here because there are ears everywhere. Let's get lunch later, and then we can talk."

Morgan agreed. She also didn't want to say anything here where their fellow editors could hear.

They went to the sandwich shop down the street for lunch, and after getting their food, they found a spot in a corner near the front windows. Jonathan had brought the manuscript along and set it on the table.

"Sarah's story completely rips apart everything that has ever been written about her," Jonathan said. "And it all makes sense now. I guess it was easy to believe the lies because that was the only opinion out there."

"Right?" Morgan said. "No one ever questioned it. Plus, the newspapers back then wrote about her being crazy, so people believed it. Why wouldn't they? It's all so sad, too, because she had a whole life before coming to California, and then they ripped her to shreds."

Jonathan nodded as he bit into his sandwich. "I have to be honest with you. This is way too important and too good for Generation Publishing. You really should seek out a different publisher. Or maybe get an agent to find the perfect fit."

Morgan sat back in her chair and thought about that. She hadn't considered getting an agent. "Do you think a bigger publisher might be interested?"

"Yes, I do. This is big. It's Sarah telling her own story. I think it would be in demand if an agent started putting it out there."

"That would be incredible. But what will that say about my loyalty to Generation Publishing and the parent company? Could they fire me for seeking out a different publisher?" Morgan couldn't afford to lose her job. And she didn't want to have to find a new one and move somewhere else.

Jonathan grinned. "That would look very petty of them if you suddenly had a bestselling book and they fired you."

Morgan made a face. "You and I both know there's no guarantee of a bestseller. Even if another publisher picks it up, it could do well or just marginally well. Not enough money for me to quit my job."

"It's worth a try, though. No one will know if you're soliciting the manuscript, especially if you can find an agent. Until a deal is made, Amanda or the parent company wouldn't know a thing."

"I don't know," Morgan said. "The publishing world can be very small when it comes to things like this. I suppose I can't submit it to the parent company without Amanda being involved, either. They're a big publisher—one that I'd want to work with."

Jonathan shrugged. "She'd hear about it, that's for sure. I really think it's worth a try to go with a different publisher. You should also write a biography of your Grandma Olivia explaining who she was and how you're related. That will add more interest to the story, too."

Morgan nodded as she picked at the chips on her plate. "My mom is sifting through the details of her life online. Olivia was very secretive. We haven't figured out if she had her baby illegitimately or if she adopted her. We do know for certain, though, through census records, that she worked for Mrs. Winchester as a secretary. So at least we have that."

"It's a good start." Jonathan smiled over at her. "Thanks for letting me read the manuscript. I'm glad you trusted me with it."

Morgan did trust Jonathan. And she valued his opinion, too, more than she'd realized. "Do you want to go somewhere for dinner tonight? Chinese food sounds good." The minute the words left her lips, Morgan was surprised at herself. But she wanted to spend more time with Jonathan, other than at work.

"Sure. That does sound good."

She took a breath. At least it seemed he wanted to be around her, too.

When they returned to the office after lunch, Amanda snagged Morgan at the door. "There you are. I've been looking for you. Can you come into my office?"

"Sure. I'll be right in." Morgan glanced at Jonathan, who

shrugged. You never knew if Amanda was going to yell at you or commend you when she called you into the office. Morgan put her small backpack in her desk drawer and headed into Amanda's office.

"What's up?" Morgan asked.

Amanda was sitting at her desk, writing something on a sheet of paper. She waved to Morgan to sit down in the chair in front of the desk but kept her eyes on the paperwork. After a minute, she sat up straight and adjusted her thick, black glasses. "Tell me what's going on with the Winchester manuscript you mentioned a while back. Are you going to let me read it?"

Morgan's mouth dropped open, and she snapped it shut immediately. Did this woman have ultrasonic hearing, or was she psychic? Why would she bring up the manuscript today? "I did finish reading it, and it's pretty amazing. We're still looking into the facts around my great-great-grandmother who worked for Mrs. Winchester and typed it for her." Morgan thought she could stall Amanda with the lack of information on the person who actually typed it.

"That can be worked out later. I'm sure it will be easy to prove she worked for Winchester. When can I have a look at the manuscript?" Amanda said in the demanding voice she used that meant you didn't have a choice.

"To be honest," Morgan said, trying not to feel intimidated by Amanda. "I was thinking of consulting an agent to see what my options are."

"That's ridiculous." Amanda stood up and walked around to the front of the desk. Her skirt was ankle-length and swished as she walked on her four-inch heels. She sat on the corner of the desk, which made her tower over Morgan, and looked her straight in the eye. "You know a good story when you read it.

What more would an agent know? And if there is a problem, I'll know how to fix it. Why on earth would you pay a percentage to an agent when you can publish it directly here?"

"Well, I..." Morgan started to defend her choice, but Amanda cut her off.

"Listen, Morgan. I mentioned this manuscript to an editor at the parent company, and they're interested. They're as big a publisher as you can get. And it would be a feather in your cap, and mine, if we let them have it. So why wait? Can you get me a copy today?"

Morgan felt trapped. On the one hand, Amanda was right—the parent company was a big publisher. But on the other hand, Morgan felt she'd lose control of the manuscript if she let Amanda handle the sale and publication of it. But if Morgan said no, she felt she'd risk losing her job.

"I have an extra copy in my desk," Morgan said. "I guess it wouldn't hurt for you to read it. I'm not ready to make any commitments with it yet."

Amanda stood and went back to her side of the desk. "Of course. It's completely your decision what happens to the manuscript." She sat down and smiled. "If it's good, I'll make sure you get a good deal. You know I have your back."

Do I? Morgan thought. *Or are you protecting your own back?*

Morgan stood. "I'll get the manuscript for you." She left and walked to her desk. She felt like she'd just been hit by a train.

"What's going on?" Jonathan whispered as Morgan passed his cubicle.

"I'll tell you later at dinner," Morgan said. She went to her desk and slipped a copy of the Winchester manuscript into a folder so Jonathan wouldn't see it. It felt wrong, sneaking it away like this. But she didn't want to explain it all right now. Then she returned to Amanda's office and put it on her desk.

"Great. Thanks," Amanda said, not even looking at the folder. She kept her head bent over her paperwork again. Morgan felt she'd been dismissed, so she left and went back to her desk.

After work, Jonathan and Morgan took the bus to China-town and entered a small restaurant Jonathan had suggested. The place was quiet, and they chose a small booth near the front where they could watch the tourists streaming by the window.

"This is a nice place," Morgan said, glancing around. "I usually order take-out from a place around the corner from my apartment."

"I do that sometimes, too," Jonathan said. "But I like to come here with friends once in a while. Their food is so much better here."

"So, does that make me one of your friends?" Morgan teased.

He looked startled for a moment, then laughed. "I hope we're at least friends. We've known each other for four years."

Morgan sobered. "Yes, we are. I was just teasing you."

They ordered their food and then sat gazing out the window while they waited. Jonathan finally broke the silence. "Do you want to tell me what happened with Amanda? Or maybe it's not any of my business."

Morgan sighed. "I'm still trying to process what happened. She asked me about the Winchester manuscript out of the blue, and I wasn't prepared for it. Then she pressured me into giving her a copy."

"What?" He leaned on the table. "What did she say?"

"She asked when she could read it. I tried to make excuses,

but she saw right through them. Then I told her I wasn't even sure I wanted to submit it anywhere yet—that I wanted to talk to an agent—and she scoffed at that." Morgan suddenly felt ridiculous for giving in to Amanda. "She said she had already told an editor at the parent company about it, and they're interested. Then she made promises about getting me the best money she could and taking care of me. The whole time, I felt like I was being railroaded."

"So, you gave it to her?" Jonathan asked.

Morgan nodded. "I felt like I'd been pushed into a corner. I told her all she could do was read it and that I wasn't ready to sell it yet. She seemed to agree to that." Morgan shook her head. "I shouldn't have let her bully me like that. Now I wish I hadn't given it to her."

Jonathan sat back in his seat and was silent for a moment. Finally, he said, "We both know how bossy she can be. It's not your fault, she pushed you into giving it to her. She does that sort of thing all the time. I've seen her treat authors that way, too. Making all sorts of promises and pushing them into rewrites they don't agree with or bad contracts. I'm sorry she did that to you."

"I should have known better, but I wasn't prepared for it. I've worked for her for seven years, and I know she does this. But I felt like there was an underlying vibe in the room that I had to give it to her or else," Morgan said.

"I get it. I really do," Jonathan said gently. He reached across the table and placed his hand on her arm. "She's a bully. But she can't sell that manuscript without your consent, so at least there's that. You still have the upper hand. Don't do anything until you're ready to."

"You're right," she said, feeling better. "I don't have to do anything. She stressed me out so much this afternoon that I wasn't thinking straight. But I can say no at any time."

He smiled. "That's right."

Their food came, and they both relaxed and ate. Morgan actually felt better now that she'd told Jonathan what had happened. She'd been afraid he would think she'd caved to Amanda, but he knew their boss as well as she did. Being reminded that nothing could be done without her agreement made everything better.

The food was delicious, and they talked about topics other than work for a change. Jonathan told her about growing up in Minnesota and then moving here. Morgan told him about her parents in San Jose and how she'd ended up working in publishing. They had a good time talking and learning more about each other.

They walked on the brightly lit streets part of the way home, and Jonathan reached for her hand. She liked the feel of his hand snug around hers. When they got on the bus back to their neighborhood, he continued to hold her hand. It was a small gesture, but she liked it.

"I'll walk you home," he said once they were off the bus.

"You don't have to. I don't live far from here," Morgan said.

"What kind of a guy would I be if I let you walk home alone at night?" Jonathan asked.

"A modern guy?" she teased. But she didn't protest as they walked along together because, in truth, she didn't like walking home alone at night.

When they arrived at the house, Jonathan looked impressed. "You didn't tell me you lived in a Victorian house."

"I never really think about it, I guess," she said, glancing up at it. "It's divided into four apartments, so to me, it's an apartment building."

"It's cool," he said. "My building is an apartment building. This one has style."

"I was lucky to get it. It's a nice neighborhood, and the other renters are decent people. But it's costly," Morgan said.

"Yeah. So is my place. I feel like I could have bought a house in the suburbs by now for what I pay in rent. But then, the commute would be too long. I'd hate that."

"I know what you mean." Morgan wondered if she should invite him upstairs, then wondered what he'd think of her invitation if she did. Then she wondered why she was making everything out to be so complicated.

"Well, I should head home," he said. "I can grab the bus at the corner and be home pretty quickly."

"Thanks for dinner," Morgan said. She'd meant to pay for her own, but he'd offered to pay, and she didn't want to fight over it in the restaurant. "Next time is my treat."

He smiled. "Goodnight."

"Goodnight."

They stared at each other another moment, and then Jonathan leaned in and placed a soft kiss on her lips. Nothing demanding. Just sweet. When he pulled away, he smiled again, said goodnight, and walked down the street.

Morgan watched him leave, her heart beating just a little faster than normal.

CHAPTER TWENTY–FIVE

1906 – 1919

After the earthquake, Sarah found herself floundering for a time. Sitting at the table on the deck of her houseboat, overlooking the San Francisco Bay, she thought about all the years of work she'd put into her beloved Llanada Villa only to see it fall to pieces before her eyes. She no longer cared to continue working on it. It had been a source of excitement and joy for her in the past, but now, it no longer was.

"You can't mope forever about the ranch house," Daisy said, sitting next to her aunt and placing a folded newspaper beside her. She filled a plate with scrambled eggs from a covered chafing dish and spread strawberry jam on a piece of toast. "It's time you get yourself a new project."

Sarah smiled at her niece, happy she was spending time here on the houseboat with her. Both Daisy and Fred had been there since the earthquake while their Palo Alto house was being repaired. "I'm not moping," Sarah said, although she knew she had been. "And I'm too old to start a new project."

"You? Too old? Since when?" Daisy teased. "Have you seen

the morning paper? Everyone is excited about the possibility of the new Panama Canal bringing ships and boats from all over the world to San Francisco and our little bay. It will revitalize the city and bring fortune to everyone around."

Sarah picked up the newspaper and read the article. It was an interesting concept. With San Francisco and many surrounding towns in ashes after the earthquake and fires, this exciting news was just what the people needed to get motivated to rebuild quickly. Many San Franciscans had already started buying property out of the city to build homes in the many tiny towns around Burlingame. They feared another earthquake and thought living out of the city was safer. But, the leaders of San Francisco needed to motivate the people to rebuild, and the promise of future ships coming to port from the Panama Canal seemed to be doing the trick.

"Hmm," Sarah said, setting down the newspaper. Her mind was already forming an idea. She owned over one hundred acres directly on the bay. She could create a new harbor right here, where visitors could dock their boats.

"I can see it in your eyes," Daisy said, grinning. "You're already planning a new project."

Sarah smiled but merely sipped her coffee.

Once Sarah put her plan in motion, there was no stopping her. She wasn't the only one to think of creating a safe harbor for incoming boat traffic. Others were building wharves and docks and dredging marshland to develop waterways. She drew up her plans, hired a contractor, and was on her way to owning her own harbor.

Not one to let others supervise, Sarah bought a small Tudor home near Burlingame. She visited the worksite each day, driven in her buggy by Frank Carroll. For months, she went back and forth between the house and the bay, watching over the progress. There were a few problems, and she ended up in a lawsuit with someone dumping sewage on her property, but she continued her project.

Meanwhile, the newspapers had a field day attacking Sarah for not rebuilding her ranch house. They said she had truly gone mad by leaving it damaged as it was. Articles stated she'd lost her mind and that the earthquake had finally pushed her over the edge, and she'd had a nervous breakdown. Sarah tried to ignore their words, but it wasn't always easy. Being attacked constantly by people she'd never met was disheartening. So, she focused on her new project and the other problems she still had to settle. One of them being Belle's house.

Belle had been living in her farmhouse even after most of the land had been sold, and Louis was in and out of hospitals and sanitariums because of ill health. Sarah finally decided to buy Belle a nice piece of property in Palo Alto, closer to Daisy, and build her a new house.

Belle had loved her farmhouse but was excited about the new house. Sarah let Belle request whatever upgrades she wanted and hired a contractor to design and build the cottage. Within two months in 1907, despite all the new building going on in the aftermath of the earthquake, Belle's cottage was complete, and she moved in.

Living in Palo Alto was good for Belle. As an activist, she was involved with many causes, her most passionate one being the Palo Alto Humane Society, which promoted the humane treatment of animals and children. She later became the director of the Santa Clara County Humane Society and focused her attention on the abuse of children. As a Special Humane Officer, Belle investigated child abuse cases and found foster care for abused children. She went as far as bringing the children into her own home until a new home was found. It was through her mother's work that Daisy met a sweet, six-year-old girl named Margaret who needed a home after abuse allegations.

Since the Marriotts hadn't yet had a child after five years of marriage, it didn't take much convincing by Daisy to Fred to adopt young Margaret. The young girl lived with Daisy and Fred while the adoption was in progress, but then it was put on hold because the child's mother learned that Sarah Winchester was Daisy's aunt. The mother demanded a cash payment before she'd sign the official adoption papers.

"Can you believe it?" Daisy asked her aunt one day as they sat in the living room of Sarah's new Atherton house. Sarah had recently purchased a third house in the area and decided to make it her permanent home. The other two houses had been repaired since the earthquake, but Sarah no longer trusted they were safe. This newer one hadn't been through the big quake, and Sarah felt safer there.

"It takes a lot of nerve to ask for cash for a child. In fact, it's illegal," Sarah told her niece, utterly astonished by the mother's demands. "But unfortunately, that's the price we pay because my last name is Winchester."

"What am I going to do?" Daisy said, nearly in tears. "I don't want to lose Margaret. She's been with us for three years and is safe and happy. I can't let her go back to those awful people."

Sarah agreed. The abuse Margaret had been subjected to at the hands of her father had been terrible. They couldn't let her go back. "I'll take care of it," Sarah offered. Because that was what Sarah did—she took care of her family's problems no matter what the cost.

A meeting was held between the mother, Daisy, and Fred, with lawyers present, and the papers were signed. No mention of money passing hands was written down, but it seemed plausible. Daisy could now keep the young girl safe, and Sarah had once again come to her niece's rescue.

* * *

Sarah was tired. She was tired of moving from house to house, tired of the problems building her harbor in Burlingame, and tired of the slander from the many area newspapers. In 1909, she was seventy years old. Her arthritis was damaging her arms, hands, and legs to the point that doing simple work was impossible. She wasn't sleeping well either, which motivated her to study a healthier way of eating in the hope of curing her insomnia. She stopped drinking coffee and eating other foods she loved because of digestive problems. In letters to family back east, she complained about her minor health issues. The truth was that age was creeping up on her, and she didn't want to succumb to it. Her mind was just as clear and busy as it had always been, and what she enjoyed more than anything else was to have a project.

When her driver, Frank Carroll, died suddenly in late 1909, Sarah was devastated. His driving her around in her buggy had been her escape from becoming completely housebound. He'd worked for her since living in New Haven, and he was more of an old friend than an employee. Sarah paid for his funeral and offered to buy his widow, Mary, and their young children a home and send them support payments for as long as they needed. Mary was thankful for the money and used it to start her own successful orchard.

Without Frank to drive her around, Sarah shut down the harbor project in Burlingame, docked the houseboat in the water, and hired a caretaker to watch over it. She'd lost interest in the great San Francisco rejuvenation project. Perhaps it was time to just settle down into old age.

While staying for a time at Llanada Villa, Daisy brought Margaret for a visit, and soon, the yard was filled with the laughter of children at play. Sarah's foreman, John Hansen, and his wife had two young sons who played with Margaret, and a neighbor girl came over too. Sarah bought a pony for the children, and they had fun running around the yard and fields.

Sarah stood at the window, watching the children play some make-believe game out in the yard. "It's nice having children here, isn't it?"

Daisy smiled and nodded. "Yes. Margaret loves coming here. There's so much land to play on and things to do. She loves collecting the eggs from the chickens for the cook in the morning and running around with the Hansen's dog."

"I'm glad to hear that," Sarah said. She turned back to Daisy. "It's nice this place finally has so much life in it. I was afraid the earthquake had killed the home's spirit."

Daisy grinned. "Don't say the word spirit aloud, or the newspapers will have a field day with you, Aunt Sallie."

Sarah chuckled. "Yes. I suppose they will. Well, let them have their fun. Once I'm dead, maybe they will leave me alone."

"Don't talk like that," Daisy admonished her. "You have years ahead of you."

Sarah sighed and sat down on the green velvet sofa. "I don't feel that way, though. There is nothing anymore that excites me like building this house used to. When you have nothing to look forward to, you feel lost."

"Then find something that excites you," Daisy said. "I won't have you talking about death when there is still so much more life inside you." Daisy sat forward and poured herself some more tea. "Maybe it's time you reorganized your finances and will. When did you last do that?"

Sarah puckered her face as she thought. "Not since I left New Haven."

"Really?" Daisy looked shocked. "So much has changed. You really should update everything."

Sarah nodded. "Yes, I should." She smiled. "That will be a project. Maybe it's time I hired a new secretary now that you're busy with your family. I can no longer write figures or letters with my hands the way they are. Plus, I need more staff. All these houses of mine need more attention."

"Another good project for you. Hiring staff." Daisy smirked. "Fred suggested something the other day, and I agree with him. Now that you don't have Frank to drive you around, maybe it's time to buy an automobile and find a driver. You know how much Fred loves autos. He'd be happy to help you choose one."

Sarah took a sip of her tea, her brows raised. "Yes, I'll bet he would like that. He'd probably be fine with borrowing my automobile sometimes, too."

Daisy laughed. "I wouldn't doubt that one bit. So, you may have to buy two."

Sarah thought it might not be a bad idea after all. Carriages and horses were long out of style. Perhaps it was time she stepped into the modern world.

With Fred's help, Sarah began her collection of automobiles. She didn't stop at just one. She purchased a 1909 green Renault limousine with all the extras so she could be driven around in style. But her favorite was a gray Pierce-Arrow with a lavender stripe down the sides. It was so distinctive that everyone knew Mrs. Winchester was out for a drive when they saw the beautiful car.

Sarah hired a new driver, Fred Larsen, who could not only escort her places in her autos but also maintain and fix them. And as she predicted, Fred Marriott borrowed her vehicles quite often.

Sarah also began the process of rewriting her will. For a woman as detailed as she, writing a will was more fun than work. She worked on her investments as well and continued to purchase land around Atherton. But the project that excited her the most that year was when she'd read in the New Haven newspaper that the General Hospital Society of Connecticut was asking for donations to open a tuberculosis hospital in New Haven. This piqued her interest. Sarah had long been looking for a way to honor her beloved husband, and she saw this as an opportunity to help her old community and do something generous in William's memory.

Not wanting her name connected to her large donation, Sarah sent three hundred thousand dollars to the hospital through her lawyer. She didn't need the recognition, she just needed to know she'd be helping others who required medical treatment for the disease that had killed her beloved William. This, she felt, would be her greatest accomplishment to date.

* * *

Olivia paused her writing as Mrs. Winchester stopped to sip her water. Because the widow hadn't felt well that day, they'd met in her bedroom to work. Sarah lay on her bed, on top of the comforter, and propped up with pillows while Olivia sat in a cushy chair next to the bed. The curtains were open, letting in the sunshine, but the room was a bit stuffy. Olivia supposed Sarah's body temperature ran cooler than hers, and she needed the room to be warm.

"That was quite generous of you, donating so much money," Olivia said. "But I know all too well how generous you can be."

"That's kind of you, dear. I ended up giving three times that amount in the end, and the hospital found out it was me donating it. I generally don't like the attention, but they offered to name the facility after William, and I decided it would be a fitting tribute to him. In fact, it was dedicated to William last April in a ceremony, and my brother-in-law and William's sister, Thomas and Jennie Bennett, were able to attend. They wrote to me, telling me all about it. I'm very proud I could do this one thing in William's memory and help those suffering at the same time."

"You're an amazing woman, Mrs. Winchester," Olivia said, then felt awkward for having said it. She was always worried she was overstepping her boundaries. But Sarah only chuckled.

"Again, that is kind of you to say. I believe those with money should spread it around. And I've certainly done that, haven't I?"

Olivia smiled. Yes, Sarah Winchester had spread her money around quite successfully.

"I think I'll rest a bit before lunch," Sarah said. "Will you please tell Henrietta not to bother me for the next half hour?"

Olivia stood. "I'd be happy to. Have a nice rest." She headed out the door and practically ran into Miss Sivera.

"Oh! Miss Sivera," Olivia said, startled. "I didn't see you there. Mrs. Winchester said she'd like to rest for the next thirty minutes before lunch."

"Thank you," Miss Sivera said. "I'm sorry I startled you."

"No harm done. My mind was still on Mrs. Winchester's story. She's had such an interesting life."

"Yes, she has." Miss Sivera studied Olivia for a moment. "Do you think, after all this time, we could call each other by our given names? Please call me Henrietta."

Olivia was surprised by this. But she had been living there for a year, and they'd come to know each other quite well. "Yes. Call me Olivia, please. I think we've been through enough together to at least be on a first-name basis."

Henrietta smiled. "Yes, I guess we have."

They parted ways, and Olivia left her notepad in her room before going downstairs to lunch. She always enjoyed the meals with the staff, especially with her daughter, Rose, joining them.

Hurrying her pace, she headed downstairs.

Chapter Twenty-Six

1919 – 1920

Mrs. Winchester's health was declining as the year wore on, and Olivia spent less time with her working on her story. Olivia felt they were nearing the end of the story, and she hoped she'd get the chance to finish it before Mrs. Winchester grew too ill.

Despite that, Olivia was the happiest she'd ever been. She and Daniel were spending more time together, and her little Rose was blossoming into a toddler. Rose was walking by her first birthday and was spoiled by Mrs. Winchester, Henrietta, and the rest of the staff at Christmas. For Olivia, her Atherton house family felt like a real family.

Daniel escorted Olivia to a New Year's Eve party at a friend's house in San Jose, where the guests wore silk and satin gowns with beading that sparkled underneath the chandeliers as they danced. Misa had made Olivia a lovely gown of blue satin and had hand-sewn tiny crystal beads on the thin straps, around the waist, and the hemline. Mrs. Winchester had loaned her a mink wrap to wear with it, and Olivia wore the lovely solitaire diamond necklace Daniel had so generously given her as a Christmas present. With her hair pulled up into a sophisticated French twist, Olivia felt like a princess who'd been allowed out until midnight.

"I hope my coach doesn't turn into a pumpkin," Olivia said to Daniel as they glided around the beautiful ballroom. "This all feels like a fairy tale."

He smiled at her. "It's all real, I assure you. And someday, hopefully, I'll have a house like this where we can have fairy tale dances like this, too."

His words startled Olivia. "We?"

Daniel continued to lead her around the dance floor until they made their way to one of the small outdoor balconies. They stopped under the moonlight, the stars glittering above them. Without hesitation, he kissed her deeply, right there for everyone to see if they were so inclined.

Breathless, Olivia looked up into Daniel's warm brown eyes. "My goodness. What's gotten into you? What will everyone think?" she said. But her heart was beating rapidly, and she wished he would kiss her again with that same passion.

"They'll think I'm a man in love," he said. He looked so handsome in his black tuxedo with tails and his shirt as snowy white as a winter's day. The gold buttons on his jacket sparkled under the full moon.

Olivia didn't know how to respond to his words. She loved him too—oh so very much. But was it proper to say so? When he knelt on one knee in front of her and reached for her white-gloved hand, she was stunned.

"Dear Olivia," he said softly. "I love you, and I adore little Rose. I want us to be a family. Will you accept my offer of marriage?" Daniel lifted his other hand, which held a small leather box. He snapped it open to display a beautiful diamond ring set in platinum.

"Oh, my," was all Olivia could manage to say. The ring held three round diamonds, with the center stone twice the size of the other stones. It glittered as he held it, even under the dim outdoor lighting.

Daniel stood. "Is that a yes?" he asked, smiling wide.

After all that had happened to Olivia over the past two years, she'd never thought she'd find this kind of happiness and have a happily ever after. She loved Daniel so much. He was the type of man every woman hoped for.

"Olivia, sweetheart. You're scaring me," Daniel said, his eyes meeting hers.

"Oh, Daniel," she said, still feeling breathless. "Yes. Yes. Yes. A hundred times yes."

His face lit up, and he gently took ahold of her hand and slipped the ring over her gloved finger. She lifted her hand up and gazed at the ring, still unable to believe that a man like Daniel wanted to marry her. When her eyes met his again, she smiled.

"I'm so happy," Olivia said. From inside the room, the orchestra had stopped playing, and the crowd was counting down the last seconds to midnight. Daniel pulled Olivia into his arms, and when the clock struck twelve, he kissed her so passionately Olivia knew that she'd found her forever.

That night, as Olivia lay in bed, she couldn't help but think about the night and how magically perfect it had been. She'd worn the gorgeous engagement ring to bed because she hadn't wanted to part with it. It felt cool and heavy on her finger. She loved Daniel, there was no doubt. And she knew he loved little Rose as well. Her life couldn't have turned out any better.

Yet, there was an uncomfortable niggling inside her. Daniel truly believed Rose was the product of her first marriage. He hadn't doubted her for a second. But the story of her having a husband was a lie. How could she start their life together with that big of a lie between them?

Above all else, Olivia loved her daughter more than anything in her life. She'd do anything to protect her and give her the best life possible. But lying to a good man like Daniel seemed so wrong. What if, years from now, he found out she'd lied? How hurt would he be, knowing their marriage was built on a lie?

Olivia arrived at breakfast the next morning, exhausted from her sleepless night. She'd hidden away the engagement ring, not wanting to announce it to everyone yet. Alice just assumed she was tired from her big night out and didn't ask her why she looked so worn down.

"It's 1920; can you believe it?" Alice said as the group at the table served up their breakfast from the many platters of food. "How the time does fly. Did you enjoy your fancy party last night?" she asked Olivia.

"Oh, yes," Olivia said, barely touching her scrambled eggs and biscuit. She buttered half of a biscuit for Rose, who greedily ate it. "It was a beautiful night. The women were dressed up lovely and glittered like stars under the lights in the ballroom."

"That sounds dreamy," Mae said, sighing. "I wish I had a beau to take me to something like that."

"I hope you do someday," Olivia said, smiling at the housekeeper. "I have never been to such a fancy affair before. It was lovely." She tried to sound cheery about her night out because it had been an incredible evening. But her thoughts were weighing her down.

After breakfast, Olivia asked Elaina to watch Rose so she could talk to Henrietta. Then she went upstairs and knocked softly on Mrs. Winchester's door. She assumed Henrietta was there, having breakfast. Henrietta opened the door and smiled when she saw who it was. She stepped out into the hallway.

"How was your evening last night?" Henrietta asked.

"It was wonderful," Olivia told her. "We had a good time."

"That's good to hear," the secretary said.

"How is Mrs. Winchester today?" Olivia asked.

"She's feeling quite well, actually. We've just finished eating breakfast. But she told me to tell you not to worry about working today. It's a holiday, after all. She's hoping you can continue tomorrow or the day after."

"That sounds fine," Olivia said, but she was disappointed. She had hoped to speak to her employer about her problem. Mrs. Winchester was the only other person who knew the husband story was a lie. She'd wanted to ask her advice.

"Is something wrong?" Henrietta asked, seeming to pick up on Olivia's mood.

"I had just hoped to speak to Mrs. Winchester for a few minutes. But I don't want to disturb her."

Henrietta looked thoughtful. "I'm sure she wouldn't mind speaking with you. Give me a moment, and I'll ask her if she feels well enough to visit with you." She disappeared back inside their employer's bedroom.

Olivia wondered if she was being ridiculous about this whole matter. Maybe she shouldn't bother Mrs. Winchester. Still, she felt she owed Daniel the truth. Olivia wrung her hands as she waited, wishing now that she hadn't asked to speak to the older lady.

Henrietta returned. "Mrs. Winchester said she'd love to

speak with you. Go ahead in. I'll give you two some privacy."

"Thank you," Olivia said, then steeled herself as she walked through the door and closed it behind her. Mrs. Winchester was sitting in a cushy chair at the table and had folders and papers strewn in front of her. She was dressed as usual in a long, black gown with a beautiful cream crocheted shawl around her shoulders.

"Good morning, dear," Mrs. Winchester said, smiling at her. "Come in and sit down. I was sorting through all the investments and trusts I've set up for family members. They seem to get more complicated as the years go by."

Olivia approached the table. "If I'm interrupting, I can come back later."

Mrs. Winchester waived her curled hand in the air to brush aside her words. "You are not interrupting. This will still be here after you leave and the next day, too." She chuckled. "In fact, I'll probably still be refining all of this on my deathbed."

"Then let's hope that is a long time from now," Olivia said. She dreaded the thought of Mrs. Winchester's passing. She'd come to care very much for the older woman.

Olivia pulled out one of the chairs by the table and sat, smoothing down her striped skirt. "Can I ask your advice about a problem I have?"

Mrs. Winchester set down the paper she'd been perusing and gave her full attention to Olivia. "Of course. What is the matter?"

Olivia took a deep breath, then let it out. "Daniel proposed to me last night."

The older lady blinked several times, seeming to consider what she'd said. "That is something to celebrate, is it not?"

"It is. Or at least, it was," Olivia said. "I was very excited and told him yes, I would marry him. But now I find myself in a moral dilemma."

"Ah." Mrs. Winchester nodded her understanding. "You feel he needs to know the truth about Rose."

Olivia nearly broke down in tears of relief over her employer's understanding of her problem. "I would hate to start a marriage on a lie," she said. "He's such a good man. What if he learned I'd never been married before and that I'd lied to him? It would ruin everything."

"So, you think telling him the truth before you're married would be better?" Mrs. Winchester asked.

"Yes. But no. I don't know what to do. If I tell him the truth now, I might lose his respect and him too. If I don't, I'll always wonder when the truth will come out, and I'll lose him anyway. I don't know what to do." Tears filled her eyes, and she reached into her pocket for a handkerchief.

"Dear. Personally, I doubt if Daniel will ever learn that you weren't married before, and your secret would never be found out. But I can see it would eat you up inside knowing you lied to him." Mrs. Winchester reached out her hand and placed it over Olivia's. "The real question here isn't if you can keep the secret. It's whether or not you can live with yourself if you don't tell him the truth. You are an honest, caring person. You love those around you deeply. If you feel you need to be completely truthful with Daniel—even at the risk of losing him—then that is what you must do."

Mrs. Winchester was right. Olivia had already known she needed to tell Daniel the truth. She just needed someone else to confirm it was the right thing for her to do.

"What would you do?" Olivia asked, her voice barely a whisper.

"I can't answer that for you," Mrs. Winchester said. "Because you and I are two very different people. I believe in being honest, but if I had to choose between lying or risk losing my beloved William, I think I would have lied." She gave her a small smile. "But when I was your age, I wasn't as strong as you are. Or even nearly as strong-willed as I am now."

"Thank you, Mrs. Winchester," Olivia said. "I needed to talk to someone who'd understand." She stood and pushed the chair back in place.

"Are you going to tell him?" the elderly lady asked.

"I have to. It's the right thing to do."

Mrs. Winchester nodded. "Doing the right thing isn't always the easiest thing, though."

Olivia knew that was true. But she also knew it was the only way she could live with herself. She hoped Daniel would be able to understand.

* * *

Two days later, Daniel came to the Atherton home to deliver a letter and more paperwork for Mrs. Winchester from Frank Lieb and to pick up the notes she'd made about her trust funds for relatives. He came right before lunch and surprised Olivia on her way down to eat with the staff.

"You should have told me you were coming," Olivia said, hiding her hand so he wouldn't see she wasn't wearing her engagement ring.

"I wanted to surprise you," he said, smiling. "Do you think we can make up a basket of food and have a picnic outside? It's a beautiful day."

"Let me go upstairs for some proper shoes, and then we can

go," she said, hurrying up the back stairs. She ran into Elaina on the way to her room and asked her if she'd feed Rose lunch. Then, she entered her room, changed into flat shoes, and pocketed her engagement ring.

Once downstairs, Olivia filled a basket with food from the table, and she and Daniel headed outdoors. The day was warm, but a breeze stirred through the trees and cooled the air. They found a shady oak tree and sat underneath.

"Was everyone excited when you announced your engagement?" Daniel asked as he helped himself to a ham sandwich, and Olivia poured glasses of iced tea from a small pitcher.

"I haven't told anyone yet," Olivia said quietly. "I wanted to keep it to myself for a while." She reached into her pocket and slipped the engagement ring on her finger. Luckily, he hadn't noticed it was missing yet.

Daniel's face creased. "Oh. I thought you might be eager to tell everyone, especially Alice and Mrs. Winchester."

"I did tell Mrs. Winchester," Olivia said. "But only because I had to ask her advice."

"About what?" Daniel pulled a bowl of red grapes out of the basket and popped one in his mouth. "I hope you're not having second thoughts." His face creased with concern again.

Olivia felt like she was going to cry. She reached out her hand and covered his. Her beautiful engagement ring sparkled between them. "No, I'm not. But I hope you won't have second thoughts after I share something I must tell you."

Daniel set down his food and turned to look at her. He grasped her hand in his. "What is it?"

Olivia's mouth went dry as she tried to form the words. She hadn't had time to prepare for this. But maybe it was better this way. The longer she led him on, the worse it would be.

Finally, she said, "I've been lying to you. Actually, to everyone, but it wasn't meant to hurt anyone, only to protect me.
Mrs. Winchester and Frank Lieb were the only other people
who knew the truth. But I can't accept your marriage proposal
unless I tell you the truth, too."

Daniel frowned. "What truth?"

"I'm so sorry, Daniel. I wasn't married before, and my
husband didn't die. It was a lie to protect Rose and me. You
see, I was compromised by a man I worked with at the law
firm. He made me believe he was in love with me and then took
advantage of my inexperience with men. I thought he wanted
to marry me. It's partly my fault, partly his. The result was my
pregnancy with Rose, and he abandoned me." The words were
out. She searched Daniel's face for his reaction, praying that
after he'd thought about it a moment, he'd understand and still
love her and Rose. But the crease between his eyes grew deeper.

"You lied about being married? Rose is illegitimate?"

"Yes," Olivia said, dropping her eyes. "And I am deeply
ashamed for having made up the lie. But Mrs. Winchester
understood my predicament, and she and I decided it best to
tell everyone that I was a widow."

Daniel stood and walked a few paces away, running his
hand through his hair.

Olivia stood also and went to him. She wanted to reach
out and touch him but held back. "I'm sorry, Daniel. I never
thought I'd meet someone as wonderful as you and that the lie
would grow so big. It seemed innocent at the time. But I could
never live with myself if I didn't tell you the truth before you
married me."

Daniel spun and faced her. He looked hurt. "You lied to
me. All this time, you lied to me. And my boss, Mr. Lieb, knew

too. And Mrs. Winchester. Were they trying to pawn you off on me all this time? Sending me here so I'd fall in love with you. Was all that a lie, too? Were we a lie?"

Olivia felt like she'd been slapped. "No. Not at all. No one planned for you and me to meet and fall in love. It just happened."

"Can I believe that?" he asked, sounding angry. "Can I believe anything you say?"

Olivia's heart broke into tiny shards at that very moment. "You can believe that I fell in love with you. And that I do love you. And Rose loves you, too. Those things are true. But I have no other way to convince you than with my words."

When Daniel didn't respond, Olivia knew she'd lost him. She slipped the ring off her finger, took his hand in hers, and pressed it into his palm, closing his fingers around it.

"I'm sorry," she said, her voice cracking. "I'm so, so sorry."

He opened his hand and looked at the ring, then back up at Olivia. Without a word, Daniel strode off across the lawn toward his motorcar. He didn't look back.

Olivia dropped to the ground and wept.

Chapter Twenty—Seven

Today

It had been two weeks since Morgan had handed the Winchester manuscript to Amanda, and still, she hadn't heard a word from her. Maybe Amanda hadn't thought it was good. Or maybe the editor she'd suggested it to hadn't liked it. It would be easier if that was the case because then Morgan could try to sell it to another publisher, and her job wouldn't be in jeopardy.

Over that same time, she and Jonathan had become closer. They were seeing each other nearly every evening after work, and he'd even gone to her parents' house for dinner that past Saturday. Her parents liked him, and they all had a good time. Jonathan had been comfortable around her parents, which surprised Morgan. She'd always thought of Jonathan as awkward around new people, but that was just at work. She was learning that his work persona was quite different than his home personality. Maybe it was the stress at work, constantly worrying about what Amanda was going to say or do, that made him more cautious there. She knew that she was also on edge at work most of the time.

The Monday after they'd had such a great weekend together, Amanda's assistant, Gabbie, buzzed Morgan's phone and told her Amanda wanted to see her. Taking a breath, Morgan left her cubicle but stopped at Jonathan's first.

"This may be it," she told him in a hushed voice. "Amanda just asked to see me."

"What are you going to tell her if she offers you a contract?" he asked.

"I don't know. But I'm not going to jump into anything. I've sent out a few copies of the manuscript to agents these past two weeks, and I want to see if any are interested first."

"Well, good luck with Amanda," he said, rolling his eyes.

This made Morgan smile. She liked his sense of humor, especially when he was sarcastic. They were two of a kind in that respect.

She headed to Amanda's office. Gabbie was sitting outside it at her glass desk. "Go on in. She's waiting for you."

Morgan entered, and Amanda looked up.

"Great. Morgan. Come on in and sit down."

Morgan did. She saw the Winchester manuscript on the desk and a folder beside it.

Amanda was all smiles, which was unusual for her. She wore a red dress with red heels and a colorful scarf around her neck. Morgan knew that Amanda subscribed to the idea that red was a power color and she could sway people her way by the colors she wore.

"I have good news," Amanda said. "I loved the Winchester biography, and so did the editor at the parent company. They want to publish it."

Morgan's brows rose. "They do? Which imprint is interested?"

"Our imprint, of course," Amanda said. "They gave me the go-ahead to publish it through Generation Publishing. And they're going to invest a lot of money in it. There'll be a big advertising budget, which is unusual for us. Isn't that great? This book will save our imprint and put it on the map."

"That's nice to hear that they liked it, but I haven't decided if I'm going to sell the manuscript yet," Morgan said.

Amanda's lips curled down momentarily, but then she forced herself to smile again. "You haven't had a chance to see the deal yet." She slid the manila folder toward Morgan. "This is the contract with the offer. It's a pretty sweet deal."

Morgan lifted the contract out of the folder and looked it over. She'd given contracts to authors dozens of times, so she knew what was standard and what was a good deal. As she read the percentages, she knew this was a good offer. It was better than what most debut authors were given. Still, she wasn't in any hurry to accept it. Morgan knew that the Winchester manuscript was more valuable than her own company wanted to pay her for it.

She set the contract back on Amanda's desk and looked up at her. "It's a good deal. But I'm not ready to sell it yet. I'd like some time to think about it." Immediately, she saw that Amanda's patience was wearing thin.

"What do you mean you need to think about it?" Amanda demanded. "This is a better deal than most of our authors get—even authors who do well with us. Don't you understand how important this manuscript is?"

Morgan forced herself not to be intimidated. "Yes, I do understand how important and valuable this manuscript is. That's why I'd like some time. I don't want to jump into anything."

Amanda narrowed her eyes. "Are you asking for more money? Because if that's what this is about, then I could probably offer a little higher on the up-front money. I'm sure the company would agree it would be worth it."

"I'm sorry, Amanda. It's more than just the money. I want to make sure the right publisher works with this book. I appreciate the generous offer, but I don't think our imprint is the right place for this manuscript. We deal in mid-list authors. I think this book could do so much better than that." Morgan wasn't sure where her strength and confidence were coming from, but she stood her ground.

"I thought you wanted to publish this manuscript," Amanda said, standing up behind her desk. "Why did you give it to me to read if you didn't want to publish with our company?"

"You asked to read it. I had only talked to you about it prior to that. You were the one who asked to read it and who told the editor at our parent company about it before I'd even decided what I wanted to do with it."

"You came to me first," Amanda said.

"Yes, I did. But I didn't force you to read it."

Amanda's jaw clenched, and Morgan could tell she was grinding her teeth. "Okay," Amanda said, trying to sound calmer. "If you don't publish with us, then who do you think you'll publish with? You work for us. You found the manuscript while you were under our employ. Do you think it's fair to bring it to another publisher?"

Morgan frowned. Amanda was twisting everything around. "I found the manuscript at my mother's house in a box of my grandma's personal things. I didn't find it here, in the office. I have a right to try to find the best home possible for it."

"Not while you're an editor here, you don't. How will it

look for our company if you work here but sell the book else-where? Are you trying to get me fired? Or maybe you're trying to get yourself fired." Amanda stared hard at her.

"What are you saying?" Morgan asked, shocked by her words.

"I'm just pointing out that you can't be an acquisition editor here but sell your book somewhere else," Amanda said tightly. "So, make up your mind. Do you want to sell to us or no longer work for us?"

Morgan couldn't believe that the conversation had turned so quickly. But there was no way she was going to give this woman the rights to her grandmother's manuscript. She stood, making sure to pick up the manuscript from the desk. "I guess my choice is very clear. I'll clean out my desk right now. Good-bye, Amanda." She turned and walked out the door.

By the time Morgan made it to Jonathan's desk, her legs were wobbly. Had she really just quit her job? How would she pay rent? How would she live?

"What happened," Jonathan asked the moment he saw her. "You look like you're going to be sick."

"I think I am," Morgan said. She quickly walked to her chair and sat, afraid she might throw up or pass out right there. "I was given two choices—publish with Generation or quit. So, I quit."

Jonathan's face twisted up with anger. "Are you kidding me? She can't do that. What's wrong with her?"

"It's probably for the best," Morgan said. Her heart rate was slowing down and she didn't feel nauseous anymore. "I refuse to be pushed into doing something I'd regret."

"She can't legally fire you for refusing to publish a book with the company," Jonathan said. "You could sue them for blackmail."

Morgan sighed. "Suing them won't endear me to the publishing world. I'd never get another job because they'd be afraid I'd cause trouble."

"I'm going to talk to Amanda. She can't do this to you." Jonathan turned to leave, but Morgan grabbed his hand and pulled him back into her cubicle.

"No. Don't risk your job for me. Please."

His shoulders slumped. "You don't deserve this. Someone needs to say something to her."

"It's okay. She probably thinks I'll rethink this whole thing and cave in. But this time, I won't. She's pushed me around for the last time." Morgan stood and looked around her cubicle. There was a banker's box that held old files on the floor behind her desk. She pulled the files out and laid them on the table behind her. Then she started filling the box with her personal items.

"What can I do?" Jonathan asked, looking helpless.

"Just keep doing your job. I have a feeling that Amanda is on her last leg here, and that's why she is so desperate for me to sign. Maybe they'll fire her, and then they'll be looking for a new managing editor."

"Wishful thinking," Jonathan said.

This made Morgan laugh. She'd finished putting the few personal items she had into the box and placed the lid on top. "I'll see you tonight, okay?"

He nodded, and she walked out the door without speaking to anyone else.

Later, at her apartment, Morgan looked at her finances to see how long she could live without her income. If she was careful, she could pay her rent and essential bills for at least four months. That didn't give her much time to try to sell the manuscript or to find a new editor job. And it wasn't like there were that many publishers in San Francisco to begin with. Finding a job was going to be tough.

She called her mother, who was immediately upset for her but told her she'd made the right decision.

"You don't want to work for someone like that," Annie told her daughter. "She was blackmailing you! What kind of person does that?"

"She does," Morgan told her.

"I think you should call her supervisor and tell them what happened," Annie said firmly. "I'm sure they don't know that is how this woman conducts business."

"It won't help, Mom," Morgan said. "I think it was time I left there anyway. I'll just have to be creative and come up with a new plan on places I can work."

"You can always come home until you find a new job," Annie said. "You know we'd love to have you here."

Morgan knew they would, but going back home after years of being on her own seemed like a step backward. "It's good to know I can, Mom. But for now, I'll be fine."

Jonathan said practically the same thing that evening when he brought pizza for dinner. "Maybe you should move in with your parents to save money."

Morgan rolled her eyes. "I love my parents, but I don't want to move in with them. I'll be fine for a while. Maybe I can find a job at a newspaper or freelance as an editor. I'm sure there's something I can do. But first, I want to go through this book again and make sure it's perfect before I send out more queries to agents."

"Amanda didn't even have the decency to tell the staff that you were no longer working there," Jonathan said, sounding disgusted. "Not long after you left, she walked out and didn't come back to the office."

"Maybe she thinks I'll give in and come back."

"Then she's in for a long wait," Jonathan said. "If there's anything I've learned about you over the past few weeks, it's that you stick to your guns."

Morgan grinned. "Are you telling me that I'm stubborn?"

He leaned over and gave her a sweet kiss on the lips. "Yes. You're stubborn. But in a good way."

Two days later, Morgan was surprised to see a call on her phone from the parent company of Generation Publishing. She hesitated a moment, wondering if she should answer it, but then was too curious not to. "Hello?"

"Hello. Is this Morgan Connors?" a female voice asked.

"Yes," Morgan replied.

"I'm Kristen Reynolds, the Executive Director of Cornice Publishing. We're the parent company of your former employer, Generation Publishing."

"Yes. What can I do for you?" Morgan said. She was surprised someone so high up in the company would call her.

"Actually, I'm calling to ask what we can do for you," Kristen said. "It came to my attention that you were let go from our employ for unfair reasons. I want you to know that Amanda Janowitz is no longer the Editorial Director at Generation Publishing. She is no longer in our employ."

"Really?" Morgan was stunned.

"Yes. I'm sorry about the way she treated you. But that was just one of many things that helped us make our decision to go in another direction."

"Well, I'm not sure what to say," Morgan said. She felt vindicated by the fact that the company sided with her, but on the other hand, firing Amanda wasn't something Morgan would have asked them to do.

"I'm in town this week going over the books at Generation Publishing and ensuring all is running smoothly there. Would it be possible for you to drop by tomorrow around nine so we can talk?" Kristen asked.

"Yes. I can come by," Morgan said.

"Wonderful. I'll see you tomorrow. Have a nice evening," Kristen said before hanging up.

Morgan wasn't sure what Kristen wanted to talk to her about. She wondered if Kristen was the person Amanda had mentioned the Winchester manuscript to. She quickly called Jonathan.

"Did you meet Kristen Reynolds yet?" she asked the minute he answered his phone.

"Wow. That was fast. Yeah. I was going to call you. She came to the office today and started going through everything in Amanda's office. She introduced herself to everyone, said she was reorganizing the imprint, and Amanda was no longer with the company. It was so weird."

"She just called me," Morgan said. "She wants to meet with me. I wonder if she wants the Winchester manuscript."

"Maybe," Jonathan said. "What are you going to do if that's the case?"

"I don't know. It's so weird that they fired Amanda, and she said the way I was treated by Amanda was one of many reasons they let her go. I can't even wrap my head around it."

"To be honest, I'm glad they got rid of Amanda," Jonathan said. "She wasn't running the imprint properly, and she was always so volatile. I get that her job was demanding and stressful, but that's not the way to treat people. But she'll never change, so she'll act that way in her next job, too."

"Probably," Morgan said. "But I feel kind of bad, too. She wasn't the nicest person, but to have to find a new job right now would be hard."

"Which was the exact position Amanda put you in," Jonathan reminded her.

"True."

"Do you want to meet up and grab some dinner? Or I could bring by some takeout," Jonathan offered.

"Thanks. But I think I'll stay home and try to digest all of this," Morgan said. "I want to work more on this manuscript, too. I'll see you tomorrow at the office, okay?"

"Sounds good. I can't wait to hear what she wants."

"Me, too," Morgan said. She was very curious to know what Kristen wanted.

* * *

Morgan arrived at the office a few minutes before nine. She didn't want to be late, although she wasn't sure why. It wasn't like this was a job interview, and she needed to impress Kristen. When Morgan walked in the door, several of the other editors ran up to her and said hello and expressed how sorry they were that she'd been let go. It was nice hearing she was missed around there.

Gabbie came out of her office and smiled at Morgan. "I'm glad you're here. Kristen said to bring you in as soon as you arrived."

Morgan was surprised Gabbie was still there, considering she had been Amanda's right hand. "Were you surprised when they let Amanda go?" she asked Gabbie.

The young woman shook her head. "Not really. Between you and me, Amanda wasn't a very nice person. But I did my job as best I could and put up with her. I hope the next person will keep me on as their assistant."

Morgan smiled. "I'm sure they will."

Gabbie led her into Amanda's old office. Behind the desk sat a slender woman with cropped dark hair and brown eyes. The red top she wore with her cream slacks accentuated her golden-brown skin tone. She looked up and smiled warmly at Morgan.

"Ah, you must be Morgan," Kristen said, offering her hand to shake. "Can I get you anything before we talk?"

Morgan shook her hand. "No, thank you."

Kristen nodded to Gabbie. "Thank you, Gabbie. If we need anything, I'll let you know."

Gabbie turned and left, and the glass door made a soft swishing sound as it shut.

"Please, sit down," Kristen said as she sat. "I'm sure you're curious why I've called you in here."

"I am," Morgan said.

"I've been going through Amanda's files to get a feel as to which editors here are having the most success bringing in writers," Kristen said. "I already knew most of this information from managing Generation Publishing's yearly reports. You've worked here the longest of all the editors, have you not?"

"Yes, I have. We tend to have a high turnover rate here. Jonathan has been here four years, and the rest have been here under that amount of time."

"Yes," Kristen said, glancing at a sheet that had Jonathan's name printed on top. "He's quite good at finding successful authors as well. The whole team seems to be doing well, but you stand out the most. You've brought in the most successful novels over the past few years. You seem to have a good eye on what will sell."

"Thank you," Morgan said. "I'm always looking for good authors. But to be fair, we don't always get to bring in all the authors we feel will do well. I've had to turn away some very talented writers who've gone on to other bigger publishers."

Kristen frowned. "Really? Why?"

"Amanda didn't always agree with our choices. Like our cozy mystery editor, Lila. She has found so many wonderful mystery writers who have done well on their own and are looking for a publisher. But Amanda shot her down every time. I assumed it was because Cornice Publishing wasn't interested in cozy mysteries, but then, why hire an editor for the sole purpose of finding cozy mystery writers?"

"Hmm. Cozy mysteries are very popular right now. I'd like to see more good series from your imprint," Kristen said. "Amanda told me there were no good writers coming up in that genre."

Morgan shook her head. "That's not true. I think Amanda just didn't like cozies."

Kristen smiled. "See what I mean. You have a good eye for good books. You have the experience and the education, and most of all, you have a feel for the market. I think you'd make the perfect managing editor for Generation Publishing."

Morgan had to let those words sink in a moment before she realized what Kristen had just said. "You want me to apply for Amanda's position?"

Kristen laughed. "No. I'm asking if you'd like to have Amanda's position. I think you'd make a wonderful managing editor. What do you think?"

"I don't know what to say," Morgan said, still stunned. "I don't even work here anymore."

"We can take care of that right away," Kristen said. "It will be like you were never let go. You just moved up into a higher position." Kristen took a yellow sticky note off the pile, wrote something on it, and handed it to Morgan. "We can offer you this as a beginning salary."

Morgan stared at the number on the paper, and her eyes widened. It was twice what she'd been making as an editor. She could finally rent a bigger apartment. Or better yet, start saving for a downpayment on a house. She couldn't believe this was happening.

"What do you think?" Kristen asked. "Are you interested?"

"Yes. I'm very interested," Morgan said. Then she remembered something. "Amanda let me go because I decided against publishing my Winchester manuscript with Generation Publishing. Did you know about that?"

Kristen nodded. "Yes, I did. She sent a copy of it to me to read. And, to tell you the truth, I'm still interested in publishing it if we can make a deal. But my offer for the job of managing editor has nothing to do with that manuscript. You have the job if you want it, regardless of what you do with the book. I only ask that you let me make you the first offer. If you like it, great. If you want to see what other options you have elsewhere, that's fine too."

Morgan thought she sounded sincere. This wasn't a play for the manuscript, like Amanda had been doing. It was a genuine job offer. She smiled. "Yes. I'd like to be the managing editor here at Generation Publishing," she told Kristen. "Nothing would make me happier."

Kristen smiled broadly. "Wonderful. Welcome to the team,

Morgan. I think you're going to do a great job."

Both women stood and shook hands. Morgan couldn't wait to tell Jonathan the good news.

CHAPTER TWENTY–EIGHT

1920

Olivia didn't hear a word from Daniel over the next few weeks. She finally gave up hoping he'd change his mind and put all her energy into working on Mrs. Winchester's biography and raising Rose. Mrs. Winchester had given her notes on several pages of the manuscript, adding more details of her life so Olivia could add them to the pages. She was happy for the work because it took her mind off her broken heart.

When Mrs. Winchester heard about Daniel's reaction to hearing the truth, she was very upset for Olivia. "He seems like such a down-to-earth man," the elderly lady had said. "I thought he'd understand. Men! They are the ones who put us in difficult positions, but then they are holier than thou when they think women should be saints."

Olivia understood what she meant. Women were supposed to stay pure while men sewed their wild oats. Unfortunately, men used women to sew their wild oats. It was a terrible double standard, but what was a woman to do?

Frank Lieb and Daniel had come by the Atherton house

several times over the past weeks, and on those days, Olivia made herself scarce. Olivia didn't know all the details, but a company was taking over the Winchester Repeating Arms Company, and pressure was being put on Mrs. Winchester to sign away her stocks for a third of their net worth. She refused, and Frank Lieb was working hard to figure out how she could get around losing so much money. But Thomas Bennett was adamant that he no longer wanted to be president, and since coming home from the war, his son wasn't healthy enough to take over. So, Mrs. Winchester, Lieb, and Daniel had multiple meetings about the predicament.

Between the problem with the company and the fading health of her sister, Belle, Mrs. Winchester, despite her own poor health, was dealing with a lot of stress. Everyone in the household did what they could to make her life comfortable. Daisy had recently taken her mother back to her Palo Alto home after Belle had spent a lot of time in a sanitarium. Belle's mental health continued to decline, but Daisy felt that she needed to be in her own home.

In May, Mrs. Winchester received a telegram from New Haven that her husband's sister, Jennie Bennett, had passed away. Jennie had already signed over all her stock shares to the holding company, and that left Sarah as the last stockholder left to sign hers over. Despite being saddened by the death of her sister-in-law and not feeling well herself, Sarah still stood firm against signing over her stock options.

"They think they can cheat me out of my money after all these years," Mrs. Winchester told Olivia as they sat in her room one morning going over parts of the biography that needed work. "Oliver Winchester worked hard to build that company, and now they just want to give it away."

"I'm sorry to hear that," Olivia said. She wasn't sure why the company was failing, but she understood why Mrs. Winchester was so angry about it. It had provided well for her all these years.

"I'm sorry to complain to you, dear," Mrs. Winchester said, her anger subsiding. "Everything feels so difficult these days."

"I don't mind you bending my ear," Olivia said. "Even though I can't help with your problems, the least I can do is listen. After all, you've had to hear my problems from time to time."

The elderly lady laughed softly. "And I've never minded that either. You've been such a blessing to me. And I love having little Rose in the house. She's a breath of fresh air."

Olivia smiled at her employer. She knew Mrs. Winchester enjoyed having Rose around, and it warmed her heart.

"On a serious note, dear," Mrs. Winchester said. "I want you to keep adding to this biography up until the day I pass away. Even if we can't work on it together, or if I'm too ill to tell you anything. The day I die will be the day it is complete."

"I hope that is a long time from now," Olivia said. "But I promise I will continue to add important events until then."

Mrs. Winchester nodded. "Good. Thank you, dear."

Much to everyone's surprise, Belle passed away in her home that June. Daisy had gone to check on her and found her. She called her aunt at the Atherton home to tell her Belle was gone.

"I never thought my younger sister would pass before me," Mrs. Winchester told both Henrietta and Olivia after she'd heard the news. The women had been in Sarah's room with her, having tea, when the news had come. "She was so strong and lively all her life. Now, I'm the last of the Pardee children. All my siblings are gone."

Olivia felt sorry for Mrs. Winchester. It must feel odd to be the last one left in a family so large.

"You still have Daisy and Margaret, and of course, all of us," Henrietta told her gently. "We all love you like family, too."

Olivia felt the same way but was surprised to hear Henrietta express her feelings so openly.

"Thank you, dear," Mrs. Winchester said. "I'm lucky to have you all at my side."

Sarah helped Daisy plan Belle's burial and paid the expenses. Soon afterward, she sold Belle's home. There were still nieces and nephews strewn around the area, including Saidee, who, along with her husband, were now the caretakers of the houseboat, her brother George, and Daisy's brother William. Sarah once again changed her will, leaving trust funds to all her nieces and nephews and great-nieces and nephews. She also included her most treasured employees in her will.

Olivia wrote down new events as they occurred and added them to Mrs. Winchester's biography. The rest of the time, she tried to make herself useful in the kitchen or helped Henrietta with office work or typing. Olivia also sat with Mrs. Winchester when Maud or Henrietta were busy, but other than that, she felt like she wasn't doing enough to earn her wage. Mrs. Winchester kept her on, even when Olivia told her there wasn't much for her to do.

On a warm July day, Henrietta came into the playroom where Olivia sat with Rose to tell her she had a visitor.

"Who would be visiting me?" Olivia asked.

"It's Daniel Stanley," Henrietta said. "He asked if he could speak with you."

Olivia's heart pounded. Why on earth would Daniel want

to speak to her?

"I see you're surprised," Henrietta said. "I'm not sure what happened between you two, but he looked so pitiful, I hated to tell him you didn't want to see him. I can stay with Rose while you go talk to him."

"Thank you," Olivia said, standing up and smoothing her skirt. She glanced in the mirror and ran her hand over her pinned-up hair. Then she decided it didn't matter how she looked; she and Daniel were no longer together.

"I'll be right back," Olivia said. She straightened her shoulders and walked out the door and down the hallway. Her resolve to be strong, however, faded quickly when, at the top of the stairs, she saw him standing in the entryway, his hat in his hands. His shoulders were slouched, and he looked so sad. As she walked down the staircase, his eyes met hers, and she tried hard to keep the tears from flowing. She'd missed him terribly.

"Miss Sivera said you wanted to talk with me." Olivia tried to stop her voice from trembling. "What can I do for you?"

Daniel glanced around, looking lost. Then he nodded toward the living room. "Could we go in there to talk? It might be more private."

Olivia nodded and led the way into the living area. She perched on one of the settees and gestured for him to do the same. But Daniel continued to stand, fingering his hat brim nervously.

"How is Rose?" he finally asked, staring down at his hat.

"She's fine. She's grown so much over the past few months. It won't be long until she's two years old," Olivia said.

"And you?" Daniel asked, still not meeting her eyes. "Have you been well?"

"I've been fine," Olivia said. She didn't add more. She just wanted Daniel to get to the reason he was here.

"I'm happy to hear that," he said. He stood there, silent, for what seemed like an eternity.

"Is that all you wanted to ask me?" Olivia said, rising from the settee. "Because I need to get back to Rose."

Daniel finally raised his eyes to hers. "No. I mean, that wasn't all I wanted to say." He took a deep breath. "I came to apologize. I just didn't know how to say it. But I came to tell you that I was stupid and insensitive and inconsiderate of your feelings." He walked over to stand in front of Olivia. "I'm so sorry. You opened up and told me the truth, even though it had to have been difficult for you, and I just walked away. Again. And aside from the first time I walked away from you, the second time was worse. Because it hurt me deeply, so I can only imagine how much I hurt you."

Olivia clenched her jaw to stop herself from crying. She wanted desperately to fall into his arms and cry with relief over his apology, but she wouldn't let herself do it. He was too close, and he looked so good, yet so sad and sorry. "You did hurt me. Deeply. But I had to tell you the truth. I couldn't marry you with a lie hanging over us."

Daniel reached for her hands and held them in his. "And that proves that you're the most honest, strongest person I've ever met. You could have kept your secret, and I would never have known. But you are too good of a person to do that. I'm so sorry, Olivia. Please say you forgive me. Who am I to judge you? We all make mistakes. I've made mistakes. And the biggest mistake I've ever made was walking away from you."

Tears trailed down Olivia's cheeks. She couldn't hold them back any longer. "I do forgive you. I just hope you forgive me, too."

"There's nothing to forgive you for. I love you, Olivia. And I love little Rose with all my heart. If you can find it in your heart to forgive me enough to love me again, I'd be the happiest man alive." Daniel searched her eyes with his, waiting for her to answer.

"I do love you, Daniel. I never stopped. I thought I'd lost you forever."

He pulled her to him and held her tightly. "I will never leave you again. I promise. No matter what happens, we'll always work it out together." Pulling away, he reached into his jacket pocket and took out a small box. "Will you marry me, Olivia? Please say you will."

"Yes," she said through her tears.

Daniel took the ring from the box and slipped it on her finger, then hugged her close again. When he finally pulled away, he handed her his handkerchief, and Olivia wiped the tears from her eyes. Taking her hand, he led her to the settee so they could sit down.

"I'm so sorry for all I've put you through," Daniel said. "All I could think these past few weeks was that I didn't want to live without you and little Rose in my life."

"You'll make me cry again," Olivia said.

"I promise to try to never make you cry again," Daniel said. And he kissed her sweetly on the lips to seal his promise.

* * *

Olivia and Daniel were married in September in the backyard of Mrs. Winchester's Atherton estate. Sarah had requested they have the ceremony there so she could attend, and Olivia was more than happy to comply. Frank Lieb gave the bride away, and Henrietta was Olivia's maid of honor. Little Rose was adorable as the flower girl.

Mr. Nakmo made a lovely luncheon spread for after the wedding, and Alice created the most beautiful and delicious wedding cake. It was an extraordinary day for everyone, and Olivia knew she'd never forget Mrs. Winchester's generosity for giving her such an unforgettable wedding day.

"You won't leave us completely, will you, dear?" Mrs. Winchester said before the bride and groom left for their honeymoon. They were spending a week in San Francisco at the Palace Hotel, courtesy of Mrs. Winchester. "You still have a job here for as long as you'd like."

"I'd be happy to still work for you," Olivia told her. "After all, we still have to finish your biography."

"Yes," Sarah said. "We still have our project to finish."

Daniel and Olivia had already made plans for Olivia to go to the Atherton house at least three times a week, bringing Rose along on the days that she worked with Mrs. Winchester. Daniel had bought a small house on the outskirts of San Jose, and Elaina was going to live with them as Rose's nanny. He wanted Olivia to be happy and knew that her close relationship with Mrs. Winchester and the staff was an important part of her life.

For their week in San Francisco, though, Elaina was going to watch Rose at the Atherton house so the couple would have a worry-free vacation.

After changing into a traveling suit, Olivia stopped at Mrs. Winchester's room to say goodbye. "Thank you for everything you've done for me," she said, daring to gently hug the elderly lady. "Everything good in my life is because of you."

"No, dear. Everything good in your life is because you

deserve it," Mrs. Winchester told her. "Never let anyone tell you otherwise."

Olivia's heart warmed at her words. Mrs. Winchester had given her a second chance at a good life two years before, and she'd always be grateful to her.

"Are you happy, Mrs. Stanley?" Daniel asked once they were in the car, driving to the city.

"More than you'll ever know," Olivia said, smiling at her husband.

Chapter Twenty-Nine

1922

Sarah Lockwood Pardee Winchester passed away quietly in her bed at her beloved San Jose home, Llanada Villa, on the evening of September 5, 1922. She'd been ill for some time, her body twisted with arthritis, but her mind was as sharp as ever in those last days. Henrietta was with Sarah when she passed and called Daisy with the news.

Family, friends, and staff gathered at Daisy's home on September 8th to say goodbye to Sarah. Among them were Sarah's many nieces and nephews, Frank Lieb, his wife and son Roy, Dr. Clyde Wayland, and the many dedicated staff members from the San Jose and Atherton homes. Olivia and Daniel were in attendance also, bringing along little Rose, who had brought Sarah much joy.

Afterward, they all climbed into cars and carriages and made their way to the cemetery where Belle and Estelle had been laid to rest. Olivia knew that Daisy would eventually bring Sarah and Belle's remains back east to New Haven to be buried near their family.

A reception was held in Daisy's home after the funeral. Everyone was still in shock over the loss of their most beloved employer, aunt, and friend. Tommie Nishihara, who'd been Sarah's gardener for years, was inconsolable, and Henrietta seemed dazed. She had worked and cared for Mrs. Winchester for over ten years and looked like she'd lost her closest friend.

Olivia understood how Henrietta felt. Mrs. Winchester had given her a chance at a new life and had been nothing but kind and encouraging to her. Losing her was like losing a mother or grandmother. Olivia was thankful to have Daniel by her side, as well as Rose. She hoped that Sarah was now with her beloved husband and their little daughter, who she'd lost all those years ago.

Olivia had spent a great deal of time with Sarah over the past couple of years as both her biographer and as a good friend. She was there the day Sarah signed over her stock certificates to the holding company, losing a third of their value. Frank Leib had advised her to do so, or else she, as the only stockholder left, would be responsible for the company's debt. While it upset Sarah to lose so much money, she understood it was her only option. Olivia had personally mailed off the certificates for Sarah.

As the mourners began to disperse, Olivia asked Daniel to bring in the box that sat in their car. Catching Daisy alone in the parlor, she handed the box to her. "Mrs. Winchester's last project," Olivia told her. "She asked me to finish the manuscript after she passed away, adding what I could about her death and funeral arrangements."

Daisy opened the box and looked at the pages within. It held everything Sarah could remember about her youth, her relatives, her move to California, and all else that had happened in her life. It was a last tribute to an incredible life lived by an extraordinary woman.

"Thank you," Daisy said, setting it down on a table by the sofa. "My aunt cared about you very much. I hope you know that."

"I do. And I cared about her, too. She was an inspiration to me," Olivia said, holding back tears. "I feel like she saved my life."

Daisy lifted a brow. "That is quite a testament to how she treated those around her."

Olivia nodded. Daisy looked tired. She and her husband, Fred, had reconciled two years prior and were living together again, and Margaret had just married that spring. But Olivia knew the stress of losing her aunt had taken a toll on Daisy. "Miss Sivera said that you'll be selling off the contents of Llanada Villa. If you need help going through everything, I'd be happy to pitch in."

"Thank you. That's very kind of you. It'll be a big job. Henrietta said she'd help, and the Hansens will also. But I'll remember your offer if we need more people to help."

Olivia offered her hand to shake, and Daisy shook it. "Take care of yourself," Olivia said. "Perhaps we'll see each other from time to time."

"I'm sure we will," Daisy said.

Olivia turned and left and met up with Alice in the entryway. They spoke for a few minutes, saying goodbye. Alice was already looking for a new job, as were most of the staff, and hoped to find one soon.

"But it won't be like working for Mrs. Winchester," Alice said sadly. "She was one of a kind. A very special lady."

"I agree completely," Olivia said.

Alice nudged Olivia and pointed to the parlor. "It's sweltering outside. What on earth is Daisy doing, starting a fire in the fireplace?"

Olivia turned in time to see Daisy dropping the manuscript she'd just given her into the blazing fire. One by one, the pages curled and turned black as the fire destroyed them. She gasped, stunned at what she was seeing.

"What is she burning?" Alice whispered. "Hopefully not the will."

Olivia moved out of Daisy's sight, closer to the front door, pulling Alice with her. "Whatever she's doing is no business of ours," she said, and Alice nodded.

Olivia hugged Alice goodbye and left the house. Daniel and Rose were waiting for her by their car.

"You look like you've seen a ghost," Daniel said as they all stepped into the car. "Are you feeling all right?"

She turned and looked at Daniel. "I gave Daisy the manuscript, and before I left, I saw her dump it into the fireplace and burn it."

He frowned. "What? Why on earth would she do that?"

"I don't know. All that work. All those years of typing and rewriting to get it perfect. And she just destroyed it." Olivia's eyes filled with tears. "It was Mrs. Winchester's last project. She wanted to share her story with her family. It was her legacy to pass down to everyone so they'd know the truth and not believe the lies the newspapers told. And now it's gone."

Daniel reached over and hugged Olivia. Her tears spilled on his dark suit, leaving stains. "I'm so sorry, dear. I know how hard you worked on it. Daisy must have her reasons for not keeping it."

Olivia couldn't think of one reason to destroy the

manuscript. Daisy could have put it away with Sarah's photo albums. She wouldn't have had to share it with anyone. But it would have been nice to keep it for future generations.

"I guess there's nothing I can do about it," Olivia said, accepting Daniel's handkerchief and dabbing at her eyes. "I feel like the last four years were for nothing."

Daniel smiled. "Not nothing, dear. You have me now. And little Rose. And we have our whole lives ahead of us."

This made Olivia smile. "Yes. You're right. And I have so many great memories of working for Mrs. Winchester. Her story may have been destroyed, but my memories cannot be taken away from me."

That night, after Olivia had tucked Rose into bed and Daniel was downstairs in his study, reading a book, Olivia went to her little office next to their bedroom. On the desk sat the black Underwood typewriter that Mrs. Winchester had insisted she bring home with her to work on the manuscript. Olivia ran her fingers over the dark metal, remembering the first day she'd started working for Mrs. Winchester and how thrilling it had been to have a new typewriter all to herself. Since then, she'd typed many pages on it.

Sitting in the chair, Olivia opened the bottom drawer and pulled out a box. It looked exactly like the box she'd handed to Daisy earlier today. She set it on the desk next to the typewriter and carefully opened the lid. Inside sat a thick manuscript of pages, the title page reading, "Mrs. Sarah Lockwood Pardee Winchester, Autobiography, 1922."

Olivia smiled. She knew the carbon copy would eventually fade and smudge. So, she made up her mind to retype it so she'd have a clean copy of her own. Daisy may have destroyed the original, but Olivia would always have hers.

With loving care, Olivia placed the lid over the box and slid it back in the drawer. She, at least, would never forget the true story of Sarah Winchester's life.

CHAPTER THIRTY

Today — One Year Later

Morgan sat at her desk at Generation Publishing, admiring the advance copy of *Sarah Lockwood Pardee Winchester An Autobiography*. The cover was simple—done in a slate blue with a photo of Sarah as a young woman with a pixie-like smile. The type was embedded gold. At the bottom of the book, the type read *As told to Olivia Collins Stanley*.

Morgan loved how professional the hardcover book looked, and also the dust jacket, which included a photo of Sarah's San Jose mansion, Llanada Villa.

It had been a year since Morgan had accepted the position of managing editor, and she hadn't regrated one moment of it. Under her management, each editor had begun to shine, bringing in talented authors and bestselling books. The only editor who'd quit after she'd accepted the position was Patrick. He'd refused to take orders from someone younger than him. But Morgan hadn't been bothered by that. She'd hired a new editor to take his place, and they had successfully published two incredible memoirs since then and had many more waiting to be published. Likewise, Lila had finally been allowed free reign to take on new cozy mystery authors, and her authors' books were doing wonderfully. Lila's confidence in herself had grown, and that made Morgan happy.

Six months into her new position, Jonathan had accepted an editor's position at another publishing company. He hadn't had a problem with her being his boss—in fact, they'd worked well together just as they always had. But he wanted to pursue publishing books in the science fiction genre, and that didn't fit with their brand. He'd been hired immediately by another publisher that was happy to have his experience and expertise on their staff.

Again, Morgan hadn't minded his leaving. Their relationship had grown stronger throughout the months, and it was even better now that they didn't work in the same office. When they got together in the evening, they both had interesting things to talk about, and she loved hearing about his latest acquisition or the new author he was considering. They'd both moved up in their careers, and it was exciting to see where they would end up.

After a little negotiation, Morgan had decided to publish the Winchester manuscript with Cornice Publishing after all. They'd given her an even better offer than the one Amanda had presented to her, and they let her make all the final decisions about the project. After several edits of the manuscript, the only thing missing was information about her great-great-grandmother, Olivia Collins.

Morgan and her mother had gone through all the information Annie had collected on Olivia and decided that she had probably been unmarried when Rose was born. Whether or not anyone else knew, they had no idea. Perhaps she'd lied about having a husband and becoming a widow, or it was true, and they couldn't find a record of the marriage. No matter how it happened, Olivia had kept it a secret.

"In the end, Daniel Stanley had adopted Rose as his own daughter, and that's all that matters," Annie had told Morgan. "I feel we shouldn't air her dirty laundry now after she kept it secret for so long."

Morgan had agreed. So, she wrote the following for Olivia's biography in the back of the book:

Olivia Collins Stanley worked for Mrs. Winchester as her typist from 1918 until 1922. She assisted Mrs. Winchester in compiling her autobiography during that time. In 1920, Olivia married lawyer Daniel Stanley, and they had one child, Rose Sarah Stanley. They eventually moved to San Diego, California, where Daniel opened his own law practice, and both he and Olivia lived there until their deaths. Mrs. Winchester's manuscript was found by Olivia's great-great-granddaughter, Morgan Connors.

It was simple and to the point, giving credit to Olivia for helping Mrs. Winchester tell her story in her own words.

"How does it look?" Gabbie asked, poking her head into Morgan's office.

Morgan smiled up at her assistant. "It looks great. Come in and see."

Gabbie walked in and reached for the book Morgan handed to her. "They did a great job on it, didn't they? It looks incredible."

"They did. I can't wait for it to get out to the public," Morgan said. "I just hope people will read it, and finally everyone will know what Mrs. Winchester was really like. Her character has been maligned for too long."

"Over a hundred years," Gabbie said, handing the book

back to Morgan. "I can't wait to read it." She smiled and returned to her desk outside Morgan's door.

That evening, Morgan, Jonathan, and Morgan's parents met at a nice restaurant halfway between San Francisco and San Jose. They were seated in a booth, and Jonathan ordered a bottle of champagne.

"We're celebrating tonight," Jonathan told Annie and Dean as the waitress walked away.

Both parents looked at him expectantly until Morgan realized what they were thinking.

"No, Mom and Dad. Not that! No one is getting married yet." She pulled the autobiography out of her oversized purse. "The Winchester book is ready for publication," Morgan said. She handed it to her mother.

"Oh, honey. It's beautiful," Annie said as she studied the cover and then opened the pages.

Dean leaned in so he could see it also. "I'm so happy for you, dear," he said, smiling proudly. "What a wonderful accomplishment."

"Well, it's not my book," Morgan said. "But I'm happy I was able to finally get it out there after all these years. Maybe someday I'll write something worth publishing."

"It's still a big deal," Annie said. "I don't know what happened to the copy Mrs. Winchester had, but I'm glad everyone is finally going to be able to read the truth about her."

"Me, too," Morgan said.

The champagne came, and they poured glasses all around. Jonathan raised his glass. "To Morgan, for making it possible for the world to read the true story of Sarah Winchester." They all clinked their glasses.

Annie spoke up. "And to Olivia for saving the manuscript

all these years." All four glasses clinked in the air.

"But most of all," Morgan chimed in. "To Sarah Winchester. For living such an incredible life in a time when women didn't have the freedoms they do today."

"To Sarah," Annie and Dean said.

"To Sarah," Jonathan said. And the foursome toasted the woman who'd lived her life to the fullest no matter what anyone else thought.

- END -

Book Discussion Questions

1. Sarah Pardee grew up around her father's woodworking business and loved it. Unfortunately, because she was a female, she wasn't allowed to work there. How do you think her early years affected her choices later in life?

2. Sarah was raised by open-minded and compassionate parents who felt that every opinion should be valued and new ideas were accepted. Even though Sarah was shyer than some of her other siblings, how do you think her upbringing influenced her throughout her life?

3. Sarah and William lived in the Winchester home after they were married and spent a great deal of time with William's father, Oliver. He was a strong, outspoken man with a good business sense. Do you think some of his business ethics were mirrored by Sarah later in life when she was running her own household and investing in property?

4. Knowing what you do about the real Sarah Winchester, do you think if she'd met Olivia Collins in real life that Sarah would have been open-minded enough to hire her and help her through her difficult time?

5. Olivia felt she couldn't marry Daniel without telling him the truth. But when she did, she almost lost him. Do you think she should have told him the truth or should she have kept the truth to herself? What would you have done?

6. After Olivia gave Daisy the manuscript of Sarah's autobiography, she was shocked to see Daisy burning it. Why do you think Daisy destroyed the manuscript that had been so important to Sarah?

7. In the story, Morgan decides to publish Olivia's copy of Sarah's manuscript. If a true manuscript dictated by Sarah had been found, do you think Morgan should have published it? Knowing how private Sarah was, do you think she would have approved?

Author's Notes

This novel is a work of fiction, however, there are many real-life characters portrayed in this book. I tried my best to portray them as historically accurate as possible. All the characters in the historical portion of the novel, except for Olivia Collins, Rose, Daniel Stanley, and Alice Murphy, are real people who either worked for Mrs. Winchester or were associated with her.

What we do know for certain is that Sarah Winchester was a well-loved sister and aunt, and her employees adored her. She treated people fairly and went over and above to help those who needed it. She was a good sister who took care of family members. She had the money to do so, and she wasn't stingy with it.

So, why write about Sarah Winchester? Because I found her true life story interesting. The first forty-two years of her life she was the dutiful daughter, wife, aunt, sister, and friend. After the death of her husband, William Winchester, she decided she needed more than a life of widowhood and charity work. So, she set out on an adventure to California, built a huge mansion, invested in real estate all over the bay area, and just lived her life on her own terms. Not many women did that in a time when they didn't even have the right to vote.

Perhaps her freedom and wealth are what made the men who owned the local newspapers angry enough to write lies about her. Whatever their reasoning was, Sarah ignored them and continued doing what she loved.

I hope you enjoyed this novel about Sarah Winchester. I spent a year going through books about her and researching her family history. I also spent hours reading newspaper clippings about Sarah and the letters between her and her lawyer, Frank Lieb. There is a lot of information out there about the true Sarah Winchester if you are interested in learning more.

If you'd like to learn more about Sarah Winchester you can read the following books or check out the following websites:

- Sarah Winchester: Beyond the Mystery by Bennett Jacobstein
- Sarah Winchester, My Neighbor by Edith Daley
- Captive of the Labyrinth: Sarah L. Winchester by Mary Jo Ignoffo
- Sarah Winchester's Letters: History San Jose Website: https://historysanjose.pastperfectonline.com/archive/A070F342-96E7-4543-BDFC-008481515425
- Samuel Lieb Papers: Sarah Winchester Series (1865-1922): https://archive.org/details/hsj1979-171leibwinchester/1979-171-265/

About the Author

Deanna Lynn Sletten is the author of THE SECRETS WE CARRY, THE ONES WE LEAVE BEHIND, THE WOMEN OF GREAT HERON LAKE, MISS ETTA, FINDING LIBBIE, and several other titles. She writes heartwarming women's fiction, historical fiction, a murder mystery series, and romance novels with unforgettable characters. She has also written one middle-grade novel that takes you on the adventure of a lifetime.

Deanna is married and has two grown children. When not writing, she enjoys peaceful walks in the woods around her home with her beautiful Aussie—Miss Etta, traveling, photography, and relaxing on the lake.

Deanna loves hearing from her readers. Connect with her at her website: www.deannalsletten.com